The Trouble Causer

Solomon Kabushenga

FOUNTAIN PUBLISHERS

Kampala

Fountain Publishers
Fountain Publishers Ltd.
P.O. Box 488
Kampala, Uganda

© Solomon Kabushenga, 2007
First published 2007

ISBN 978-9970-02-538-1

Dedication

To my twin sons: Wilson Kakuru and Keneth Kato.

To all those who suffer as a result of other people's conflicts.

Chapter One

It was a very hot afternoon. The heat could go through even the hard head of a dog. The herds of cattle were very thirsty. The lucky ones already lay resting on the bare hump of a gently sloping hill. This was the resting ground, just above the communal troughs where the animals were watered. The watering place was open to all families of all the clans around. When it was time to water the animals, those who were close by brought them to Nyamiringa ridge, to this special watering place. The water did not belong to any clan. It belonged to Kazooba Nyamuhanga.

The lucky herds had already been watered. They had come earlier. There were hundreds of others still gathered around the three large troughs. They were trying to get at the water all at once. At such a time, even the many young men who came to help the herd-boys water the herds could not quite control them. There were yet other herds stampeding down the hill. A cloud of dust followed them. They were all going down to the troughs to join in the big struggle, to get their rightful share of water. This was special water, with natural salts in it.

Nobody could control them at such a time. It was all the many young men could do to keep pouring water in the large troughs faster than the cattle could drink it. They used big dug-out wooden containers to scoop the water from the well. Some three strong men would be down the well. They would be expertly throwing the containers to the young men up above. These would pour the water in the troughs and throw the containers back for a refill. If these people were slow, then the cattle would be drinking mud before another container came up from the well.

It was a beautiful, tumultuous, healthy confusion. Many voices could be heard above the general noise. The herdsboys were shouting orders, restrictions and instructions to the herds. The smaller voices were drowned by the lowing of the herds. The hollow sound of hundreds of horns randomly knocking on each other provided a musical accompaniment to the general noise. Many old men could not miss this beautiful confusion. And indeed quite a few could be seen around. They were not taking part in the watering. They were only moving around watching and listening. One could not even be sure that they owned any of the cattle because they never associated themselves with any herd. The elders say: He who does not have associates himself with what he does not have.

Amid this confusion, a small herd rushed down the hill raising a thick cloud of dust. A massive bull was in the lead. A few cows and young ones confidently followed close behind. They belonged to the herd. There were no calves around. The calves always grazed separately.

This small herd checked its speed as it got to the crowd. The cows and the weak bulls fell back. But the bull did not stop. It went forward head down. The stout short horns jutted forwards in a classical challenge. It moved forwards slowly, snorting at the ground, puffing up dust and pawing the ground with its front hooves. It moved its head from side to side, daring any bull to take up the challenge.

Seeing none, it snorted loudly twice and raised its head on a heavy neck that was stretched forward. Then it gave an impressive bull roar. The first bellow pierced through the noise around and petered out in a deep-throated tone. It was kept up for twenty full breaths. This was followed by one that was deeper and shorter. And then another and another and another...

'*Gamba, gamba Ruhogo rwa Ruteeramareingwa. Gamba,*' the small boy looking after the bull could be heard chanting praises to the bull. As if it could understand that the boy was urging it to go on, it kept up the bellowing. It ended up roaring almost like a lion. It gave twelve distinct bellows in all. The echoes of the bellows could still be heard resounding from the opposite hill.

When the bull stopped there was an unusual quietness, only punctuated by an occasional horn accidentally knocking on a neighbouring horn. Then about fifteen strides away, another bull broke the silence with a challenging bellow. It was equally impressive. But it did not have the time to go through the whole scale. The other cows and weaker bulls in between were already scuttling off to give them way.

The two bulls faced each other, heads down. They snorted louder and dug up the earth with their front hooves. Two herd-boys came at them waving sticks and shouting commands at them. The bulls ignored the intruders. The older men did not even bother themselves. They knew that to separate the bulls would make them hunt out each other until they had settled the matter once and for all.

The two bulls met head-on with a loud bang of horns. Each dug its heels into the ground and shoved. Each would move its head to get its horns into a better position but the other one would make an appropriate counter move. Neither moved the other from its position for very many breaths. The muscles of the neck, the forelegs, the hind legs and the back stood out like stout ropes in a tug-of-war. Then the first bull, Ruhogo, did something very fast. It brought its front right knee to the ground and threw the other one off balance. Then as suddenly it got up. It started pushing the other one very fast. As the second bull moved backwards, a path was cleared through the crowd of cattle. Soon the weaker bull found an escape route.

The first bull, Ruhogo, followed by the cattle in its herd, snorted loudly and puffed its way to the drinking troughs. Their young herd-boy followed them to the water, proudly chanting praises to the bull.

A short while later, this same bull, followed by its herd, made its way to the higher resting ground. They had bulldozed their way to the water. Now they could rest before they started on their second round of feeding. They had to rest until it was cooler.

There were always hundreds of cattle lying around. The bigger bulls were moving around smelling and licking at the behinds of the cows. They were looking for mates. Younger and more energetic bulls were also moving around. But these did not stop at smelling the behinds. They also attempted to mount some of the cows. Thus they picked quarrels around. Then they would continue the rounds after throwing or being thrown off by an agemate. Very occasionally, the big old bulls would also fight, particularly if there was a potential mate around.

Ruhogo stood facing the opposite ridge, Kabisha, and repeated its bellowing. Even better this time. It made thirteen distinct bellows. The boy to whose father the bull belonged dutifully sang praises and danced around it. This time he flavoured the chant with something about his clan:

Gamba Ruhogo rwa Ruteeramareingwa.	Roar, Ruteeramareingwa's Ruhogo
Owa Nyamiringa ya Nyabigyi	Of Nyamiringa in Nyabigyi
Gamba rutaasya obarungyi	Roar. He who marries beauties
Nkobutwaza mubaaseeri	Like when we went across
Nkariimayo Keirigyirwa	I admired Keirigyirwa
Naamusimba akakumu	I jabbed a finger in her ribs
Yaashashaamwa kunanurirwa	She moaned sweetly
Ntinaakutaasya owa'Bajura.	I decided to marry her, a Mujura.
Gamba.	Roar.

The boy and the bull stopped at the same time. They turned and looked at each other as if in mutual admiration. Then Ruhogo lay down in the middle of a crowd of fat well-fed cows. It absent-mindedly started chewing cud from the morning meal.

Chapter Two

I

Bugeiga was one of the richest men in the whole of Nyabigyi. His home was on top of the ridge called Kabisha, separated from the ridge called Nyamiringa by a wide valley with papyrus swamp in it. In the rains the valley was difficult to cross and his cattle would not be taken to the communal watering place. They would have to drink the ordinary stream water and their milk would be very watery. Now, in the dry season, crossing was easy.

Bugeiga believed that in Rusiina he had the best bull in Nyabigyi and all the ridges around. He happened to be passing by the watering place when a bull gave a fierce bellow. It was beautiful. He listened as it bellowed twelve times. He subconsciously praised it as it went through the twelve bellows. This was the best. He had never heard Rusiina do that well. Only one other time had he even heard it give ten. It only gave eight or nine. He attributed this classic performance to the presence of hundreds of admirers. And, probably, there was a cow on heat around.

Soon after it had stopped he heard another bull answer. It had as powerful a deep-throated bellow but it did not match the first one. He knew that the two bulls were going to fight. It would be almost a contest between himself, a Mugirakwe, and the owner of that other bull, whichever clan he belonged to.

Some while later he heard his bull again. He had crossed the valley and was on his home ridge, Kabisha, opposite the resting ground for the cattle. This time, when the bull's bellow started, he praised it aloud:

Gamba Rusiina rwa Bugeiga.	Roar Bugeiga's Rusiina.
Gamba gamba rwa Bugeiga	Roar, roar Bugeiga's
Omugwisa 'kagwe wabagyirakwe	The trouble causer of the Bagyirakwe
Ba Nyabigyi	From Nyabigyi
Nkarahira enumi yangye	I swore by my bull
Abataziine babwerabwera.	Those who had none looked down with shame.
Gamba.	Roar.

That could not be any other bull. It had to be Rusiina, his powerful bull. Of that he was sure. He started reminiscing. His departed father could not have boasted of a better bull. Nor could his grandfather, for that matter. His father had had a bigger herd all right. But his bull had no equal. He knew that his brothers, let alone the rest of the clansmen and the other clans around, envied him for this bull.

And indeed it was a wonder bull. Bugeiga himself was a big and tall man. He had to bend his head when passing through any door. Neglect of this had resulted in his head hitting the lintel even when going through the highest doors. And yet the bull Rusiina reached to the level of his armpit. He always liked to caress it in the evenings when the herd gathered around the fire to keep away from flies. Then when it was relaxed he would rest against it, his arm stretched out, the elbow resting on its back.

As its name suggests, it was black. But our cows are not described as black, brown or red, even if they are. Such are not suitable descriptive names for animals which are used in paying bride price.

If anybody had watched Bugeiga as he walked home thinking about his bull they would have seen the expression on his soot-black face change as the picture of Rusiina went through his head. The short furrowed face with thick horns barely an arm long. The small eyes almost hidden by the thick furrows. This gave it a furious, powerful look. The large muscular neck and the chest which went down to the elbows. The big hump which moved from side to side majestically as the bull moved. Yes, it was a beautiful bull. He scratched his black curly hair.

Bugeiga stopped thinking about his wealth and his bull. He had got to the big cluster of houses. This was his grandfather's homestead. And all the descendants of his grandfather lived on this ridge. Except the women, of course. They went away to live with their husbands. And of course in different clans.

His grandfather, Rwabugyirakwe, had claimed land for himself on this ridge Kabisha very many years back. The neighbouring ridge which his grandfather had similarly acquired had become too small to sustain all the grandsons. The more daring ones had therefore moved to the unclaimed ridges and hills around. Some had been claimed, but by weaker people. And these had been chased away to look for more distant and often poorer land. It was not quite through bloodshed that Rwabugyirakwe had acquired Kabisha. But it had often required bloodshed to keep it, as some people thought they could uproot him.

Bugeiga entered his own compound on the edge of the large cluster of houses. It was surrounded with a cactus fence which enclosed the whole collection of houses. There were only three gates leading to the outside and two of those would be closed at night.

A visitor would know this was a large and well-to-do family. Looking at Bugeiga one could guess it from his general appearance and the confident way in which he carried himself. He wore two big goat skins. The strap passed over the arm and the skin under the opposite armpit. One was worn hanging from the left shoulder and the other from the right. The hairless side was treated with a special type of red earth and then smeared with ghee. This was done often to keep the skins properly and softly tanned. Like all skins, the other side had beautiful patterns made on them with beads. The two skins did not hide much. They were not meant to. Only those who have something to hide, like a disease or a deformity, needed to cover their manly endowments.

On each arm he wore a thick copper bangle. On the ankles he wore many small bangles. Around his neck an amulet dangled conspicuously. And if anybody could have checked in the mongoose-skin pouch hanging around his neck, he would have found a more powerful talisman and other safeguards. His walking staff was long and pointed on both ends. On one end it was driven into a sharp small spear. He carried a sharp curved matchet in his left hand, resting it on his shoulder.

His first wife, Keigwisagye, could see that he was in his especially good mood as soon as he came through the gate. She looked at him expectantly with a smile lingering on her face. She had harvested sorghum some forty odd times since she got married to him. That was over forty years. She knew his moods very well.

He did not greet her. That was not necessary. Even when he was addressing her, it was as if he was addressing someone else. He drove his staff into the softer ground where there was grass and leaned on it. He then talked quietly looking elsewhere, at nobody.

'Where are the goats eating from?'

'I overheard the boys saying that they would take them to Nyamiirima.' The wife knew what this enquiry meant, so she answered enthusiastically.

'Where is your last born?'

'He has gone to split firewood. Should he be fetched?'

'Yes. And tell him to go and fetch that *Mushere* he-goat. It has started climbing the females. It is not a strong one and will spoil the offspring.'

He did not even enter the house after this. He walked off with long confident strides. Despite his age and tallness he was still very straight-backed. He disappeared deeper into the cluster of houses. Keigwisagye looked after him with a grateful smile. She was a plump elderly woman. Her face spoke of peace, gentleness and motherhood. Even the way she went about her work was casually peaceful.

II

As her husband disappeared round the corner, Keigwisagye became busy. She headed for the granary. There was the millet to grind. There were some other ingredients to collect. They would go into preparing a special meal tonight. When a man has been so considerate as to skin a whole goat for his wives and children, no wife should have any excuse for putting a meal in front of him which is lacking in anything.

But first she had to have Rwecurenga called home. He was her last born. She was lucky that her last born was a son and she had somebody to perform these small but important traditional chores.

Rwecurenga was very fast and also very thoughtful. He was a favourite of very many adults around, a child who could be sent by anybody on any errand. His uncles and most elders around agreed that he would grow into a good and important man. It was only fifteen harvest seasons since his birth but already he was a man. He had his father's stature. But, again many agreed, he did not have his father's conceit and his often ill-advised judgements and actions. He had his mother's handsomeness and dark brown complexion.

When he went for the goat his mother sent a message to her husband's other wives. She did not have to give them orders or instructions as such – though as the first wife she could – but she had to inform them.

Passing by the three houses not so long afterwards, one could hear the grinding stones in all the three houses crying. In one of the houses the young girl grinding the millet recited a common accompaniment to the stone:

Osagamagingo aseeraki	Why should anybody be grinding at this time?
Aseera kitanga neejuga	She grinds because Kitanga is bleating
Kyosa juba baatubaagira	so grind faster Kitanga is to be slaughtered for us
Tugikoze tuhirik'amabondo.	We eat and fill our stomachs

And very soon Mushere could be heard bleating. Rwecurenga had just tied it behind his mother's largest granary. He was sharpening the knives now.

Bugeiga came back as Rwecurenga finished his part of the job with the goat. He had had three small stepbrothers to help him. He had long mastered the art of cutting the goat into the appropriate pieces. But he could not do that when his father was around. His mother had already taken the special parts for roasting. Those included the last bit of the large intestine, the liver, the kidneys, the heart and the part of the chest which includes the breast-bone. These would be nicely roasted for the man, the head of the family. And according to tradition women – where they were allowed to eat goat's meat – and children did not eat such parts. They would have caused some long-term effect, like children becoming stupid and lethargic from eating liver.

Bugeiga's family was one of the exceptional ones. The women in his family ate goat's meat and even mutton. Very few other families like his – the families of rich people – existed. But women eating chicken was unheard of, even among the rich ones. All the others had to make do with game meat and beef which was very rare.

The father would now apportion the goat among his three wives. He would also distribute to the younger children their respective bits and pieces for roasting. Those who were not there, like the one grazing the goats and the cattle boy, would have their special pieces kept for them. Fire was already roaring in each of the wives' houses.

A goat is a very exacting animal. No woman would attempt to skin or even apportion it. Even if she was a widow or alone in the home, the custom would not allow it. As such a woman could not know which parts to give to which children and which parts to give to this or that wife. This work was meant for a man. And to him it was very easy. As a matter of fact, the goat divides itself into many specific parts. Almost as if each part is labelled. The parts for women only; the parts for cousins and in-laws; and the parts for all, which were certainly the fewest. Naturally, if there are no cousins or in-laws around then their specific parts revert to the common pool.

Bugeiga was just finishing apportioning the goat when the cattle came. Each wife had taken her share. Each child had a small stake with pieces speared on it. Even the family dogs had had their share, things like the pancreas, gall bladder, genitals but not testicles, and others.

He did not notice that as Rusiina approached home it made only six bellows instead of its usual eight or nine. Nor did he notice that they were rather dull. He was in too good a mood to notice such trivia. He went through his own gate to the cattle's fireplace outside. He started piling more dry cowdung and green, undried grass onto the fire. A lot of smoke was needed to drive away the flies. A grandson brought him his special stool. He was of Keigwisagye's house.

'Go and ask your grandmother whether your uncles are there.' This request would now get to all the houses. All sons would come. The young boy ran off, the wind puffing the small goatskin behind his back. Despite the evening cold, this was the only attire he had on.

The cattle had now come through the gate nearest to his compound. Bagyenyi, the young son who grazed the cattle, came behind them, whistling one of the melodious cattle songs. He was the fourth son of the second wife and a few seasons younger than Rwecurenga. With him was one of Keigwisagye's grandsons.

'Your mother must have something waiting for you,' his father said as the two young boys got to him. 'Go and see her and come back soon.'

III

The cloudless sky was a beautiful blue-black. But for the uncountable stars which shone so brightly, it would have been black. The moon had not come yet. It would be coming soon. It had passed its fullness some four days back. The cattle had been ushered into the kraal soon after milking. Another smoky fire had been made there. Very many dry big branches had been piled into the gate of the kraal. These went up to the level of the high fence. Even if a predator managed to enter the kraal, it could not possibly get out with its kill.

Now Bugeiga sat by the fire, *hakikoome* the semi-permanent fireplace. He sat on his traditional stool with a leopard skin glued to its seat. He leaned his back against the big kitooma tree. His oldest sons from all the houses, as well as the older of the grandsons, sat around him. Normally they would be listening to interesting stories about their ancestors. But tonight somehow no good bloody story was forthcoming. The young boys and the girls were in their mothers' houses. Such stories would give them sleepless nights full of ghastly nightmares.

They had just finished a big and varied delicious dinner. Each of the wives had done her best to outdo the others. And no panel of judges could have given a true verdict if they attempted to find a winner. Each had attempted to satisfy a particular taste of her husband's. The special dish that, he had confided at some intimate time, she prepared better than anybody else he knew.

Bugeiga's home being reasonably harmonious, they quite often all ate together. The women, with the help of their daughters, had brought their dishes to the men. They were sitting around the now roaring wood fire. This had been built in the same place where the grass fire for the cattle had been. This fire would not die out until morning, unless it rained in the night. They had all eaten well. The young men were full and pleased with their father. Whereas a goat skinned for the family was not a rare occurrence in Bugeiga's home, this one had not been expected so soon. Only a week back he had skinned a very big castrated billygoat when a friend had visited him. They were not only friends. They had also married together, that is from the same house.

The young men wondered why he had suddenly skinned this one for them. And yet, looking at him sitting there and leaning against that tree, he was far from being happy. He had not even enjoyed the meal. He had swallowed only four medium-sized balls of millet bread properly filled with soup. Then he had pulled over the basket of mashed matooke prepared by his youngest wife;

taking a big lump he deftly rounded it up into a big ball with his right hand; he dug the thumb into the ball, creating a big deep hole; he then scooped the ball full of soup from the clay bowl he was using for soup and threw it all into his mouth. He tonguipulated the large bolus of food to the back of his mouth and swallowed it. It landed into the stomach with a loud thud. Three more such balls he pushed away the basket of matooke. He then picked at the roast meat, specially done by his first wife. Soon he had stopped that too and started passing it over to the sons. He called them one by one as he passed chunks of meat to them. The last chunks – and decidedly the best – went first to the boys who had grazed the cattle and then to the goat boys. Water was poured for him as he washed his hands.

He picked up his long-necked gourd and drank the sweet *bushera*, prepared from sorghum flour. He leaned against the tree again and held his head between his hands as if it throbbed with pain.

When Bagyenyi had gone to his mother after bringing in the cattle, Bugeiga had gone to meet his bull as usual. Rusiina had been very restless. Soon he had noticed the big weal on its stout neck. The skin was razed off part of the weal, about two fingers long. When his son came back, Bugeiga had got the whole story out of him. He had taken the truth very bitterly. He could not quite believe that his son had told him the truth. He shook his head sadly.

Again he asked quietly as if in a dream, 'Tell me again, son, so that I may understand properly. How did Rusiina get that welt?'

'It fought with Ruhogo rwa Ruteeramareingwa,' Bagyenyi answered calmly.

Bugeiga looked down between his feet. 'But Rusiina always fights other bulls. And it has never received such a welt.' He stopped dreamily and looked towards the kraal. 'And it has never come home so restless and in such low spirits.'

'But it always beats the others,' Bagyenyi replied defensively.

'You mean this other one beat Rusiina?'

'Eeee.'

'How can another bull beat Rusiina?' Ndemire asked quietly. He was a son to the third wife. He was a few moons older than Bagyenyi. His agemates sometimes called him 'the black-hearted one'. But of course they called him this only behind his back. His comment was ignored by his brothers but it did not escape the father. Indeed after thinking about it for many breaths, he asked the same question.

'How, indeed?' He banged his fist hard on his thigh. 'How can it beat Rusiina? How did it happen?'

The boy then described the fight again, rather too vividly for his father's liking. It was as if his own son was praising this other bull for beating Rusiina.

'And where were you to allow that to happen?' Bugeiga asked accusingly, when the son finished describing the fight.

'You know very well, taata, that I could have done nothing.'

'And you say that it belongs to whom?' he asked, gnashing his teeth. His eyes glared around in the dull, yellow light from the wood fire.

'To Ruteeramareingwa, the Mujura from Nyamiringa,' one of the older sons volunteered. He had been there to help water the cattle.

'And you still insist that it was not Rusiina that made those twelve powerful bellows when you were watering.'

'No,' Bagyenyi said, timidly now. He was starting to wonder why this should have affected his father so much. 'It was Ruhogo rwa Ruteeramareingwa.'

Bugeiga went quiet for some time. He picked up the gourd of *bushera*. He sucked at the tube meditatively and put it down again. He stood up and took his long staff. It had been leaning against the big tree. He stood there lost for a brief moment. Then suddenly he drove the staff into the ground hard.

'No,' he protested loudly and slumped onto the stool again. 'Ruhogo! May it be struck by lightning!' He gnashed his teeth loudly. 'And Rusiina, may it be killed by cowpox!' Then, more quietly, 'How can I, Bugeiga, stand in front of men and swear by a bull which cannot defend itself against another bull, in public?'

'But father these are only bulls. I do not think that you should let their fight disturb you,' Kyereeta said, trying to calm his father down. He was the third wife's first son. He had only recently married his first wife.

'No, it is not just bulls,' the father protested vehemently. 'Can't you see that that was Ruteeramareingwa, a Mujura, fighting me Bugeiga, a Mugirakwe? Can't you see that the small powerless clan beat us down there, by the watering place?

'No, taata, that is not true. It is not like someone sent that bull to come and fight with ours. Rusiina could have fought with any other bull,' his oldest son, Karwemera, argued.

'As such, I do not think that we would be fair at all if we tried to create a human quarrel out of a normal bulls' scuffle. Bulls always fight. But we never see their fighting as the owners' fight. Why so now?'

'Men always fight, too, son. And it is not always that their fight results into anything. But sometimes the smallest thing may spark off a terrible bloodshed. I can assure you, sons, that this is the beginning of doom.'

The sons were tongue-tied for some time. They could not see any connection between two bulls fighting and doom. The father stood holding his staff. For a few moments he listened to the darkness around them as if there was someone out there talking to him. Then he started moving off towards the first wife's house. Only there could he sleep without being disturbed by anything, if he wanted to. A few paces away, he stopped and looked back at his sons. Then, quietly, he broke the dark silence that had followed him. 'Caution, my children. Where everything is going wrong, even a rat will scare a cat.' As he finished saying that, a big yellow three-quarter moon broke out from its hiding place at the edge of the world.

Chapter Three

I

Bugeiga turned in his bed for what must have been a millionth time that night. It must have been nearing the first cockcrow. He tried to scratch himself in between the shoulder blades. He could not reach the exact itchy place. When a man fails to find sleep, even the imaginary fleas and lice make sure they suck him where he will not reach them.

Bugeiga knew that the fleas and lice in Baanuza's bed were imaginary. Baanuza was his second wife. He had found lice in her bed a few seasons after he had married her. Without telling her why, he had skipped her in his rounds for a full phase of the moon. When he went back the lice had gone and, he hoped, for good. That was many harvest seasons back. But this night they appeared most numerous. He knew that they were imaginary but they gave him a hard time nonetheless.

He turned onto his back again and closed his heavy eyelids. He was once again on the verge of sleep when, this time, a mosquito passed his ear. It went away and settled somewhere. Hopefully it had settled down to suck his wife's blood and he would escape it. Maliciously he thought of staying motionless so as not to disturb its feeding. As if it could read his malice the mosquito came for him. It settled on his bare shoulder. He hit his shoulder hard with anger and hoped that he had squashed the little sucker.

He turned onto his left side and pulled the big soft skin blanket over his head. He closed his eyes to coax sleep. Instead he saw the cause of his current misery in the black abyss which resulted.

He had slept equally badly the previous night.

He had got up in the morning determined to go and look at the two bulls together. He had hoped to find some consolation like Rusiina being a better bull in some other way. He had gone down to the watering place. He had come away most disappointed.

Ruhogo was certainly a much better bull. Bigger, more muscular, more majestic, a few years younger and even cleaner. When Ruhogo bellowed as it got to the watering place, only young bulls replied. They were not challenging it but imitating it, learning from it.

He had followed the herds to the resting place and spent some time comparing the two bulls. His Rusiina had become completely cowed. He had gone home struggling to hide his anger and frustration with difficulty. He

13

had found himself losing his temper with everybody at home for no particular reason.

Fortunately his stepbrother's son had come by with a message that morning. Bugeiga was to go by sometime that evening. He already knew why. His brother's young wife was pregnant with her first baby. She had brewed for her in-laws, not quite but almost to celebrate. And if Bugeiga knew his brothers well, her husband had to skin a goat to go with the booze. But being who he was, Bugeiga could not get there early.

Anyhow, the day had been a very bad one. Miserably he hung his mongoose skin pouch on his shoulder. There was his tobacco smoking pipe. The other things inside were known only to himself. He collected his matchet and staff and set off for his brother's compound four compounds away. When he got to the gate he stopped for a brief moment. His eyes went to the area on the inner side of the fence where a strong family talisman was buried. In his heart he prayed for his family. Then he looked up at the sun. This time he mumbled the words, 'Kazooba Nyamuhanga'. In his heart again, he prayed quietly for the family and himself. The sun was god the creator, the most powerful god.

He had taken the longest route. On the way he had attempted to analyse himself. He, Bugeiga, rich, lucky with his three wives, and strong sons many of whom were promising to be great on their own. How could his peace be disturbed by a mere bull, belonging only to those Bajura? No, he had to do something about it.

'But how can such a small weak clan own such a strong powerful bull?' he asked himself loudly. 'And where has it been all this time anyway?' Maybe it was the turn of rats to chase cats, after all.

II

At his stepbrother's place Bugeiga was welcomed in the big way he deserved. Many of his brothers were there. There were also a few cousins and brothers-in-law. They were all sitting outside the young wife's house in a big semi-circle. In the middle stood a large wide-mouthed pot. It was half full of fresh frothy booze. A number of long drinking tubes stood in the pot. He did not greet all the men one by one. He was too moody for that.

One of the young cousins, one who became easily drunk, had felt deprived of the women. Just before Bugeiga arrived he had sent for his wife. She had left the other women who were drinking the dregs indoors and was now kneeling at his side. He put the tube between her two hands. She drank deep from the pot.

Bugeiga was aware of the genial conversation, laughing, joking and serious talk. He had not followed much of it until someone had mentioned the bull fight.

'Did I hear that a bull from the ridges across fought with Rusiina?' Mboneko asked. He was a younger stepbrother to Bugeiga's father. So he was Bugeiga's younger father.

'Yee,' suddenly everybody answered. Each one was trying to contribute something to the discussion all at once. They had all heard about the fight. Bugeiga did not say anything. He wondered whether any of them had spent a sleepless night thinking about the fight.

'That bull, Ruhogo, has been growing very rapidly. It is not yet six full moons since it started bellowing like a proper bull. But already it is the finest bull that has grazed in all the ridges of Nyabigyi and around in our time,' Kalebya said.

'But, Kalebya, you have been here barely thirty years. How do you know what went on in our time before you were born?' an older uncle asked.

'How do I know anything that happened before I was born?' Kalebya retorted. He was not a Mugyirakwe but he was Bugeiga's cousin. 'If you tell me that there once was a better bull at some time in your life, I will know so. If you tell me that there never was, I will know so too. But so far everybody I have heard talk about it says there never was a better one.'

'I hear that bull originated from our clan,' another old uncle said. 'Do you remember that cow Kahogo, which was paid as part of the price for my brother's fourth wife many, many years ago?'

'Eee,' the old ones answered in unison. They remembered the cow clearly.

'It is the grandmother of the father of this bull.'

'No wonder it is so good,' the older uncle said. 'I do not think that they could have such a bull produced in their herds. And for that matter, how could they have anything else to compete with what we have?'

'I do not agree there,' Busaahu said in his calm old voice. 'Why do we not have the same number of wives from each of the other clans around?' He paused a little for effect. 'You also forget their medicine men and their gods. That Migayo is certainly the strongest medicine man in all the countries around. People come from far and wide to consult him. I think it is simply a progressive clan.'

'That bit about Migayo is true enough. Maybe he has given his brother's bull a potent drug to …'

'Could be,' the older uncle quickly interjected. 'I would not put anything beyond those Bajura. If we are not careful, they may soon attempt to dislodge us from these ridges.'

'Yes.' Bugeiga spoke for the first time, shaking his head. 'These things spell doom. I suggest we take some action as a precaution. I say that this small clan is advancing too fast. We should curb them when they are still far. Our forefathers said that "a tree is only easily bent when it is still young."'

'What kind of action can we take? And precaution against what?' Busaahu said. 'No, children of my father and you, sons of my brothers, we are not cocks or dogs which try to pick a quarrel at the slightest chance, even when there is no provocation. You do not take precautions by provoking. And if any Mugirakwe pokes a finger in the eye of a Mujura just because bulls fought, then the gods will judge. He will have "planted millet on his own shin" and it will be him to weed the millet.' He stopped and looked at the many eyes looking at him attentively. 'The fool who persistently refused advice, "I will not be told", attempted to cross a lake in a canoe made out of clay.'

'But,' Bugeiga persisted, 'Do you not think that they will give us trouble?'

'Why? And how do you know that they will start anything?' Busaahu asked more vehemently. 'Will any of you put himself in the place of Kazooba Nyamuhanga who creates and gives all? Will any of you do his work for him and direct his wishes?' He stopped and glared around. 'If anybody is going to oppose the wishes of the gods let him do so on his own as an individual. Let him not involve the clan. This case is very straightforward. Those of us who see doom in this are the ones who are going to bring doom on us. Even the blind can see this. As our fathers said, "If you really wish for a bad smell you use somebody's buttocks for your pillow. Particularly after he has eaten a lot of beans."'

After delivering his advice the old Busaahu seized a tube and concentrated on drinking. He was a very respected old man. He was the oldest Mugirakwe in all the ridges around but he could still throw the spear a very long way. And very few would challenge him at shooting with a bow. And although he was very old, he would not stay at home if the other men went to war. He was Bugeiga's older young father. He was the second son of Rwabugyirakwe's third wife.

The tube coughed in the big pot. The beer had reached the bottom. A young man from the home quickly went into the house of the hostess. Soon he came out staggering under the weight of another pot. Talk stopped while he poured the thick frothy *muramba* into the bigger wide-mouthed pot.

Talking resumed on a less heated tone. They continued to talk about the fight for some time. Most of them saw nothing in it. Quite a few opposed Bugeiga openly about doing anything about it. He was personally determined though. For consolation he decided to drink a lot. He had sucked longer every time the tube came to him. But soon he realised that the more he drank the more he became depressed. Even the roasted meat did not improve his state of mind.

He left as soon as the moon broke out from its hiding place. The night was still very young. Under normal conditions he would have started to enjoy the drink and the togetherness. As it was, the women had just started dancing. The men would soon join the women and real fun would start.

Walking home, he decided to go it alone. He would, somehow, have to hit at the source of his misery. When he got home he went straight to his second wife's house.

III

Sleeping with Baanuza had always soothed him. Whenever he went to her bed depressed, she would soon get him out of it. But tonight it had not worked. She had understood his mood. Right away she had set out to calm him. She had tried hard; indeed she must have gone beyond her previous best. And when he had lain motionless for some time, she had believed him to be asleep. She had just started falling off to sleep when he started turning round. Not wanting to embarrass him she pretended to be asleep herself. But his turning went on and on endlessly. Several times he mumbled a curse. Then he sighed long and deep and Baanuza realised that she had to try another tactic.

'You have not slept at all, my lord. What is bothering you so much?' she enquired quietly and gently.

He sighed deeply again before he answered. 'If it was only bothering me I would not fail to find sleep. It is graver than that. Most unfortunately my brothers and clansmen do not see it.'

'My lord, I know I am only a woman. But if I may say anything, I would say that you stick with your clansmen. Take their advice and do what they say. They are your lifeblood. You know how much importance you have always attached to that.'

'You are also siding with them, eh? I was forgetting that the Bajura are your mothers.' He sounded genuinely hurt.

'Not so, my lord. You know that I would stand by you in any difficulty.' Her mother was a Mujura of the Ruteeramareingwa sub-clan.

'Would you?'

'But of course yes, and you know I would, my lord. You are my father, my mother, my brother, my sister, my uncle, my everything. You are my husband.'

Bugeiga sighed again, but this time with relief. 'Then stay by me my sweet Baanuza. I do not know what, but I am going to do something.'

'Be careful, my lord. And may Kazooba Nyamuhanga protect and guide you.'

Thus comforted he was soon feeling drowsy. Later, in semi-sleep, he could vaguely hear one of his cousins singing drunkenly on his way home. He was going to the next ridge, Kaabya. A big family of the Baamungwe clan lived there. His mother, like many other wives to the Baamungwe, came from the Bagirakwe.

Bugeiga tried to listen to everything he sang and said. Here, he recited a chain of funny rhymes. There he abused an in-law, regardless of whether her husband was in the house or not, for having refused to open for him some time back. There he called an uncle and informed him that he was passing on his way home and asked whether he had abused him. There he abused a dog which barked at him unwarrantedly. And right through the valley he continued, not stopping at all. Fortunately there was a big moon. Not that it would have mattered to him if it was dark.

Somewhere far off in the rocky hilltops a leopard roared. A dog nearby barked timidly. It ran to stay closer to its owner's door in case the leopard came that way. On the ridge across, the drunken cousin could be heard singing even louder, undeterred by the leopard in the hills.

Bugeiga in a deep daze wondered why the man had decided to go all the way to Kaabya. Certainly, anybody around would have given him a bed. If anything happened to him, like if that leopard killed him, which was not unlikely, then the Bagirakwe would be blamed. Then, just before he fell completely asleep, he recalled that the Baamungwe and the leopard belonged to the same clan. Leopards would never attack the Baamungwe. If a leopard made a mistake and showed signs of attacking a human clansman, then the man would use the passwords *ndi mungwe*, I am a leopards man. Then the leopard would escort him all the way home to make sure he got there safely. To show his gratitude, the man would give the leopard a present of a small goat.

Chapter Four

I

Nyabigyi was very big. It occupied the whole of that cold mountainous region at the heart of Rukiga. Indeed, Nyabigyi was the heart of Rukiga. To walk from one end to the other end of Nyabigyi, you would start at cockcrow and arrive with sunset. Walking the full length of Rukiga would take not less than five days taking the straightest route possible.

Many clans of Bakiga lived together not quite in disharmony. One clan occupied these two ridges. The next three would be occupied by another. Across the valley there would be yet another clan; and the same clan would be found occupying another ridge some ten ridges away. It all depended on who staked the first claim, on which place in the long past. Sometimes people left such places, more often than not unwillingly.

All clans in an area shared many things communally, apart from cultivable land. These included water, paths, grazing areas and all social recreational grounds. Nyabigyi was becoming thickly populated. Some extended families owned as much as a whole ridge. But individual men in the family did not have enough land for themselves and to give to their many sons. And these sons would also have to apportion their land to their sons. Some people, therefore, would have to migrate to distant places. Land was therefore a major source of disagreements even among brothers. One would spear a neighbour for using as much as two strides of his land.

Rukiga was surrounded by wilderness, jungle and forest for long distances in most directions. Beyond that in the direction from which the sun greeted Nyabigyi, there was Mpororo. Beyond the lakes lived the Banyambo, Banyarwanda and Batwa. The Bakiga have always wondered whether the Banyarwanda were the ancestors of Batwa or the other way around. In the direction of sunset was Rwangaminyeeto, which meant hater of youth. Between there and Mpororo lay Butumbi, which meant place of the dead. Both these two countries were very severe, with many hostile spirits, gods and witches. Indeed if any families migrated to these places without the backing of equally powerful spirits, gods and medicine men, they would soon realise their folly. In less than one moon there would not be enough members left in a family to make the trip back. And beyond these two was an even worse place, Kyangwe kya Mbiribiri.

Kyangwe kya Mbiribiri, that distant place of witches, lay far beyond Rwangaminyeeto. Indeed it started from the other side of the salt lakes and

Rwitanzigye, the lake which cannot be crossed even by locusts. People there have managed to tame thunderbolts and bring them to their land. They are readily available to the people in case one wants to send one on an errand, like striking an enemy. Passing through, you would see some people chasing them out of their gardens. However, it is very difficult to find anybody who has been there. But, true enough, if you looked in that direction on a cloudless evening, you would see many cubs of thunderbolts playing in the lower skies, just above the horizon. Looking at them you would think that they were numerous small lightnings. The edge of the world is just beyond Kyangwe kya Mbiribiri.

All these places are very far away from Nyabigyi. It would take many days to make the journey. But it was not unusual for people from Nyabigyi to go to those countries around them and vice versa. A number of brave men would of course be needed to make the trip. There were many wild animals and hostile tribes on the way. Even the bravest people would reinforce themselves with powerful talismans. There were too many dangers on the way for anybody to feel completely secure.

For many different reasons families from Nyabigyi had migrated to these places. Some went looking for adventure. Others hoped for more and more fertile land. Yet others had actually been disowned by the clan for a serious crime they had committed. These had to go far away to a place where they were not known at all. Others still would go because of some war with another clan. The defeated clan would have to migrate. Some of these people got to the new places and prospered. These would invite their friends and relatives to join them and try their luck. And hence the not uncommon traffic between these places.

II

Ruteeramareingwa sat just outside his gate, *heirembo*, relaxing. His equals called him Ruteera for short. He had had a hard day in the garden with his youngest and fourth wife. He was sitting in the shade of the huge kitooma tree. This tree was a characteristic feature of the long established homes. It was in the mid-afternoon. The sun was at its hottest and it was the hot season soon after the harvest. His son, Kubiriba, found him there. He was coming from the cattle watering place. He was the second wife's fourth child.

'Have you spent the day well, taata?' the young man asked meekly, coming closer.

'Yeego,' the father answered suspiciously. Normally his son would have gone on to the inner compound. 'Other news?' he asked.

Kubiriba did not answer right away. He sat on a big stone nearest to where his father sat, in the shade. He looked up at his father and looked down again.

He did not know quite how to start. He was still disposed to be shy when he talked to his father.

'What is it?' the father asked encouragingly. 'Is there something disturbing you?'

The young man cleared his throat and looked up at his father again. 'It is …' he started. The lump which had lodged itself in his throat stopped him. This time he coughed hard and dislodged it. 'It is Rwecurenga.'

'Which Rwecurenga?'

'Bugeiga's son, the last born to his first wife.'

The father looked at the son with a furrowed forehead. Rwecurenga was certainly known as a good boy around. But he was Bugeiga's son. Right away, the bull fight he had forgotten came to his mind. But he dismissed it as nothing. 'What did Rwecurenga do?'

'We had just finished watering the cattle. He called me aside and told me troubling news.'

'That what?' The father was evidently worried now.

'That his father is planning to do something to us.'

'What could Bugeiga do to us? He is our relative. His second wife is my sister's daughter.'

'He says it is because Ruhogo fought and beat his bull, down by the watering place.'

The fight he had just dismissed as nothing came back to his mind. It was just over a week after the fight. In his household, and indeed among the Bajura, the fight had not caused ripples. It was not even a topic worthy of any discussion. As a matter of fact, Ruteera had not heard it from his own home but from some old man who had heard about how Bugeiga felt about the fight from the Bagirakwe. He had in passing asked Ruteera what he knew about the issue. Finding that Ruteera knew nothing about it, he had gone on to tell him. That is how he came to know that there had been a fight. And he had forgotten about it almost right away. The fight did not deserve to rouse the feelings and thoughts of a respectable old gentleman.

But now the situation had changed. What was happening to the world? Surely a man of Bugeiga's standing and wealth could not mar his position just because two bulls had fought? People had always seen bulls fight. All other household animals fought; even men, women and children did fight. So, what was so exciting about bulls fighting? Only Bugeiga had seen anything in it. To all other clans, including Bugeiga's own clan, the Bagirakwe, it was looked upon like the normal thing that it was.

'Why did he tell you?' Ruteera asked, sounding rather distant. 'Was he sent to pass on the message to you?

'No. He overheard his father talking about it. He also says that his father had discussed it with his older sons before. That they had tried to make him see that it was a normal thing. But he says he wonders whether they succeeded at all. So he is planning to do something about it alone if possible. So, when Rwecurenga overheard him saying so, he thought he should warn us.'

Ruteera considered this news briefly. Then he shook his head in wonderment. The world was getting confused. 'All right, son, you have done very well to tell me about it. Kazooba Nyamuhanga will help us.' Kubiriba moved on to the inner compound.

Ruteeramareingwa, left alone now, wondered about Bugeiga. Would he, Bugeiga, want to live alone, isolated? No, it was not possible. Different clans have always lived together in all the regions of Rukiga and the countries around. No clan could ever live by itself. Where otherwise would they get wives from? No man ever married a woman from his own clan. Even if they were generations and generations apart, they were still brother and sister. Nor could a boy lust for a girl of his clan and vice versa. This sin would be punished by exiling the offender, after other and more painful punishments they would be forced to leave the clan. In this way marriages brought about interclan relationships. And it was in that way that Ruteeramareingwa was Bugeiga's father-in-law. Any wonder then that Ruteeramareingwa sat outside his gate, worrying about the disturbing news his son had just brought him?

III

He was still sitting in the same place an hour later. Two old men had just joined him. They had been passing by, coming from watching the cattle being watered. Seeing him sitting out there they had come to chat with him. The old men went to sit on the big logs lying around and planted their staffs in the ground. They refused his offer of more comfortable stools. They were not going to stay long. He called a young daughter who was near.

'You go and tell your mother to bring for these men some little water to wet their throats. They must be dying of thirst.'

She ran into her mother's house, the third wife's. She is young but good, he reflected. If he still knew how to tell, she would make some young man a good and dutiful wife, and not in the far-off future.

Soon the young girl came back with a calabash of water. She had not told Keshakama, her mother, because she knew where to get the drinking water from. Seeing it to be plain water, the father reacted before she handed the water to the elders.

'Did your mother give you that water to bring?' he asked, not too harshly.

'No, taata, I got it from the pot myself.'

'I meant the water with flour in it, you girl. That is why I told you to go and tell your mother.' He choked on a teasing laugh. He was not exactly rebuking her. 'Do you think that I do not know where to get plain drinking water from in your mother's house?' The young girl gaped with big eyes. Her father's message was getting to her.

One old man rescued the young girl, against Ruteera's objections. 'Give me that calabash,' he said grabbing the vessel. 'Water is the best for quenching this type of thirst.' So saying, he tilted the calabash and poured the cooling water into his mouth. The other old man also reached for the calabash and drank.

'Away with your water, girl,' Ruteera barked at the girl teasingly. 'Do you think we are frogs to drink water? Go and tell your mother quickly.'

The girl ran off with the half-full calabash. She was laughing at her father. She had won over the water. Even the two elders had agreed that water was better for thirst. The elders joined in and laughed with the disappearing girl.

'She will grow into a good woman,' one elder said.

'So you say! You do not know how much of stupidity is in that head of hers,' her father objected. He knew that this was unfair to the girl. But he could not join the public in praising his own children.

'You are too harsh, Ruteera my friend. Do you know that you can kill a child's spirit of initiative by disapproving of everything he does?'

'Do you mean to tell me that I should approve of everything they do? Even if they bring plain water to serve to visitors?'

'By no means,' the other elder said. 'But at least try to give credit where it is due, as often as possible. This girl of yours is young. You should not have disapproved of her water so strongly.'

'Here she comes again,' the father said, glad to change the topic. He knew they were right, but he did not want to give in to them so easily. 'I hope she has brought the right thing this time.'

It was the right thing. She had a big calabash full of *bushera*. It had been brewed some three days back from sorghum flour and had a sweet strong taste. It was not quite intoxicating and it was not meant to be. But it had quite a kick. One felt it as it settled comfortably in the stomach.

With the girl gone again the elders resumed their general conversation. Conveniently enough there had been this talk about the bull fight. The older of the two men, Zikanga, brought it into discussion.

'That is a very fine bull you have there, son of my mother. Very few of that fineness have roamed the earth.'

'Yes, indeed,' the other elder remarked. 'We have just been looking at it.' Ruteera looked at the ground between his legs. Ruhogo's fineness was the cause of his troubling thoughts and anxiety.

'I wish it was half as fine. Then I would not be in such a troubled state.' He looked down again. The elders let him thrash it out with his inner self before commenting. 'Providence is an over-exacting benefactor,' he resumed thoughtfully, 'He gives you your portion of luck. But he makes sure that the amount of headache that comes with it is in direct proportion to the luck.'

'It is funny, indeed,' the other elder said, 'but he provides a proportionate way of finding a cure for the headaches.'

'True enough,' Ruteera persisted. 'But sometimes the headache is out of proportion to the luck that caused it.'

'Maybe,' Zikanga observed. 'But never incurable in one way or another. Have you, for instance, ever heard of an elephant growing such big tusks that it could not carry them?' He looked at Ruteera quizzically.

'Never at all, son of my father. But this bull of mine might turn out to be a bit "too big tusks" for this elephant to carry,' Ruteera completed, poking an index finger at his chest. They all laughed.

'Take it easy, friend, it will not be. Bugeiga's meditations will bring him to no good end.'

'You do not know that I have just received a message from across there, this afternoon, do you?' They did not. So he told them the full message as his son had given it to him.

'Tsu-tsu-tsu,' Zikanga started shaking his head. 'This Bugeiga and his conceit and bad intentions! Maybe he thinks that he is made out of special human materials.'

'His heart is as black as he. It is like the soot scraped off a cooking pot,' the elders agreed. 'One of these days his makers will desert him. You cannot abuse the generosity of the gods and expect them to shut their eyes against your evil deeds for ever.'

'You can all talk,' Ruteera put in. 'It is not your headache. As we say, "a spectator at a wrestling challenge told his friend to throw his challenger quickly so that they could go." Bugeiga could be thinking of doing something beyond all our imaginations right now.'

'What can he do?'

'And indeed what can he not do? And do you know that whatever he does, I have to answer back?'

'That is right. But we hope that you will not hesitate to call upon the elders at once,' Zikanga persisted.

'I certainly will. But you know Bugeiga well. Once his dirty mind sets him out to do something, he will not stop short of total war until he has achieved his end. And you know what that would mean to me and my family.'

'Oh, but time for such wars is past and gone for good,' Zikanga said.

'Not according to what I heard from one Mugirakwe,' the other elder objected. 'I have been thinking that it is all a joke. But with that Bugeiga you can never be very sure.'

'And if such a war resulted from this, I would have to flee, with my clansmen, because they would have fought on my side. We would be forced to leave behind everything we have built. And, of course, we could not abandon our ancestors' graves without doing our best to defend them.' Ruteeramareingwa thought about such a possibility with bitterness.

These other old men belonged to different clans. Through marriages, they were related to both Bugeiga's and Ruteera's clans in some way. But they would not take part in any war between the two. Unless they wanted to involve their clans in a feud that was not theirs.

'May it be cursed,' Zikanga roared with anger. 'How can the unreasonableness and bad manners of one person be allowed to affect a different and innocent clan? The time has come when different clans should live together in any place in much better harmony. We are one people. Why should we eat each other all the time as if we were grasshoppers?' He gnashed his teeth.

'Those brainless creatures start devouring each other the moment you put them in a gourd. They do not know each other, even if they are related. But we do know each other.' He looked up at Ruteera's face. He stretched out his hand and touched him on the shoulder. 'Take heart, son of my father. Things will turn out well.'

So saying, the two elders got up and collected their staffs. They adjusted their goat skins and pouches.

'Tell the mother of your children,' the other elder said, 'that her bushera was very well prepared. We have liked it very much. But it would have been even better, had we drunk it looking at her beautiful face with the big smiling eyes.' They laughed heartily as they moved towards the main gate. Ruteera saw them off. He left them at the gate, which opened out to the thoroughfare.

Ruteera's third wife was decidedly the most beautiful of the four. Keshakama had been a village star at the time he married her. Even today, after producing five children, many men would gladly pay as many cows as Ruteera had paid for her. And, unlike most other beautiful women, she was not conceited; and she could really dig. Her children had never known a hungry day.

Ruteera was fully deserving of her. At over fifty-five years, he was still quite a handsome man. When he married her he had been much younger and more handsome. He was a broad-chested man of average height. His soil-brown face was starting to wrinkle on the sides of the mouth. The long pointed nose was well proportioned in relation to his longish face. He could touch the tip of his nose with the tip of his tongue. He very rarely quarrelled with anybody. His neighbours respected him for his rationality.

He was in deep thoughts when he came back from seeing off his friends. They had heartened him to some extent. But he could feel some general uneasiness in his bones. They could all do nothing if Bugeiga was really determined and meant to do something.

He started thinking about Nyabigyi again. Like everywhere else, many clans had always lived there together, peacefully. But it was not unknown for something smaller even than a land dispute to start grave disharmony. It could even lead to bloodshed. Like this recent bull fight! Who could believe that such an ignorable incident might lead Nyabigyi into a tragic catastrophe? Certainly not Ruteeramareingwa.

He decided to go into the garden. There was always something to do in his many gardens. If he stayed idle in one place, he would think too much about this issue. That would not do him any good.

Chapter Five

I

It was early morning almost two full moons since the bull fight. Everybody had already forgotten it. Nothing bad had come out of it after all. Apparently, Bugeiga had come to his senses in the end. Or so people thought. They did not know that Migayo, the powerful Mufumu, had spent almost a full day consulting with the clan's Nyabingyi. The next day he and his brother Ruteeramareingwa had offered two separate huge sacrifices to the gods. One went to all the gods, but a special one went to the Nyabingyi of the clan. Among other things, this included a large he-goat which was slaughtered in the shrine in one corner of Migayo's compound and a large pot of beer. These were left in the shrine for the gods and ancestors of the clan to feast on at leisure. Calmness and the threatened harmony had returned to Nyabigyi.

The morning was very cold, misty and quiet. The sun would not be breaking through the fog for some time. The lazy women would not be going to their gardens until then. Many would not bother to go at all. It was coming to the end of the dry season. But this place was so endowed that the dry season was actually not dry. It only had much less rain than the other seasons. As a matter of fact, it was the ideal time for planting sweet potatoes. It had to be done now, because as soon as the rains started in earnest, women would not have the time. That was the time to plant beans and maize in the fields from which they had harvested sorghum. After that there would be so much weeding that the women would have time for nothing else. And sweet potatoes are a very important crop to people. To a family which does not have gardens of these, each ready within about a moon of another, famine is almost a certainty.

Keshakama, Ruteeramareingwa's third wife, had woken up very early. She was planting this year's potatoes on their contour patch up in the hills. She was glad that she had a daughter who was old enough to help her. Otherwise she would not have managed the burden this morning and many other mornings like it.

As it was, she was heavily loaded as she went to the field. Her first son had remained at home. He would be going to graze the family's goats with a boy from another house. Her daughter, the one who had brought water for the elders, carried the youngest baby. This one was just under one year. Her third child, a boy, was old enough to walk on his own. He even carried his own small hoe. The mother was heavy again, pregnant with yet another child. On her head she carried a big basket. This contained the food they would eat in the field. Three hoes and a matchet tied in a bundle were strapped across the mouth of the basket. She pulled three leading goats on long ropes. Some seven more followed behind.

The untied goats kept running into the gardens near the path. Her son, who still lisped with childish speech, went around chasing them out. He never had a moment to rest. He called their names in earnest entreaty, shouted commands at them and hit them with his small hoe whenever he caught up with them. But they could not heed his entreaties.

'You, you will break that goat with that hoe and we shall be sad,' the mother rebuked. He struck another one, a pregnant one this time. It bleated painfully. 'Hey! You will make that goat miscarry. Have you no eyes to see that it is heavy and it will be putting down soon?'

'But maama, why do you not tell thee the goath-t altho to thtop going into the gardenth, if you do not want me to beat them?' the boy asked, running after another goat. Well, he thought, if the goats were not going to listen to him, he was not going to listen to his mother either.

Keshakama had refused to surrender her personal goats to her husband's herd. Her husband's herd belonged to them all: children, four wives and the husband. But these belonged to her and her children only. Of course if her husband required one from her herd he could help himself. They belonged to him. Everything that belonged to a woman belonged to her husband. After all, she also belonged to him in the first place.

When they got to the garden she tied the goats where there was a lot of luxuriant grass for them. Next she prepared a place for the baby in the shade of a tree. It was at the top of the contoured stretch she was working on. She first inspected the area around to make sure that her small son was safe from things like caterpillars and snakes. Even then she had to keep constant watch. Snakes were most numerous at this time of the dry season.

If the baby had not developed any teeth yet, she would not have bothered. No snake can harm a baby who has no teeth. Even if the baby falls on it, even when he is totally unprotected. Before a snake decided to do harm to a baby, it would first rub its tail between his gums. If there were teeth it would bite him. She had smeared him with the snake repellent potion. But all the same the watch was necessary. Some snakes were especially stubborn.

Several times the baby cried from hunger. Then she would use this time to rest while she suckled the baby. Meanwhile, her older children would go to the fire where some sweet potatoes were roasting. These were eaten during the hours before the main lunch. Otherwise, the last two children would be playing under the tree.

At this time, the youngest baby ate a lot of soil. That was good for him. Without eating soil a child cannot grow. The soil we eat when we are young gives us a required connection with the earth. It is an unbreakable bond with the earth, mutual and everlasting. And that is why we get buried in it – to go and join our ancestors living within the protection of the earth's womb.

II

Just before the midday meal a woman friend came by. She came from the same ridge, Nyamiringa. Their husbands, brothers, belonged to the same sub-clan. She was coming from her gardens higher up the hill. She had only gone to inspect her garden to see how the crops were doing.

'You have worked, Keshakama,' the neighbour complimented.

'Yeego,' Keshakama replied with a smile. Her friend was coming nearer to shake her hands in greeting.

'Have you spent the day well?' she greeted.

'Yeego,' Keshakama replied.

'What other news?'

'It is good.'

The friend inspected the stretch that had been dug that morning with admiration. 'Their bows!' she swore, by the bows of her husband's clan. 'So you have dug all this only this morning?' She turned to the children and shook their hands in greeting.

'Yee,' Keshakama replied gently with a wide smile.

'Did you have any help?'

'Yes,' she said gently, pointing at her young daughter and even smaller son. 'I had those two there,' smiling proudly.

'Cho, cho, cho. It is as if you had two women giving you a day.' The friend picked one of the hoes which every woman took to the garden for that purpose. They moved to the bottom of the patch and started again. She would not go until they had got to the top of the contour. It was some twenty strides to the top.

'Your husband and the children are there?' Keshakama asked as they started digging.

'Yeego.'

'How are they?'

'They are well. Except my husband. He is suffering from a swelling in the upper eyelid.'

'Oh! That is bad.'

'The eyelid is so swollen that it cannot open at all.'

'Have you gone across to Kabisha, to see Mboneko the Mugirakwe?' Keshakama advised. 'He is the nearest person who has killed a Munyarwanda.'

'No. But yesterday a woman suckling twins put her milk in his eyes.'

'I know. Most of us use that cure. But if he does not improve, go to see Mboneko.'

'Yes. Actually I meant to go there this afternoon.'

Keshakama remembered taking her daughter to see another man who had killed a Munyarwanda. The child was taken into the house and the door was shut; then she had to put her eye right on the floor. The man came chanting self-praises on how brave he was and how he killed the Munyarwanda. He danced a war dance with his spear. He speared the door in front of where the bad eye was, taking care that the spear did not go through the door. The swelling disappeared overnight.

Naturally, the two women gossiped about many things in the ridges around. But they could not talk very freely. The two children nearby were old enough to hear and understand. So their gossip was restricted within the limits of decency. By and by they got to some more serious topics. And as they talked they subconsciously dug faster and faster.

'Does Bugeiga's son still have an eye on one of your daughters?'

'Which son and which daughter of mine?' Keshakama asked, feigning ignorance. 'Mine is not yet old enough to get married as you can see.'

'You and your pretence,' the friend continued teasingly, casting a sideways glance at Keshakama. 'I mean Rwecurenga and Kenyangyi.' This was Ruteera's second wife's daughter. She followed the boy who followed Kubiriba. She was the sixth child. Rwecurenga had been following her around for quite some time. He loved her. And those who knew her believed that the girl reciprocated this feeling. He always managed to find her in places where he could talk to her. Somehow he always managed to find out where she would be, where there were no elders to prevent some verbal exchange. That was all he wanted for the time being.

'Ah, that one?' Keshakama started. 'She is still very young. Thirteen years is too early. Both of them would outgrow each other's love and break their marriage.'

'But her brother is marrying at a very young age,' her friend observed. 'Why were the two of them not thought too young?'

'That girl is older by more than a full season. And Kubiriba is older than Rwecurenga.' Keshakama was determined to defend her husband's household.

'Supposing that the two young lovers do not change when they grow up. Do you think Ruteera will accept to give his daughter to Bugeiga's son, considering what has been going on?'

'Oh, but that is nothing to my husband. I am sure that he has forgotten everything. After all, nothing came out of Bugeiga's threats. My husband is not a man to keep a feud at heart. When it ends it has ended. So I suppose he would accept.'

'That is good, then. You know,' she looked at her friend pleadingly, 'that boy is going to grow into a very good man. Unfortunately, if the situation could be reversed, and it was Bugeiga's daughter and Ruteera's son, Bugeiga would not consent.'

'Now, look here,' Keshakama attacked with pretended surprise. 'You talk as if you have been asked to impart a message to us. Has the boy sent you to put in a word for him?'

'Certainly not. I am only talking, open-heartedly, about what I know to be true. But I would, willingly, carry a message for him to any girl if he asked me. I would only need to believe that she would make him happy.'

'I see.' Keshakama looked sideways with a smile lingering on her face. She knew she would do the same for most of her husband's sons. 'I was forgetting that you are his aunt.' They laughed loudly, with mutual understanding. Which woman would not like her son to be happily married? Only witches and those who were unhappily married themselves would not wish another's happiness.

'That reminds me,' Keshakama resumed. 'We have visitors the day after tomorrow.'

'Swear!'

'Their bows! And I want you to help us to cook.'

'From where?'

'From Kaabya. They are coming to see the cows.'

'Oh, so Kubiriba is actually bringing home his first wife that soon? I thought it was still some time away.'

'She is coming soon. And a real beauty too.'

'I have heard about it. And do not blame me for wanting to do the same for Rwecurenga.' She fixed an accusing eye on Keshakama. 'You went back to your clan and picked one as beautiful as you and marked her for your stepson.' Keshakama blinked rapidly, almost with guilt. 'You are really lucky, you women of Ruteera's household. The way you help each other!'

'We are lucky, indeed, and happy too.' Her voice became very quiet, almost as if she was talking to herself. 'We are almost like sisters.'

'It is very rare indeed,' her friend commented. 'Not that I am particularly complaining.'

'No, indeed. I should call you a liar if you said that you had any serious problems in your family.'

'Not very serious ones. We only get some to remind us that we are alive. But your husband's home is truly rare,' she persisted. 'In some homes you find the wives eating each other. One wife will set fire to where the other one has passed. In other cases a wife will feed witches' potions to the children of the other, if she gets the chance.'

'Imagine! As if sharing a husband should separate them instead of bringing them together! Anyway,' Keshakama continued proudly, 'we are lucky that our husband is most considerate. I think a good husband would bring harmony in any home, even if there were ten wives.'

'Not if there was a witch among them, even if they were only two.' The two women considered that quietly, briefly.

'No,' Keshakama said between her teeth. 'A witch is a curse. Can you imagine your husband's wife killing off your children one by one, as you produce them?'

'A witch is a curse indeed. The gods of our ancestors were very right to dictate that witches should be burnt alive whenever they were caught.'

'Anyway,' Keshakama confided, 'if witches and match-killers do not interfere, that beauty will be part of our family in one or two full moons' time.'

'Ha, and it is all right for your husband to give his sons wives when they are still young!'

'Yes. He claims that that is the best for them both. If the husband and wife grow up together, they will find it difficult to forsake each other when they are old. They are almost like brother and sister.'

'Thank you for giving me that knowledge,' she said mischievously, 'I will pass it over to my nephew, Rwecurenga.'

The two women got to the top of the contour. Keshakama turned around and admired the large piece she had dug with her friend. 'Thank you very much,' she said, moving towards the shade. 'You have dug a very big piece for me.'

'It is not very big.' She was offered water to wash her hands. Keshakama had also brought out food and a calabash of *bushera*. 'But I am going straight home,' she complained. 'You go on and eat. I will eat at home.'

'And where will it be heard of? How can you leave without eating the food which is already put out?'

'All right. But ...'

'There are no buts.' They washed their hands and fell to it. The young children who had already eaten many roasted potatoes were not particularly hungry. They drank a lot of the *bushera* and ate very little of the food.

III

That day Keshakama got home earlier than usual. She got there before the cattle came home. She had a lot of work to do. This time the big basket she carried was even heavier than it had been in the morning. It contained an assortment of foods. There were greens picked from her garden, potatoes, two pumpkins, and even three giant mushrooms. She also carried a small bundle of firewood, tied together with the three hoes. They were again tied across the mouth of the heavy basket. The two older children went home the way they had come, the son chasing and hitting the goats all the way home.

'Mama,' he asked just before they got home 'a goat which ith alive and dithturbing me and the one which ith in the bowl with thoup, which ith better and thweeter?'

'The one in the bowl with soup.'

'Why then do you not let me kill thith Katobo which dithturbth me motht, and we have it with thoup tonight?' and so saying he bashed a big fat spotted one. Katobo was its name. He rarely managed to catch up with it.

'No, my son.' The mother was amused. 'Your father will work on that.'

'I hope he doth tho thoon. My back teeth are shaking for want of eating meat.'

'No wonder your ears are falling off. They are sore at the back.'

They laughed as the boy dashed through their gate, still bashing at the goats with his small hoe. He stepped on a rope trailing behind a running goat. He staggered dangerously but managed not to fall down, then chased after another goat to give it a bash.

'Eh! Slowly, slowly my child,' Ruteera said to the boy as he staggered. 'Did you not almost fall down?'

'Have you spent the day well?' Keshakama greeted the men as she passed them.

'Yeego,' they answered. She continued to her house to put away what she carried. Then she would come and greet them proudly.

'That boy looks like a sharp one,' Tibeijuka commented.

'He is too quick for my liking. He does everything hurriedly.'

Ruteera sat under the big kitooma tree in the inner compound. He was with Migayo, Tibeijuka, a younger father and Mazima. They had come to help him put final touches to the preparations for the coming feast. They had finished deliberating on the arrangements. They were now relaxing, chit-chatting. They stopped talking when they saw Keshakama coming to them. They did not hide their admiration. She had finished putting away what she had been carrying.

Keshakama knelt beside her husband's younger father and proffered both her arms to him. The old man grabbed the arms and greeted her, caressing them. Next she went to Migayo and Tibeijuka. These were in-laws. She could not offer only arms to them. She offered her open chest and they hugged her most lustfully. Ruteera and his son Mazima looked on, amused. Tibeijuka did not release her immediately after the greeting. He lingered on, caressing her shoulders.

'But you, Tibeijuka,' Migayo rebuked jokingly. 'Where will you end, with lusting for your brother's wives?'

Tibeijuka broke into a song: 'A beautiful woman is that one who is not yours, ye ye ye,' and released her. She hurried off, laughing. All the others laughed good-humouredly. 'A very good woman, Ruteera, son of my father,' he continued. 'How did you always manage to pick the best?'

'He was born lucky,' Migayo commented. 'And his eye was especially keen for good women.'

'You could not be more right,' the younger father said. 'Look at Keirigyirwa! Many men battled for that woman when she was a girl. And Ruteera snatched her from them all. No wonder he called her Keirigyirwa, "the lovable one".'

They all thought of Keirigyirwa. Ruteera's first wife was a beautiful woman. She was almost copper-brown with a thick mat of greying hair on her head. If she took a full month without cutting it, it would defeat her attempts to keep it smart. She was slightly taller than average. She was almost as tall as her husband. Throughout her married life she had been beautifully rounded, with enough flesh to suit her height. But now with old age she was getting fat. She was gentle, impressive but sometimes stubborn. She almost always got her way, whenever she wanted. Neither she nor her husband had ever regretted their marriage. They still enjoyed each other's company very much.

The men continued talking about wives for some time. They talked about the lucky ones and the unfortunate ones.

'Like that Oribariho,' Ruteera said.

'Aha! Yes, that man was really lucky,' Migayo said. 'To inherit that woman.'

'Surely that was so long ago. Has he not had four children with her already?' the younger father rejoined. 'Yet you still talk about her and his luck, as if it was yesterday.'

'But that is only natural. That which is good,' Migayo continued, 'does not stop being talked about.'

'Ah, that woman was really contested. Many in-laws and some older stepsons were trying to win her favour,' Ruteera said. 'One really wonders what Oribariho gave her to get her from all the others.'

'Actually, it was quite easy for him. Let us see! Who were really vying for her?' the younger father started quizzically. 'The deceased actually left no old sons. Those would have had the first right. But since they were too young, the next in line were the first brothers. And who were they?' He stopped as if he expected an answer. None came so he continued. 'Kibande is one. That man started beating his wife the day he married her. They have had many seasons together but he still beats her every other day.' He stopped for that to sink in. 'Then the older brother, he could hardly support the two he already had. And all the others were either equally eligible – second brothers – or even more distant - sons of younger fathers.'

'Yes, actually she made the nearest best choice,' Tibeijuka observed. 'Ha, it is good that our custom allows the woman to have some liberty in choosing the man to inherit her from among the brothers-in-law. And any woman in her position would have made the same choice. Can you imagine such a good woman being inherited by one like that Kibande?'

'But,' Mazima asked, puzzled, 'why didn't Oribariho take the widow's land with her?'

'He is not from the same mother,' the younger father answered, matter-of-factly.

'But he paid no bride price,' said Mazima.

'Of course he paid no bride price,' the younger father continued. 'He and his brother had the same father and he had already paid the cows for the bride price for the first marriage. Another bride price would only have been paid if Oribariho belonged to another father altogether. And even then, the bride price would have been paid to the brothers of the deceased, not to the widow's family.'

'So then if the land she brought with her originally belonged to the husband's father, not to the husband, why could it not pass to Oribariho?' asked Mazima.

'Because it belonged to a different house already,' said Ruteera. 'The father had allocated it to the dead brother's mother's house. Oribariho had a different mother, remember. The land could not change houses. That cannot be. It would be a sure way of bringing hatred between the houses. The only case when it can happen without turning son against father is if the wife is divorced or dies, leaving no sons.'

'But surely, considering that Oribariho had his brother's children, including a son to look after, he should have taken at least a portion to help him feed the children! Now where will the deceased's sons get land from?'

'Oh, yes. That is the point. Strictly, that land does belong to the sons. As you are all aware, women cannot inherit land. But in the long past, whoever inherited the woman would inherit the land also if she had a son, even if he was from outside. It was hoped that the man would give the land to the rightful owners, the sons of the brother. But some men turned around and either gave them a very small portion or none at all. So the elders intervened.

'The first brother of the deceased, together with their mother, now takes back the land. If the brother left no son, they share it. If he left young sons, then the mother and the first brother take it as caretakers.'

'So in Oribariho's case the land goes to Kibande and his mother,' said Mazima. 'I hope they act correctly.'

'In a case like this, if anyone tries to swindle the sons, then the stepfather helps them through the right channels, the elders.'

'But our custom is really good,' Tibeijuka observed. 'I heard that in Kongwe and Kyangwe kya Mbiribiri, such a widow may leave home and go to be married elsewhere, even in another clan.'

'Those people's ways of life are all crooked,' Migayo retorted. 'All they know is medicine and witchcraft and nothing else.'

'That really sounds crooked,' Tibeijuka continued. 'When you marry a wife, does she not belong to the clan?'

'Yes,' the others agreed.

'Then why should she leave, as if the man left no brothers behind to keep her in the family?'

'But even here they sometimes leave,' Mazima observed.

'That is very rare,' the younger father explained. 'But they have to be a very special case, like witches, very lazy or just very bad women. They would have been divorced by their husband if the husband had lived. And anyway, they do not leave with any children who might be inheritors. So they soon know their stand. They realise that they are rejected by the clan.'

'What happens to a deceased's wife while all the discussions are going on?' asked Mazima. 'Who looks after her and her family?'

'Young widows receive special attention,' said Tibeijuka. 'Their in-laws make sure that they miss practically nothing, apart from the physical presence of their husbands. Everybody trying to win a widow's favour tries hard to outperform the other brothers. And this continues until she makes up her mind who she will take. And then the others accept her choice.

'In most cases the whole process is difficult. But sometimes it is very easy. A very old man may have many wives, several of whom are young. Certainly, even before he dies, some of his older sons or his much younger brothers may already be visiting the younger wives secretly. When such a man dies, they start visiting the widow openly. But, although no rule is laid down, only the sons who are already married may inherit their father's young wives. And an old widow does not get inherited. She stays alone.'

The old men left just before it became dark. They wanted to get home before their cattle came home. Ruteera walked them to the main thoroughfare outside his gate. He waited outside until his own cattle had returned.

That bride price would leave a noticeable dent in his herd. They would be picking ten cows. He looked them over again. He had to decide which ones he would take away to hide.

Chapter Six

I

All Ruteeramareingwa's wives had been busy for days. What with all the cleaning and redecorating to do! The children had made countless trips to the communal chalk pit and the special red-soil pit. The dull white and red patterns were shining now. Neat red patterns were made on the walls against the new white background. The whole compound really looked smart. Most important, there was all the cooking to prepare for. And the preparations had to be done now. Many baskets of millet and sorghum had to be ground.

The feast of selecting cows for Kubiriba's bride price was very demanding indeed. They had to impress upon their new in-laws that their daughter was coming to a family which could manage itself, plus any additional visitors, however many might arrive. They had to put so much food in front of their in-laws that they could not finish it. The in-laws would also bring the heaviest eaters in their clan to make sure that they finished the food put before them. They would not be very many now. Not as many as they would be on the day they escorted the girl to her new home. But if they remembered how much food was put before them when Ruteera was marrying Keshakama, they would come prepared for a real feast. And, of course, there were Ruteera's own relatives who would come to witness the occasion. They had to be fed and boozed.

By mid-morning on the appointed day all the women were very busy cooking. They had even invited their friends to come and help them. Many pots were on the fire, in temporary sheds put up for the purpose. Many more still would be put on the fire when the visitors arrived. That would be around the time when the sun was directly overhead. Three big goats had been skinned.

Ruteeramareingwa and a few elders sat in the shade of a big kitooda tree, in the centre of his compound. It was in the place where he had built his first small house, preparatory to marrying his first wife. Keirigyirwa. These were his immediate uncles and brothers. They all wore their smartest goats skins. More younger fathers, uncles and brothers were expected. They had to be present to witness the occasion. A man could not do anything important without calling his brothers to witness it. And a marriage contract was one of the most important.

Ruteera and his brothers had already performed one small duty that morning. They had removed some twelve of his best cows from the small herd and hidden them among his brothers' herds. They had brought back some weaker ones to maintain the herd's numbers.

38

This could not be called cheating or unfair play. Everybody in the situation did it. The in-laws were given a free hand to pick the best cows from the herd. And no man could stand by and see ten or so of the best cows in his herd taken away. Not if he could avoid it. With the bulls it was different. They could not choose the best. That would be like taking a man from his home, and leaving all his wives with no man to provide for and rule over them.

One elder rummaged for a smoking pipe from his spotted wild-cat skin pouch. He followed it with a fist-sized lump of tobacco. It was wrapped in dry banana fibres. He filled the big bowl slowly. He knew he would not smoke this fill alone. He called Ruteera's young grandson who was lurking around and handed him the pipe. The brothers had been talking about recent marriages.

'A son of our daughter also married recently,' Tibeijuka said. He was some ten years younger than Ruteera.

'Which one?' someone murmured. There were hundreds of sons of their daughters.

'This daughter of ours,' Tibeijuka resumed hesitantly. 'Daughter of these brothers of ours from Kyamugaga?'

'Oh, the one who got married to Karuhize?' the owner of the pipe said, taking it from the young boy. The small boy had come puffing at it rapidly to stop the fire from dying. He was still too young to smoke a pipe. But he could light pipes for the elders and continue puffing until they caught properly. That could not be called smoking a pipe.

'Yes, that one,' he continued. 'But the way in which he got his wife was most interesting.'

'Ehe, what happened?' Migayo the medicine man asked.

'He tried to marry her in the traditional way but when his uncles went to woo, her parents refused. He even attempted to steal her but failed.'

'Why?' Ruteera asked. 'Did he not have enough cows for the bride price?'

'He had. And in fact they were well off.'

'Then what was the problem?' Ruteera insisted, unable to understand.

'They said there was a feud involving the house of a close brother of Karuhize's and a close brother of the girl's father. Apparently, a daughter of theirs who had been married to the Baamugyesera had died during childbirth. They later claimed that she had been bewitched. And that the wife of this close brother of Karuhize's had done the bewitching.'

'But that was easy to confirm,' claimed Migayo, whose medicinal and divining powers were known about everywhere. 'Did they not bring a medicine man to make her talk in her sleep?'

'They did but she denied knowledge of any witchcraft.'

'Then she was innocent,' Migayo rejoined, amid general assent, 'unless the medicine man employed was a charlatan.'

'And what did the midwife say?'

'That it was witchcraft.' He stopped and looked around. 'You see, the child brought the side first and, though she did all she could, with all her knowledge, the midwife could not make the child come straight. Later, she said that someone did not want that wife to produce at all.'

They all agreed that this was a result of witchcraft indeed. All such cases were attributed to witchcraft. Why otherwise do all other children come head first and yet some few choose to come side first, and even legs first? And in many such cases the midwife manages to straigthen things out and deliver the child safely. How does one, then, explain those few cases where the midwife, with her expertise and medicines, fails to deliver the baby?

'Yes, indeed,' another elder retorted, 'that was the result of witchcraft. They only picked on the wrong person. Why did they pick on her, anyway?'

'She had failed to produce herself. And the two were not friends. They had always quarrelled.'

'That is the problem. Nobody is ever believed to have died a natural death. Whatever the circumstances, we say that he has been bewitched. Then we start looking for the bewitcher.'

'That is true, son of my father,' another old man put in. 'How otherwise does one die? Even the very bad spirits will not pick a victim at random. They will have to be directed to you by your enemies or, at least, your evil deeds.'

'So how did he marry her in the end?' Ruteera asked.

'That is the interesting part of it. Karuhize's real brother is a blood-friend of the brother of the girl's father.' The elders nodded their heads, starting to see it. 'You know, after they cut each other on the stomach, mingle the blood which they collected and drink it, they take oaths which, naturally, are broken only by death.'

'Or very involved and expensive cleansing rites,' Migayo put in.

'And so?' someone asked impatiently.

'Karuhize called his brother. They went to his blood-friend and importuned him to help. To cut a long story short, they gathered eight good cows and twelve goats. Led by the two blood-friends, they camped at the gate of the girl's father, uninvited.'

'That is very interesting indeed.'

'Yes. They tried to chase them away but they refused to leave. For four days they refused even to eat, unless they were called in to eat food provided by the home.'

'That was very tricky,' an old man observed. 'The girl's family could not send them away by force because the blood would hound them. They could not call them home because then they would enter with their cows. And once the cows entered, they could not be sent away. They could not refuse them food indefinitely. Again, that blood the two friends drank ...' He shook his head in resignation.

'So for four days they stayed there. Apparently they only smoked their pipes. But at night the friend smuggled food for them to their fireplace. Twice it rained but they stayed in the rain.' He laughed.

'On the fifth day they saw a handful of elders enter the compound through another gate. Their friend assured them that he had talked to two of these elders on their behalf. And sure enough, they were called home not much later. To eat first and then talk. The men, dancing and jumping happily, drove their cows through the gate. The wife was as good as married.'

The elders started talking, trying to express their mixed reactions. They would all have had something to say. But they did not have the time. Their visitors had arrived. Some thirty strong men were gathering at the main gate. They were waiting to be welcomed home. Ruteera had known that they could not be fewer. He was glad that he had prepared for many more than that. He nodded with a knowing smile to himself.

Soon the in-laws filed through the gate following Kubiriba, their prospective son-in-law. He took them to sit in the temporary big reception hall. It had been constructed near his mother's house, specifically for this occasion. The sticks were collected from the visitors and taken for safe-keeping. If any stick got lost, it would be paid for with a goat. As soon as the visitors were settled and greetings completed, small calabashes of *bushera* were passed around. They could not be served with beer until after they had completed the process of selecting the cows. The girl's father was never present at these occasions. He trusted his delegates completely.

Meanwhile, Ruteeramareingwa had sent a message to his sons grazing the cattle to bring them home for their noon rest. To make this possible, he had instructed the young men to water them early.

The full bride price had been agreed upon, at a previous ceremony at the home of the girl's parents. Altogether the girl's people were going to pick nine cows, one bull and fifteen goats. The ninth cow was a special one and would be picked first. It was the traditional fine. The parents of the girl always looked for a fault so as to exact this fine. If there was no fault then they would invent it. So this fine, *ekiiru*, had been traditionally accepted as part of the bride price. No man who paid any bride price escaped it. And no man failed to marry because of it.

The bellowing of Ruhogo as the herd approached their fireplace aroused the new in-laws. Together with the elders they went out to meet them. It was a simple, straightforward exercise. And it would take a very short time. Anybody could tell a good cow from a bad one. Once or twice they asked about the history of a cow before they selected it. Several times Ruteera also pleaded with them to drop their choice and select another one.

'You cannot take that one,' he would say. 'I am only part owner of that one. I share it with that brother of mine there.' Or, 'That one, as you can see, has got a very young calf. If you take it, you will be obliged to take the calf also, and count it as a full cow.' In this way he saved all the cows that had been brought in from his brothers' herds and one or two of the remaining best. As they set out towards the goats pen the two groups were both satisfied with the deal. After selecting the goats they went back to the reception hall. The beautiful bull had impressed them all very much. And for quite some time conversation centred on it.

II

When they got back to the hall they found the calabashes of *bushera* gone. A large, wide-mouthed pot stood in the middle. Three ordinary pots full of *muramba* must have been poured into this one to fill it. This beer had been specially prepared, with honey added to it. A young man was stirring the beer with a bundle of drinking tubes, to stop the potent brew from frothing over. There was another pot of beer without honey in it. Some people knew themselves to be weak drinkers. They would drink this one.

The elders and the immediate brothers of Ruteeramareingwa would sit with the in-laws. Another place, which would be served as well as this one, had been prepared for the other invited guests. Not everybody would sit with the in-laws. The uninvited guests would be given some *bushera* but they had to wait for the in-laws to finish before they could start eating.

It was around this time that Keshakama managed to break away from all the cooking. She came to greet the people from her home. They were her younger fathers and brothers. She came beaming, showing good health and general well-being. She went around offering her hand in greeting. She started from the oldest and would greet the youngest last. The elder would begin: *'Keije!'* and she would reply 'Ee!'

Buhooro?	Are you well?
Eee!	Yes!
Buhorogye?	Very well?
Eego!	Yes!

Agandi?	Other news?
Nimarungyi!	They are good!

While greeting the elders she knelt down; but she did not get up first to greet a brother and then kneel again for an elder sitting next to him. This greeting continued until she had completed the circle. At one stage she tried to greet a young boy, thinking that she was his female father. But it turned out that he was a brother. The custom does not allow a woman to ask a male the greeting questions unless she is older by relationship. She really looked beautiful, bedecked with beads and bangles. Her skin skirt and the topskin were beautifully tanned and seasoned and she had decorated them with more beads.

'So you see how well we treat your daughters?' an elder asked the in-laws, indicating Keshakama, with open admiration.

'They must deserve good treatment,' an elderly in-law countered. 'Otherwise you would not waste it on them if they were not good wives to you.' They all laughed.

'That is true, they deserve it,' Tibeijuka observed. 'That is why we find it fitting to come for more of your daughters.'

They laughed again. This trend of conversation had been provoked by Keshakama's entrance. She was taking it all very well. It was a great tribute to be openly praised by your husbands in front of your brothers and younger fathers. She felt she had to say something for her husbands also. She did not know what, yet.

'You are very right, my friend,' one of her younger fathers was saying. 'We also appreciate the way you treat them. As you can see, we are always ready to give you more of our daughters.' They laughed yet again.

'We Bajura,' Keshakama started, with a tinge of feminine shyness, 'know how to treat our wives. And I am sure your young daughter will find a lot of happiness with us.' More laughter.

'They must be very good indeed,' a younger father observed with a wrinkled forehead. 'Now you tell us, your fathers and brothers, that you are a Mujura?'

'Yes, indeed,' she replied defiantly. 'You gave me to them knowing that that would happen. Particularly as they are good. They have a bad habit of rubbing their clan into you and making it stick; in a particularly good way, too.'

'I have given you a goat,' one brother of her husband announced happily. He was strongly moved by the way she had recommended them to their in-laws.

'I give you another one,' another of her brothers-in-law said.

'Yara-ra-ra-ra-ra-ra,' she broke into a happy song, on a very high-pitched note. Others joined her, clapping their hands happily. Everybody was in a very good mood.

'I will give you a great big one,' chipped in Ruteeramareingwa, who had thus far refrained from joining the conversation, 'when we go to sleep tonight.' Everybody laughed at it.

Keshakama, who had been given two goats, was the happiest. She would have stayed longer with them if it had not been time to feed the visitors. The serving girls had started carrying in baskets of food.

Containers and containers of food continued to come. There was millet bread, mashed steamed matooke and even sweet potatoes. In front of everybody there was a big earthenware bowl. This was filled with chunks of meat. There was almost no space for soup: to get to it they had to finish the top chunks first. Two other pots had been brought. One was full of meat and the other one soup. These were on standby. The serving girls would make sure that these, too, did not go untouched.

Looking at the faces of the in-laws, one could discern a shared message. They all seemed to be saying, 'You see? I told you. We did not bring enough men to finish the food.' They did not even finish half of it. The uninvited observers would feast on this. Food would be added whenever necessary. Everybody would go away wondering what the actual wedding feast would be like.

The in-laws had to return to Kaabya. As they were many they did not have to start on the journey back early. They left just before sunset. A few long-necked gourds were filled with beer for the men to drink on the way back. Some of them, however, were too full to squeeze in anything else. Quite a few were intoxicated but jovial. Their sticks were returned and a few girls and boys prepared to see them on their way.

They did not take the bride price home with them. Custom required that Ruteera's people take the cows and goats to the in-laws. They would expect as big a feast as the in-laws had just had. Before they left, they agreed that they should take the bride price on the first day after the next full moon.

Healthy lusty laughter followed the group down the hill. The in-laws went singing drunken funny and lusty teasing songs. They were all free to tease each other. Even the girls could tease the men as much as they wanted. They only had to know how far decency allowed them to go and stop there.

And, as we say, a person is not a goat which you keep a keen eye on, to stop it immediately it starts going to somebody's garden. A person looks after himself by his own self.

For those of Ruteeramareingwa's family, the feast had just started. Those who had gone to see off the visitors came back to find everybody ecstatic. All the restraints of the day had gone with the in-laws. All those who had worked hard for this feast could now relax. Even Ruteera's wives could join the dance. Keirigyirwa, Ruteera's first wife, had been very busy for the whole day supervising the cooking women. But now she could be seen in the big circle of women, singing and providing the hand accompaniment to the dancers. She would not stay long but she would dance.

A big fire had been made in the middle of the compound. Young men and women were there dancing, expressing so much emotion. On such occasions the dances were very competitive. There were a number of elders here who could boast of several hundred goats. They had all fed well and drunk a lot. And there was still enough beer to last the strong ones till morning. When they got into the right mood, such elders gave away goats as presents, very freely. Whoever excelled in a particular dance would receive a goat. And the elders were now looking for merit to reward.

The women were looking their best now. They had redecorated themselves. They now wore beads around their necks and waists. They even wore a thin strip of hide, studded with beads, around their heads. The soft skin skirts they wore had bells on them. The beautiful patterns shaved on their heads were shiny with sweat.

Hands are a very important musical instrument. And a dance needed good hand-clappers.

Right now the woman soloist was leading in a song about Kubiriba and his bride-to-be. If she did not exaggerate, the girl was a real beauty:

> She is not big she is not small
> She is not short she is not tall
> She is all in proportion.

'Yee-ummma-ummma,' the hand-clappers answered.

> She is not black she is not brown
> She has long forehead she has black hair
> She has both skin tones.

Yee Ummmm Ummmm

> She has big eyes like a heifer's eyes
> She looks at you like she's going to give
> But she won't give you.

Yee Ummmm Ummmm

> Her legs are well proportioned, fitting her buttocks too
> Her waist is like basket-weaving grass

Her breasts are full.
Yee Ummmm   Ummmm

The soloist changed her tone, now reaching a feverish climax:.
She has made many men mad
But she is mad after Kubiriba
But she is mad after Kubiriba.

When the soloist reached the climax, the circle of women clapped their hands faster, changing the rhythm. The women and men who had been trotting around in the circle now paired up. They jumped higher and thudded the ground harder with their bare feet, in tune with the clapping hands. The young women with full firm breasts, shook them very tantalisingly in the face of their male partners. The neck beads hanging down their chests helped to enhance the tantalising power of the breasts as they moved with the women's dancing. The old women took pride in the children they had suckled, when they saw their own flat, deflated breasts jumping up and down.

It was such a lively night with lively music. Even the very old men and women sitting around shook their heads and shoulders. They clapped their hands feebly in response to the music. They proved the saying: 'A person who danced in youth will never fail to move shoulders to the tune of music'.

Some musical instruments had been produced. Tibeijuka was now playing *enanga*, the harp, and his third son, was playing *endingiri*, a one-string violin. Another young man played a flute.

The dancing went on throughout the night. Those who got tired or drunk would retire to some sleeping place. All such places would be crowded. Very wide mats had been placed on the floor and these would be used both to sleep on and to cover oneself. With so much beer in them they would not feel the cold.

Chapter Seven

I

Kubiriba's stick dropped from his hands. He picked it up quickly, hoping to escape comments.

'Ah, your in-laws have prepared a big feast for us indeed,' Oribaribo commented. 'Your stick is already falling in anticipation?' Oribariho, the man whose marriage to his brother's widow the men had once discussed, was son to Ruteera's younger father.

'They had better,' Kubiriba said pompously, eyeing his wife mirthfully. It was a good omen indeed. The others started commenting on it, too.

Kubiriba was going to visit his in-laws for the first time since the marriage, two moons back. The couple were still on their honeymoon. The scars on Kubiriba's face were just starting to darken. They were going for the ceremony of finishing ghee. All the ghee in her mother's house was to be used for the feast and the containers cleaned for the new ghee.

Kubiriba walked in front of his wife, Keishemeza. Her maiden name had now been put aside and her husband had given her a new one, as good a pet name as he could. Keishemeza for instance meant, 'She who makes one feel happy.'

Following closely behind them were some seven men and five girls. The girls wore beautiful skins, beautifully decorated with beads and bells. The many bells jingled musically as they moved. Oribariho was the elder representing Kuburiba's father. His brothers were represented by Kubiriba's father's first son, Mazima. The others were all close brothers and sisters. Two of the men carried pots of beer. All the others carried big baskets of some dry food. Kubiriba, his wife and Oribariho carried nothing. Kubiriba was taking a special present to his wife's parents – a hoe and its handle. His brother Mazima carried it for him.

Before they had exhausted talking about the good and bad omens, Kubiriba accidentally stubbed the middle toe of his right foot on a stone. The toe got badly cut. He jumped and limped to a stop with pain. This was also a good omen, and a painful one at that. He stopped, went behind a bush and urinated on his toe to stop it from developing pus.

'Cho, Kubiriba,' his brother commented teasingly. 'You must be faking all these omens. Not so long ago, you dropped your stick. And now you almost dropped a toenail. Are we supposed to believe that the double omens are genuine?' They all laughed.

'Let us see,' a younger man said, going to examine the injury. 'Oh no,' he shouted triumphantly. 'He cannot have faked this one. This cut is for real.' Kubiriba regained the lead. Right then, twenty strides ahead, a rat came onto the wide path from the lower side.

'Look at that rat, now,' Kubiriba said, giving way for all to see. The rat hesitated in the middle of the path. If it went back to the lower side, it would be a bad omen. It made up its mind and crossed the path. 'Are you going to accuse me of faking that rat also?' he asked, limping comically.

'No, my child,' his younger father defended. 'It seems you are heading for good luck. Three consecutive good omens are not very common.'

'What better luck could I have than my Keishemeza here?' he said, grabbing his wife's arm. They all started discussing the possibilities. It wouldn't be just a big feast. There had to be something more. They agreed that if nothing good came, then some very bad luck would befall them.

There were many such omens, good and bad. For instance, if you met a lone dog, you would almost certainly go home. It was one of the worst omens. Meeting a woman before you washed your face was also very bad, or simply meeting a woman first when you were going on some important errand. There were interpretations for many such everyday occurrences. And they always came true.

Kubiriba was elated by the omens. So far he was very happy with his wife and he believed her to be happy too. She certainly looked happy. His mind wandered off to their marriage again. It had been an exciting time.

When Ruteeramareingwa's people had taken the cows to their home, the two families had agreed to have the marriage ceremony sooner than usual. They wanted to have done with it before they were beset by all the work in the gardens. So the marriage had taken place only one moon after the bride price had been delivered.

Some forty men had gone to Keishemeza's home the day before she was to be officially handed over to her husband. A bull and two goats had been slaughtered for the feast at her father's house. It was indeed a feast that one could talk about. Looking at all those who came and were fed, one would think that the whole clan was there. Those Bajura from Ruteera's clan were impressed. They had seen for themselves that their in-laws were a strong family. There had been a lot of eating, drinking and dancing.

The bride, as tradition demanded, had been out of circulation for some two weeks. In that period she was attended to in seclusion, in her mother's house. One of the attendants was an aunt. During that time she was taught so many things and she was generally given encouraging advice about married life.

She was handed over the next day.

The handing-over ceremony had been long. Many elders had spoken. Both sides had pledged undying bonding. Their two children had brought them together, as some others before them had done. It was imperative that they made their relationship even stronger and never stopped eating together. Then the two children were given their share of advice. Actually only one got it. Keishemeza was still in her mother's house crying her eyes out. Then people started giving them presents. They were given very many things, including a cow from the girl's father and several goats from her uncles. Finally, the father asked two strong sons to hand over the girl.

The two strong young men went to her mother's house to pull her out. Her girlfriends started singing a special farewell song to her. In the house, her crying increased. She struggled fiercely before she was overpowered and pulled out. Kubiriba, supported by his brothers, waited for her outside her mother's house. Looking at it all, one would think that she did not want to go.

Weeping and struggling, she was pulled out of the house and handed over to Kubiriba. Right away his brothers surrounded them to prevent her from escaping. If she managed to break loose and go back to her mother's house, they would have to pay more bride price to get her out again. They had practically carried her off the compound weeping like a child. Her bridal escort followed, some of them crying too. Outside the gate, she was put into a litter and carried all the way to her new home. There more colourful feasting awaited them. They were received with dancing, speeches, presents and rejoicing. Here also, a bull and goats had been slaughtered.

II

Kubiriba and his train got to their in-laws just before the goats were taken out to graze. Their daughter who had gone away wailing had come back laughing and very happy. She even looked more brown. And, as her mother observed later, her belly was starting to show signs of swelling. Only the keen eyes of a very interested mother could see it. This was good news indeed! Only two moons …

Once the greetings were over, the entertainment started. Only one person did not come out to greet the visitors – the girl's mother. Her daughter had to find her in the house, in her room, to greet her. Tradition dictates that a man should not talk face to face with his mother-in-law. He does not see her. They never greet by shaking hands or embracing. Even when they greet verbally, the mother-in-law should be in a room while the young man is outside. In this way, no temptation of a lustful nature would develop between them. And, if a son-in-law ever entered his in-laws' compound unannounced, he would be forced to pay a heavy fine. The assumption would be that he wanted to catch his mother-in-law outside or even find her in some embarrassing situation. And the relationship between the two stayed this way. But if, after a long time in marriage, they wished to waive this custom, the man would pay the fine of a goat in advance. Then she would treat him like a real son and stop hiding from him.

The visitors had been fed. The men were now relaxing with a pot of *muramba* in front of them. The father-in-law had invited some of his closest brothers and friends to be present at the small reunion.

'Our daughter looks so well, Kubiriba,' a younger father of the girl said. 'We are glad to see that you are treating her well.' Kubiriba only smiled to acknowledge the compliment. So far, he was happy with his wife.

'I remember,' Keishemeza's father started, 'when his father came with Keshakama to thank us, the elders made the same observation.'

'Yes, indeed. And this is only to be expected. Is this one a rat and that one a mouse? They are all one: rat. We should not wonder why this young man behaves like his father.'

'As one elder said when you visited us,' Kubiriba started importantly, 'when a woman is a good wife to you, you cannot help treating her well.'

'That is well said, my son,' an elder commended. 'Good wives are hard to come by these days. And it is few who realise the folly of losing such a one.'

'And,' Kubiriba said, winking at the brother who had carried the special gift for him, 'I have brought a small present for our parents.' So saying he passed the hoe and its handle to his father-in-law. The father showed the significant handle around for all present to see. There was no hole in it for the hoe.

'You gave me a good wife,' Kubiriba continued. 'She digs for me and looks after me, probably better than I look after her. I have brought you this small present only as a small token. I am thanking you for the priceless wife you gave me.' Beaming faces looked at the new wife appraisingly. An excited murmur broke out in the gathering. Even her mother, far away in her room, joined in the excitement. Nobody doubted that she had been a virgin. But all the same, it excited them to hear her being declared one.

'Thank you very much, my son,' his father-in-law stated joyfully. 'We are very happy to know that you are happy with our daughter. And we are very happy to see her come back looking so healthy and happy. So I am also going to give you a small present.' He looked around the gathering. He seemed to hesitate before he continued. 'But I will present it to you the day after tomorrow, when you are preparing to return.'

Kubiriba's escort looked at one another questioningly. This left almost no doubt in their minds what the present would be. They expressed their gratitude profusely, clapping their hands and jumping up and down. It was some time before order was restored.

Kubiriba's mind, however, was far away. He unconsciously explored some of the scars with a finger. He was reliving the two-night struggle to break her virginity. On their first night together they had had a fierce struggle through the night. He had believed that he would overpower her before cockcrow. But by morning he had not gone beyond her knees. Extremely exhausted and bleeding from many scratches, he had collapsed and slept through the day. Only once did he raise his head, when his sister had woken them up for food. But having no appetite for food, both had collapsed back into a deep slumber.

That night the struggle had started immediately after supper. And he had conquered her just after the second cockcrow. The scratches had multiplied and some were quite painful.

Of course she had been a virgin. And hence, the hoe and its handle being presented separately. The in-laws would make a hole in the handle and fix the hoe themselves. If he had brought the handle with a hole in it or with the hoe fixed, the parents would have known that she had not been a virgin. There would have been a fine to pay for looking after the girl badly. As it was they were delighted. They were proud of their daughter. She had spared them derision. It was always painful and shameful for a father to refund the bride price, just because his daughter could not wait for her rightful husband.

III

'Titchi-he, Kubiriba sneezed loudly.

'May you survive, good Mujura,' someone wished him.

'Titchi-he,' he sneezed twice again, in quick succession.

'May it be good,' another one said.

'It has to be good,' Oribariho, the younger father, said. 'As you see, his omens turn out to be true in a big way.' He turned to Kubiriba. 'You did not fake the omens after all, my son.' He indicated the cow.

The young healthy heifer went ahead of them. A long rope trailed behind it, tied around its hind leg to restrain it. Kubiriba would return the rope on the next visit to the in-laws. He would take it with a goat tied in its noose. The group had just crossed the swamp, on their way home.

'Haa,' his brother Mazima teased. 'Now that he has been right once, I suppose his omens can never go wrong!'

'They can,' his wife commented, tilting her head to give him a sideways glance. 'As a matter of fact, this sneeze spells a cold, not good luck.' She looked straight at him and pointed an accusing finger at him with a jocose stance. 'You will not find any special party waiting for you at home.' They all laughed at him.

'Come on, my good wife. Are you jealous because your father gave me a cow?' he said, grabbing her. He wrapped his arm around her waist. 'Do not worry, we shall drink the milk together.' There was more laughter. He continued holding her, his hand playing with the beads around her waist.

'Actually, he is not faking this one, you know,' Oribariho said seriously. 'I am inviting you all to my home. There is a calabash of beer there.' They all ululated and jumped. They surrounded the elderly man and danced around him. The many bells on the women's skirts tinkled rhythmically as they danced. They all knew what he meant by a 'calabash'. 'But first we shall get home and report to Ruteeramareingwa. Then we shall proceed to my home.'

It had started raining just as they entered Ruteera's compound. They were welcomed with food and a pot of beer. But they agreed that they should leave that pot and drink it the next day. They decided to go and drink Oribariho's. They waited for the rain to stop but it went on and on and looked as if it would not stop at all. They decided that rain was not going to get between them and a pot of beer. So, when it abated only slightly, they decided to go. After all, it was not far. And they were not salt.

They got to Oribariho's home late and wet.

IV

The beer was in the house of the third wife, the wife Oribariho had inherited from his dead brother. Some five young men were sitting comfortably around a pot of *muramba*. A slow hardwood fire in a corner warmed the whole house. She had invited the young men to thresh sorghum for her. They had really worked hard. After the women helpers had finished winnowing, there were ten big baskets of clean grain.

The women had just finished the winnowing when the rain threatened. But that was not a hindrance. The Bajura were the greatest rain-making clan. The name 'Bajura' itself means rain people. One of the young men went just outside the gate and peered at the sky in the direction the rain was coming from. He removed a small black horn from his skin pouch. It was plugged at the open end. His lips could be seen moving as if he was talking to himself. He hung the horn in the main tree at the gate. The heavy cloud was already shedding big drops. The heavy drops continued to fall for a short while before the cloud passed them by.

'Hey, I thought you were going to stop it!' Bagambirelyo teased him. The young man smiled benignly. 'Is it because we are around?'

'No,' someone else answered. 'It is because the cloud was very heavy.'

'Ha, we know that a bad lover claims that the mat is slippery,' Bagambirelyo said amid laughter.

They started processing eight of the baskets for germinating. Processing sorghum requires quite some skill. The sorghum is thoroughly mixed with a small, specific amount of very fine wood-ash. It is then put in baskets lined with papyrus fronds. The basket is covered at the mouth and tied very carefully so that it does not burst as the sorghum absorbs water and swells. The full baskets are then taken down to the river and left in the water overnight. The next day it is removed from the water and left overnight. It is then taken home and removed from the baskets. It is piled in one heap and covered with grass and banana leaves and left for three days, then uncovered and spread out to dry. It will have changed to a blackish colour on the outside and is very sweet, almost like sugar cane. On the day it is spread out to dry, many children suffer from full tummies. They eat so much of it that they end up with indigestion. It is this sweet sorghum that is used to brew *muramba* and *bushera*.

The young men prepared the sorghum quickly and carried it down to the river. As they came back another heavy cloud was moving towards Nyamiringa, noisily. When they got home the man removed his horn from the tree. Their buttocks had barely touched the seats when it started raining.

'Now it may go on and rain as much as it wants, 'Bagambirelyo said. 'We are indoors, we have food,' he said, eyeing the hostess questioningly, 'I hope. And we have beer.'

'You and this greed of yours,' a friend commented. Everybody burst into laughter. 'Don't you know the saying "a child with greed never dies his own death"?'

'That is good. I would like to be really greedy and have other people keep dying my deaths for me,' Bagambirelyo responded.

'That is not the meaning, you fool. He dies the death which is not meant for him.'

'And in so doing he does not die; or he resurrects later because he has to be alive to die his own death.' Bagambirelyo was a very funny one. Those who knew him well found him entertaining. And those who did not know him took offence at first. But they soon learnt to appreciate his sense of humour. Those who had been working with him for the whole day had no more laughter left in them, or so they thought. Their ribs were aching badly.

They were served with a big meal. When they finished eating, a pot of *muramba* was put before them. They had not taken the pot halfway when the owner of the home arrived. He came with the whole group who had gone to Kubiriba's in-laws. They were all dripping wet. It was soon after sunset but it was already dark. They greeted those at home hurriedly.

'Why didn't you wait until it had stopped raining?' Bagambirelyo asked, with seriousness. He grabbed the two drinking tubes sticking out of the pot of beer protectively.

'We had to come and help you to drink that pot of beer,' Oribariho said, heading for the inner room where his wife was. 'We knew if we did not, you would drink too much and die of beer.' Everyone laughed.

'Ha! Do you think this beer could possibly kill me? It could not do me the honour. It knows that then I would die a most comfortable death, stone drunk. Then I would be the most drunken spirit in the spirit world.' Everybody laughed again. 'Anyway, I suppose you are welcome back. But not to the tubes. The beer is only for those who threshed the sorghum.'

'Do not worry about them,' the hostess said, placing seats for the newcomers. 'There is more beer than you can all finish.' She ushered the girls to the kitchen to have their share there.

'That will be the day. I suppose I am going to grow roots here, since I am not ready to go until it is finished.'

'Your younger father, the owner of the home, might decide to cut the roots before they are properly established.' She was a good woman and humorous too.

The newcomers joined in and started drinking. The half pot of beer was finished and another one was brought. Before they started drinking Oribariho cleared his throat. The young men continued with their conversation. He cleared his throat again, making his intentions clear this time. They stopped and looked at him respectfully.

'Kubiriba, my son, you are a lucky young man,' the elderly man said slowly and carefully. 'But I must count myself lucky too.' He stopped briefly and looked round at the young men paying attention to him. 'It is not every day that a man takes his son on the young man's visit to his in-laws and they come back with a cow leading them home.' Those they had found at home looked at Kubiriba with envy.

'Did they really give you a cow?' Bagambirelyo asked, genuinely serious this time.

'Yes, and we came with it. A big, healthy heifer,' Mazima said.

'In that case, you deserve the beer, even though you did not thresh the sorghum.' He grabbed a drinking tube and thrust it towards Kubiriba. Kubiriba received the tube and faked long pulls with resounding swallowings. Everybody again laughed hilariously. The elderly man cut their laughter short.

'And I, as the younger father who escorted him, I give him the goat with which he will return the rope.'

Mazima jumped up and danced and slapped him on the shoulders and thanked Oribariho. The last omen, the sneeze, had turned out to be lucky.

They continued talking jovially about Kubiriba's good luck for a long time. As they drank they talked more and more. They joked and teased and criticised and admired and their voices drowned the rain outside. They were not yet halfway through the pot when an alarm penetrated the dark rainy night and stopped their noise. A woman was wailing, crying that she was being killed.

'That is Kibande beating his wife again,' Oribariho said. His brother, Kibande, lived about three compounds away.

'The way that woman is wailing, he must be working on her really hard,' Bagambirelyo put in. 'I wonder why people enjoy beating their wives, as if they have nothing more enjoyable to do to them.'

'What is wrong with beating a wife? Is there a man who does not beat his?' This young speaker had a reputation for beating his. He had been married to her for some seven seasons.

'Why are you in a hurry to support the beating, my brother?' a friend asked accusingly.

'I forgot the saying that "where there is a leper, one does not fold fingers". I have just stepped on a sore toe,' Bagambirelyo said, looking at him squarely. 'By the way, have you been to your in-laws to return her? I hear that you almost broke her jaw.'

'That is not true. People are only exaggerating. And anyway, I still ask, is there anything wrong with that? She is my wife.'

'Oh, certainly not,' another of the same age said. 'Indeed, when you do not beat her, she may start thinking that she also has testicles. But Kibande's beating is too much. He beats her very often. And he actually threshes her as if he was threshing sorghum.'

'That is bad then,' someone else said. 'It is not the normal wife-beating. But there are some women who will not believe that their husbands love them if they do not beat them. Such a woman will become sullen for no particular reason. When you say anything to her, even the gentlest word, she will become quarrelsome. If you rebuke her she will become worse. If you do not beat her she will stretch your patience to the limit. She will even deliberately start burning your food. Eventually you will be forced to beat her. And then she will become a loving, dutiful wife again.'

'Ah, but some men really overdo it,' Oribariho said. 'For instance Kibande's wife will not get up from the mat for two days.'

'Why doesn't she leave him? Does she have no home or brother where she came from?'

'She has gone home many times. But every time, Kibande goes after her, very repentant, pays all the fine and brings her back.' Oribariho paused briefly. 'You see, he actually loves her.'

'No, that cannot be love,' a young unmarried man objected. 'You cannot beat a woman you love like that. I do not even believe that some women ask for it. Are they not humans like us? Do they not feel pain?'

'You talk like that because you have not yet married any to see for yourself. We all say that before we marry. But we soon come face-to-face with reality,' Bagambirelyo – who was not married, by the way – explained. 'And then we beat them like drums.'

'Indeed, beating should be administered regularly, in light doses like a preventative medicine,' the one who beat his wife advised. 'If the woman runs away to her parents, it is all right. That is, if she has no injury to show there. You will go and return with her. After all, carrying a pot of beer to your in-laws and keeping your wife in line is worth the trouble. If you do not beat her, the marriage will break up.'

'All the same, I disagree with you when you say that we must beat our wives "to keep them in line" as you call it,' the unmarried young man persisted. 'There must be other ways, and better ones at that, of keeping them in line. Me, I will not beat mine, when I marry them.'

Kubiriba was of the same opinion. He wondered whether he would ever beat Keishemeza. He hoped that the situation would never arise. But, he thought reluctantly, if she asked him to, he would certainly prescribe the required medication. One simply could not be sure with women.

Chapter Eight

I

Three full seasons had passed. Both good and bad things had come and gone. And Nyabigyi still lived. Not quite in disharmony.

Kubiriba's wife had produced twins first – a girl and a boy. She was revered. Mothers of twins are held in high esteem. And, as custom demands, two huge goats had been skinned for her. One, the day after she had delivered, and another one when the umbilical cords withered and fell off. The twins were quite big now. She had delayed having another child but she was now quite heavy with the third.

Bugeiga's son Rwecurenga and Ruteeramareingwa's daughter Kenyangyi had also grown up. They had got married some six moons back. It appeared that Bugeiga had not opposed the match as speculated in some circles. His health had been declining slowly. He never laughed now. He was very rarely seen smiling. His wives and children had been the first to see this marked change. But nobody knew that deep inside his black heart fought with his ribs.

The outsiders did not know the truth. When Rwecurenga had first told Bugeiga of his intention to marry Ruteeramareingwa's daughter, Bugeiga had received it very badly. He had sworn, cursed and refused vehemently.

'It cannot be,' he had said finally. 'I will not allow it. The whole of Nyabigyi is full of girls. Some are even much better than this one. How can you choose the daughter of my worst enemy for a wife?'

'But father,' Rwecurenga had pleaded meekly, 'he is not your enemy at all.' The young man had done his homework and an aunt who was married to Ruteera's close brother had reassured them: 'He has nothing against you. And I know for certain from very reliable sources that he will not refuse me his daughter.'

'He may not refuse,' Bugeiga continued slowly. He emphasised his words by tapping the floor with his staff. 'That is his business. But I will not have any son of mine marrying into that home.' He looked up at his son with red piercing eyes. 'And that is my business.'

'Father,' the young lover persisted with a shaky voice, 'I do not mean to rebel against your will. But I plead with you. I love that girl and she loves me.'

'How many times must I tell you!' the father raised his voice.

Rwecurenga realised that he could not make his father change his mind alone. He went and sought advice from his older brothers. That same evening accompanied by Karwemera, his father's oldest son, he called on Busaahu.

Two days later Busaahu and three other elders called on Bugeiga. It was all casual. Any casual observer could not have known that the visit had been planned. It appeared as if they had all been coming from some place where they had business and had to pass by Bugeiga's home. Seeing him sitting outside under the big kitooma tree, they had inevitably gone in and sat down. Busaahu and another elder came first. They were genuinely coming from the watering place. The other two had come separately. But they had joined the group in the same way.

Mboneko was the last elder to join the group. He came slowly and greeted them quietly in his low voice, without ceremony. He sat down and received the gourd of *bushera* which Bugeiga offered him. He took a long drink from the single tube, put the gourd down and looked at the ground between his feet sadly.

'You do not look happy,' Bugeiga commented. 'Why?'

'I am coming from Rukandema's home,' he said. The others looked down sadly too. They were quiet for a short time. They all knew why.

'What have you decided to do?' the youngest of the four asked.

'Did we have any alternative?' Mboneko murmured. 'We must do as our custom demands. Her brothers together with two younger fathers will take her to the papyrus swamp tomorrow and kill her.' They were quiet for a brief moment.

'Why are they not taking her to the falls?' Bugeiga asked.

'For one thing it is very far. For another, the last one to be thrown over, almost two seasons back, grabbed at the brothers at the very last moment and went over the falls with one of them. An innocent brother died a death which was not his. And the brothers inadvertently shed the blood of their own brother. You remember how expensive it was for them to cleanse themselves.'

Again they were all quiet for a long time. Their minds were thinking about many things that happened in the clans and about the rules the gods of their ancestors had laid down for them. These had to be obeyed. Bugeiga was the first to break the silence.

'The whole of that girl?' he protested, shaking his head slowly. 'Indeed, as we say, the beautiful ones will even attempt to taste steam.'

'Of course. But it burns them and spoils their beauty,' Busaahu observed. 'She still refuses to name the man who made her pregnant?'

'She has adamantly refused. Whatever tortures her brothers have put her to, she stays mute as if she has no tongue in her mouth.'

'Then she slept with him with consent. That is why she is protecting him,' Busaahu observed.

'Whoever he is, there must have been something else wrong somewhere,' another elder put in. 'Which man would not have married that girl, having spoilt her, if he was the one who took her virginity?'

'Indeed which man?' the youngest asked.

'That must be the reason,' Busaahu mused. 'He must have found her not to be a virgin. Otherwise, I do not see how any man could have refused her. Beautiful, hard-working, cheerful … Ha!'

'Why did she not try to elope?' Bugeiga asked.

'She tried. And that was how she was found out,' Mboneko said. 'Someone told her mother that the girl was moving around advertising herself. Her mother asked her. In answer she burst out crying. Her brother found her crying.'

'Poor girl! I wonder how many other girls get pregnant and manage to get married before they are found out,' the youngest man said.

'There must be quite a few. Is this not the only girl to be killed for being pregnant, in our neighbourhood? In two seasons?'

'That is true. But there are two who gave birth in only eight moons. Three others had their bride price returned to the husbands soon after the marriage. They were not virgins. They are still the laughing-stock of their generation.' Bugeiga gnashed his teeth, apparently for no deserving reason.

'I do not know what is happening to the world,' Busaahu said, really concerned. 'Not so long ago such was almost unheard of. Looseness was simply not there among our girls. Both our boys and our girls knew and guarded against the consequences. No man would touch a girl he was not going to marry. And no girl would give in to a man until he had taken her home. And even then, she would put up a last fight against the inevitable.'

'The world is turning upside-down indeed,' the elder who had not said much so far observed. 'These days even a self-respecting man may marry a girl who is not a virgin.'

'I think our customs are slackening,' Busaahu continued. 'When we were more strict, pregnancies were not there. The girls knew that a non-virgin would never find a respectable husband. Or within a marriage she might be mistreated. So, once a girl lost her virginity, she would certainly marry the man she had lost it to. If the man refused to marry her, then she would cry rape. Then her brothers would spear the man. But now …'

'I think our customs are too harsh sometimes,' the youngest one observed. 'Killing a girl for having enjoyed what everybody else enjoys? I think we should relax them somewhat.'

'It is not us. It is the gods. Had the gods not decreed such a serious retribution, then we would have had to deal with the other and more serious situation. The question of bastards. The tradition simply cannot accept bastards.'

'Certainly not,' Bugeiga said emphatically. 'If only seeing a bastard can cause some serious diseases, *amahano*, what about having one produced in your home, by your daughter?'

This was recognised in almost all clans around. And if a girl was left to give birth at home, it would bring about inexplicable illness and sometimes death. It would get into the family so deeply that some children would be born deformed. And the rites performed to rid a family of this *amahano* were too expensive for most.

'You are right, my child,' Mboneko said. 'It is better to kill the girl when she is still pregnant. The cleansing rites after killing her are cheaper than trying to uproot *amahano* from a family. You wait, you will see. Funny things are going to start happening to Rukandema. Are we not going to be here?' He looked around importantly. 'You will be telling me.'

The elders continued to talk about general affairs of the clan and Nyabigyi as a whole. A long time passed before they broached the business that had brought them. Meanwhile, a big gourd of cold sweet *bushera* went round. Then, after an exchange of proverbs and counter proverbs, one elder came to the point.

'When is your son Rwecurenga bringing that girl home? We are dying for one of those great feasts of yours.' A quick cloud passed over Bugeiga's face. The watchful elders noted it quietly.

'I do not know that any son of mine is bringing home any wife.' He was almost cool, struggling hard to keep calm. 'No one has told me that he has found a girl he intends to marry.'

'Do not lie to us, Bugeiga. We were not born yesterday,' another elder countered jovially. 'We have never known you not to be well informed about the affairs of your family.'

Bugeiga, realising for the first time that the five elders had not met there coincidentally, asked: 'What are you trying to get at?'

'Why do you not admit that you have refused to let him marry Ruteeramareingwa's daughter?'

Bugeiga suddenly lost his temper. He blinked rapidly and heaved. He wanted to tell them to go away and leave him to handle the affairs of his family alone. But he could not. It was their family also. Busaahu was his father's brother. Mboneko was his father's step-brother. Of the other two, one was his close younger father, and the other his brother.

'But you … you…' he stuttered and stopped.

'Say it, Bugeiga, we want to know your reasons for refusing,' Busaahu urged.

'Cannot a man do what he wants with his family, without having to explain to some other people?'

'Yes, he can,' Busaahu continued. 'But not if it affects other people.'

'And whom does it affect this time?'

'He who came to us very miserable and asked us to intervene for him. And, you know, you have no reason at all. That young girl is very well behaved, hard-working and beautiful. She comes from a good home. We all know her background. The two young people have been secret friends for a very long time.

'Moreover, her father is a good, self-respecting man. He should have been the one to be against the match. But, despite your threats to do him harm, he has as good as accepted to give his daughter to your son.' Busaahu stopped and stared at Bugeiga who was gnashing his teeth again. 'No, my son, you are the one who is bad. And you are failing in your duty as a father. Instead of getting your son a good wife you are barring his way. You want to see him lose a girl that all fathers are fighting to secure for their sons.'

'But why do you insist on bending my hand in this? Can I not plainly say that I do not want my son to marry her?'

'Yes, you can and we would have no right to intervene. But your son asked us to intervene for him. He says he may do something desperate if you continue to refuse. Do not think that we did not think deeply about this before we came to you. So tell us, what are your reasons?' Mboneko looked up at him quizzically. 'Is it not because of that bull fight?' The other elders nodded their heads and mumbled in agreement.

'That was over three full seasons ago,' Busaahu put in. 'And, after all, you ate your bull long ago. We talked to you soon after the fight and we thought you had taken our advice. Apparently, you did not.'

Bugeiga's anger was welling up again. Busaahu should not have mentioned the fact that Bugeiga had eaten the bull. He had slaughtered it in anger. He could not afford to see it shamefacedly coming home. People did not know this, as he had slaughtered it for a marriage feast. They did not know that he, personally, had not eaten it.

The discussion continued. In the end the elders prevailed over him. He accepted the start of the marriage negotiations. He fully capitulated and admitted that he knew of no ill intentions Ruteeramareingwa had towards him. His son was very happy with the elders and his father. Four moons later he was taking his wife home, amid happy feasting and celebrating.

Only one person did not celebrate, Bugeiga. He went through it all like a drugged man. It all came and passed painfully like a bad dream. People thought it was because of his ill-health. But that was not the case. He had given in to the pressure of the elders. But he had not blessed the marriage. And he would never feel happy about it. He looked at it all as another victory on Ruteeramareingwa's part. And, as if a general curse had befallen him, even his cows had started dying. Moreover, he had buried two children in one week because of fever.

He looked really weighed down. His confident gait and long strides had changed into something else. Watching him walk one would think that he was running away from some imminent danger. His affability had changed into a cold, unsmiling harshness. And, as he always went looking down, his shoulders seemed to be stooping.

II

The big group had put their loads down to rest. One of the men who carried the pots of beer disappeared into the bushes. He came back with a green tube, peeling off its leaves. Nobody could doubt his intention.

'You, why do you not wait and drink when we get there?' Rwecurenga reproved.

'Ha-ha,' the man responded comically. He pushed the tube through the grass on the top of the beer. Without this grass, the potent beer would bubble out. 'Are you mistaking me for a fool?' The others laughed at this. 'What if I slip and the pot breaks before we get there?' He squatted, embracing the big pot between his legs. He started drinking, sucking hard and swallowing loudly. The other envious companions wished they could gather the same guts and have a drink also.

'You remind me of a man,' he started as he got up, exaggeratedly wiping imaginary drops of the beer from his lips, 'of a man who was sent to carry a pot of beer to his master's in-laws. He did not stop on the way. In spite of the heat he resisted all temptations to put the pot down to rest and drink a little. When the thirsty fool got there he was not thanked. He was not even given a drop of the beer he had carried to quench his thirst. He only regretted it on his way back home carrying the empty pot, and thirstier than ever. He drank water from the first stream he came to.' Everybody laughed again.

'Served him right,' someone commented. 'Was he carrying a dead body? Only those cannot put down what they are carrying until they get to the rightful destination.' Laughter resounded through the whole group. Someone farted long and loud. It could be heard through the laughter. This increased the laughter even more.

'Ah, this little boy also! He has already started misbehaving,' the man who had farted complained, pointing at a youngish boy. This boy was obviously innocent and everybody knew it.

'Where do you want me to put it when it comes?' the young boy asked defiantly. 'Would you rather I pushed it back to give me a pain in the stomach? After all it is the only perfume that some of us are used to.' They guffawed. This young boy was the *mafuka*. He was taken along only to be blamed for any farting that anybody in their group did at the in-law's place. Farting was looked at as something very shameful. Particularly at the in-laws'. And such a boy was always taken along for this purpose. He was a close relative of the bridegroom. When they returned, the bridegroom would give him a goat or a sheep.

'You people, you will kill us with laughter. If you go on like this, we shall get there with no ribs left. As it is, they are already hurting,' Rwecurenga complained, fighting to stifle his own laughter. 'Get up and go. Those Bajura will be waiting for us. And we do not want to keep them waiting. Do we, my woman, Kenyangyi?'

'No, my lord. As you can see, you are not pulling a goat to pay the fine for getting there late.' Rwecurenga had given her a pet name, Keijumeeza, as was the custom. He still often called her by her maiden name.

It was some six months after their marriage. They were going to the girl's father for the final marriage ceremony, the ceremony to end their honeymoon. A honeymoon did not have a fixed period. If the husband was wealthy it could take a long time. If he was poor, it would be hurried so that the wife could start working in the gardens.

During this period the woman did nothing much. Even the little she did was in and around the house. She spent the rest of the time beautifying herself. And the result was fantastic. Even the ugly ones would look healthier, happier and lighter. They would look almost beautiful.

Kenyangi now looked brighter than the white cattle egrets she got her maiden name from. She looked even gentler than that bird. Rwecurenga was content. He knew that his in-laws were happy with the way he looked after her so far. To him, she had been a dream come true.

'You see, Rwecurenga,' one of the men pointed out as they were approaching the last hump on the ridge, 'you were hurrying us for nothing. You know that Nyamaringa is not very far.'

'I do not blame him,' the younger father with them commented. 'He is impatient to show off his star to those Bajura. They claim that they are the best at looking after their wives.'

They got to Ruteera's home earlier than they had expected. That day they were visitors. Only Kenyangyi moved around greeting the brothers and sisters. Anyway, a girl is never a visitor in her father's home, even after marriage. When she comes, she has come home. Everywhere Kenyangyi went, she was congratulated on her health and her beauty.

Rwecurenga and his male companions stayed with the men of the family. The evening was filled with feasting. There was a lot to drink and to eat.

And of course those young Bagirakwe men were looking forward to dancing with the beautiful Bajura girls.

III

The next day Rwecurenga managed to go visiting. In the last few moons his friendship with Kubiriba had become much deeper than that of mere brothers-in-law. Their friendship had started with some reservations: it was at the time when Rwecurenga warned the Bajura about his father's attitude. When some years later he had shown his intention to marry Kenyangyi against his father's wishes, they had dropped the little suspicious feeling they had had. Friendship between the two young men became deeper. And, whereas Rwecurenga knew nothing of Bugeiga's future plans, he had assured Kubiriba that he was on his side whatever happened. They became such close friends that two days rarely passed without them meeting, normally in the evenings. They would move around and then separate, usually when the cattle were returning home.

So, when he got the time the next day to move around, his feet naturally led him to Kubiriba's house. Kubiriba's wife Keishemeza received him with an affectionate hug. She was also an in-law. She had secretly prepared a small delicious meal for him and her husband.

Among the Bakiga, a man does not eat chicken at the home of his father-in-law. It is far below his dignity. The least he could expect is a she-goat. This is the dictate of custom. But there is normally so much meat that one would want a change before the end of the second day. So the man has to visit his brothers-in-law to look for this change. The tradition does not follow him there, if he hides properly. If the season is right – as it happened to be – there could even be such delicacies as fried grasshoppers. And that is what his friend's wife put before him first. Two hours later, the secret meal of chicken and millet bread was put before the two friends. Keishemeza ate in the kitchen. She had prepared a different sauce, as women did not eat chicken.

'This is very good, my friend Kubiriba. I thought my wife was the best at preparing chicken and millet bread.'

'You know, of course "a child who does not move around thinks that his mother is the best cook".'

'All the same,' Rwecurenga replied, patting his friend on the shoulder with the left hand. He pointed the thigh bone he had just cleaned of flesh at him. He pushed the bone into his own mouth. He crushed it between his strong teeth, noisily. 'This is really superb,' he concluded, grinding the head of the bone between his teeth.

Keishemeza had come out of the kitchen to serve them.

'Shee,' she said quietly, with a finger on her lips. 'Do not let your wife hear you overpraising me. She might think that I am scheming to grab you.'

'Shee,' Rwecurenga whispered, also with a finger on his lips. 'Do not let your husband overhear you thinking of it. He might think that it is true.' They all laughed, the husband tapping him on the back.

'Really, I do not know what I would do to you if it was true. I do not think that I would have the guts to kill you.'

'I wish there was another Kenyangyi in this family,' Rwecurenga said thoughtfully. 'I would marry her for my second wife, to have another pair of you for in-laws.'

'You talk of in-laws. I wish my father or any of my big younger fathers could come now and find you eating a mere bird,' Kubiriba teased. 'I would like to see you cough up a goat and a pot of beer for abusing their hospitality. And you would not be allowed to taste them. How can you leave a whole goat and come here to gorge yourself on a simple two-legged one as if you have not seen food for days?'

'Let them come. I know where to hide, where they would not find me.'

'Where? Even if you entered a rat hole the family cat would pull you out.'

'What if my lovely sister-in-law, Keishemeza, hid me in her skin-skirt?' he said loudly, for the benefit of Keishemeza's ears. 'Would you refuse to hide me, my lovely in-law?'

'I would willingly hide you,' she said, laughing shyly.

'Then I would call my sister, your wife, and we would pair up against the two of you,' said Kubiriba, also laughing. 'Then we would fetch firewood for throwing away.' Rwecurenga laughed too, rubbing his tummy. He gave himself a few strong blows on the chest and belched twice, loud, deep and long.

'Be full,' Keishemeza commented.

'You have really cooked very well.' Rwecurenga leaned back against the wall and started rubbing his tummy again. 'You see, I have sprouted a tummy like a toad.'

Chicken thus eaten in secret was more delicious than chicken eaten in the open. That night Rwecurenga did not eat much of the goat meat that was put before him. He pretended that he had a full stomach as a result of indigestion.

'I must have eaten something which did not agree with the snake in my stomach.' And as if to support his statement, some funny sounds were heard from his stomach, at a high complaining pitch.

'If it continues,' his father-in-law advised, 'tell us before it is too late so that we may give you medicine. For the time being, your wife can give you some roots. She knows them and where to find them. If she does not, she will consult her mother.' Rwecurenga feigned a painful expression. He nursed his bulging tummy. He winked meaningfully at Kubiriba.

As a matter of fact, everybody knew what was wrong with him. The married men had all gone through it. And they still did, every time they officially visited their in-laws. The drinking and merry-making continued.

The next day the young couple were officially declared to have ended their honeymoon. The ceremony was short. The wife was given all the things she would need in her home, now that she would be fully independent.

When they arrived back home, Bugeiga gave his son a specific piece of land. Naturally, it was part of his mother's land. Now it would be indisputably his. He also gave him two extra strips of land down in the valley and a small portion in the hills.

That night was the first quiet night in their house. Previously, there would always be one or two of Rwecurenga's sisters, who had been assigned to attend to the bride. But tonight they were all alone. They talked warmly as they sat around the fire after their supper. They had been taking stock of their wealth. By all standards they were not poor.

'Bugeiga does not like me but he has been generous to us,' Kenyangyi said, giggling mischievously. Rwecurenga pinched her playfully. She struggled and fell on his shoulder, still giggling.

'How often must I tell you that you should not mention my father's name? Does your mother call her father-in-law by his name?'

'But I do not always say his name.'

'Why did you decide to do so now?'

'I wanted to see what you would do. Last night you went to bed singing drunkenly at my mother's place. But you were not fined for it.'

'So you are paying me back. Or are you fining me?'

'I am sorry, my lord.'

These two were almost equal offences in the custom. It was a big crime for a man to get so drunk that he started singing drunkenly at his mother-in-law's place. A very big fine might ensue if his drunken imagination strayed. Hence, the saying that "he who had something in which he trusted, would start singing drunkenly at his mother-in-law's place". Similarly, it was a big offence for a woman to mention her father-in-law's name. She would pay a big fine if she was heard.

'I wish,' Kenyangyi continued, 'that my lord's father could know how clean-hearted the Ruteeramareingwas are. How happy with his blessing the two of us would be.'

'Are we not happy now?'

'Yes, we are. I am certainly not complaining. But imagine.'

'All right then, let us go to bed.' So saying he got up and lifted her from the floor. 'Remember we have to start cultivating that land in the valley tomorrow. And we have a lot of celebrating to do tonight.'

He carried her to bed. She went struggling in his arms. She hit him with feeble arms and complained while laughing. She had no intention of breaking free.

Chapter Nine

I

Ruteera and all his senior sons and senior grandsons sat outside at the fireplace. It was an evening right in the middle of the minor harvest season. Those who had sown their millet early had already harvested and were eating the new millet. Kubiriba's wife, Keishemeza, was one of Ruteera's daughters-in-law who had harvested her millet already. She was a very lucky woman. She had had her third child, a son, two weeks before her millet was ready to be harvested. Her millet would have gone to waste in the field if she had not had the child at the right time. And her son, who was born at the beginning of the time of plenty, would never know famine. We name our children according to the circumstances prevailing at the time of their birth either in the clan, the family or the village. This boy was named Bwezire. It meant that the millet was ripe and gave a heavy yield.

Tonight Keishemeza had given her father-in-law and her husband's immediate brothers the traditional first meal of the new harvest. Kubiriba had skinned a young he-goat to supplement the new green peas. A pot of beer had been brewed specially for the purpose. Only the home people were there. In many homes, where the brothers were not friendly – particularly if they were from the same mother – the woman would cook this meal for her husband and his father only.

The new round of seasons had started well. The harvests would be big. Even the sorghum which was already starting to flower looked very healthy. Nothing short of locusts – may the gods forbid – and recurrent hailstones would affect the sorghum much. Some pessimists said that such big harvests prophesied a catastrophe.

'Why are there so few Bajura in the ridges around, compared with other clans?' Tindikahwa, an older grandson, asked after the supper.

'That is a long story, my child,' Ruteera started, looking up at the young moon. 'But you deserve to know why.' He gave them the long story, cut down here and there. His older sons had heard it many times but they always listened to it. There was always an extra detail and they asked deeper questions for further clarification. They had to learn it very deeply and know all the details. Soon it would be their turn to tell the story to their grandchildren, who would also tell it to their grandchildren when their turn came. He stressed the bravery of his ancestors. He had seen one or two in their very old age. Even then they looked very brave. They proudly showed off the scars sustained in those wars.

Essentially, the Bajura had always been few. They had initially left home as a small group running away from famine. Their original home was called Butatuurwa. It was a bad place, towards Rwangaminyeeto, following the direction of the sun as it went to sleep. Most of the brothers they had left behind had perished in that great famine. Others, who had gone in different directions, might have survived. Nobody knew for sure. Those who came this way had belonged to one big home, bigger than Ruteera's father's home. The father of that home was Kajura. He had died only a short time back. He had been a very rich, powerful man. 'We all descend from that powerful man.'

However, being so few, they could never have defended their settlements from attacks by the bigger clans they found in the areas they tried to settle in. 'He who is greater than you will kill your father and inherit your mother, my son,' the old man observed. 'And you will do nothing about it.' So the Bajura were always on the run. They stopped when their fathers learnt very powerful medicines, to add to the wealth Kajura had left to his sons. As a matter of fact, this was the Bajura's second settlement, here in Nyabigyi. Ruteera himself was part of the fifth generation in the area.

Their movement helped the Bajura in one way. Whichever place they were chased from, a few Bajura would be left behind. These were normally men, who had made friends with the men in the indigenous clans. They would normally be blood-friends who were blood bound never to harm each other. These multiplied. And, if one retraced the trail the Bajura had followed in their long flights, one would find pockets of Bajura all along the trail. In some places there were more Bajura than there were in Nyabigyi.

'Why did they not stay and fight instead of always fleeing?' Tindikahwa wondered loudly.

'They stayed and fought, my child.' The grandfather stopped and gnashed his teeth. He shook his head slowly, remembering the bloody stories he had heard from his grandfather. 'Ahaaa! They were very brave men, I can assure you. But we have always been greatly outnumbered. Had they fought to the last, they would have been wiped out.'

Tindikahwa was a bright cheerful boy of thirteen, very much loved by his grandfather. He would very rarely be found doing nothing. If he did not know something, he would not rest until he had learnt as much about it as he could. But sometimes he became very moody and uncommunicative. Then, nobody could get at whatever he was thinking about.

II

The quarter moon was just disappearing when Ruteera concluded the story. He left his grandchildren getting more details from the senior sons. He was going to spend the night in the house of his third wife. He found her also telling the younger children – and the girls – a women's story, equally interesting. It was that sad story about Nzima and that hateful stepmother. She had got to the part where Njunju had found out about Nzima's whereabouts. Nzima was singing advice to her:

> *Njunjuwe ningyira rucwekana*
> *Sho na nyoko bakagamba kamwe*
> *Twite Nzima ahiguze Njunju akure.*
> *Njunjuwe okareka kwitwa eitesi*
> *Wabura okanywa agomate okareka kwitwa enjara*
> *Sho na nyoko tibarenda ngu mbeho.*

The man's wife had died leaving behind a small daughter, Nzima. He married another wife who also produced a girl, Njunju. This Njunju was not as beautiful as Nzima and she was always sickly. The jealous mother mistreated Nzima a great deal. The father, who could not be at home all the time, could not see this. Worse still, whenever he was at home, he showed more love to Nzima than to her stepsister. The poor girl was afraid to complain. Her tormentor had always threatened her that if she complained to her father, she would suffer greatly. Poor girl! She could imagine what 'greatly' would be. As it were, she was already going through hell.

She was always punished both for her mistakes and Njunju's, too.

Whenever her stepmother was angered outside the house, she would hide her anger, only to vent it on the poor girl later. Nzima did almost all the work at home. Most of it was much harder than others of her age could manage. She very rarely got enough to eat. And sometimes eating was a punishment to her. The woman would put boiling food, straight from the pot, into her hands. If a single bit fell down she would be beaten. And she would not see any more food for days. All the delicacies like milk and eggs naturally went to Njunju.

The two girls grew up to be very good friends. It started to be difficult for the woman to mistreat Nzima so much and so openly. Whenever she gave her daughter anything, Njunju would find a way of sharing it with Nzima. Whenever Nzima was given any work, Njunju would help her. Even the punishments lessened. Njunju would always intervene. So the woman planned to kill the girl.

She dug a pit secretly in a private space in her kitchen where no one else went. It was very deep indeed. One day when her husband was away she sent her daughter to the well alone. She dropped Nzima into the pit and covered it with a big mat. She threatened that if Nzima attempted to attract anybody in any way, she would pour boiling water down the pit to scald her. And she added that, after all, the father was in on this, so nobody would rescue her.

Njunju came back from the well to find Nzima gone. She was heart-broken. She asked her mother what had become of her sister. The mother said she did not know. When the father came that night and asked for Nzima, again she disclaimed any knowledge of her whereabouts. Three days passed and still there was no sign of Nzima. Meanwhile, Njunju had not eaten or drunk anything. She had sworn to die of hunger, unless Nzima was found. On the fourth day the mother tried to give another explanation to the father. She said that Nzima had gone secretly to get married and that, by and by, the man she had eloped with would be coming to report. Njunju rejected this as impossible. Nzima could not have done anything without telling her – they so loved each other – let alone running away to get married. This made her most suspicious.

Njunju would hide and weep bitterly, broken-hearted. On the fifth day she hid in the corner of the kitchen, weeping loudly. She prayed to the gods to bring her sister back:

> Nzima, Nzima, Nzima. I am weeping, Nzima.
> I will never eat food until I see Nzima.
> I will never drink milk or *bushera* until I see Nzima.
> I know my mother has done something fiendish to her
> I entreat all you gods to bring her back
> Or else I will die of a broken heart.

The weak girl in the pit heard her. Then she wept in answer. She sang a deeply touching song, advising her sister – and this is the stage the story-telling had got to when Ruteera arrived:

> Njunju, wee, I am talking about doom.
> Your father and mother agreed on this one thing
> To kill Nzima to give way to Njunju to grow.
> Njunju, wee, don't die of stupidity.
> You should eat and drink milk and not die of hunger.
> Your mother and father wish that I should not live.

Njunju was shocked to learn what had happened. She secretly went to search for her father. She was full of hatred and vengeance thinking of her mother.

When she told her father, he quickly summoned his neighbours and the elders of the clan. He came home with them right away. He summoned his wife to the gathering. He asked her for his daughter. The wife again denied knowledge of her whereabouts.

Tearfully he asked his brothers to grab the woman. He asked Njunju to take three elders to where Nzima was. Nzima was brought up very sick and weak. Everybody wondered at the woman's act. The elders decreed that she be burned alive.

A big fire was made. She was burned alive in the fire. The women around were called to see for themselves, in case they entertained the same feelings about their orphaned stepchildren.

III

Ruteera, having eaten well and with a settled mind, was already sound asleep when his wife came to join him. She had just finished the story and put the sleepy children to bed. On getting into the bed her body touched his. He jumped violently and sat up in bed.

'What is it, my lord?' she asked puzzled. She caressed him, held him close. He was sweating, his heart beating violently. 'What is it?' she asked again.

'It is,' he started, but realised he could not remember. It had been a terrible nightmare. He groped in his foggy mind for the dream but still could not remember what it really was about. All he could remember was that it had been terrible and had appeared as true as life. His wife had woken him up before it was through.

'I cannot remember it,' he explained. It was infuriating. He could feel it all in his mind. He could almost see it all happening with all the horror but he could not remember it. 'Well, whatever it was, it was a very bad dream. Like the gods were warning me about something, about – I do not know what!'

'Do not worry, my lord. On which side of your body were you sleeping?'

'Let me see, on the right side.' They were both quiet for a brief period.

'Then you should not have forgotten it. Whatever it was all about.'

'No, indeed I should not have forgotten it. Whatever it was all about it was not an ordinary dream.'

'Forget it for now,' the wife advised. 'Let us have some deep sleep. Maybe it will come back'

'I wish not. Our elders say that "nobody has ever refused to sleep for fear of dreaming." Tonight I might be the first to refuse, if this dream must come back.'

'When you were younger,' the wife started playfully cajoling him, 'You used to know some nice ways in which to refuse to sleep.'

'You mean I cannot do the same now?' he whispered, snuggling closer.

'It is a challenge.'

'Let us find out.'

Chapter Ten

I

The next morning Ruteera spent a long time in bed. He was trying to remember the dream but again he could not. The harder he tried to remember, the more distant it felt. And the deeper the feeling of doom it gave him. Eventually he got out of bed. He was tired and red-eyed. He had not slept after that dream. Only after the birds began to twitter in the morning had he allowed himself to doze off.

His wife had already gone to the garden. Her middle daughter had stayed behind to serve him with breakfast. She would follow them to the garden later. Breakfast consisted of cold sweet potatoes with warmed-up vegetables and fried pumpkin seeds. He washed it down with cold sweet *bushera*.

The potatoes and vegetables were part of the previous night's cooking. Our mothers say that "a person who has got a child never leaves the pot empty". So a mother always cooks so much that some must remain in the pot. But again they say that "when you feed the young child, the older ones looking on will also feel hungry". They would need to be fed too. As it turned out there was always enough for everybody's breakfast.

Ruteera did not finish what was put before him. He did not have much of an appetite. All his mind was still concentrated on that dream. He had a strong premonition that his ever-caring ancestors were trying to warn him about some impending doom. And they could not quite break through to him. So somebody had to be interfering with their efforts.

This conclusion drove him to Migayo's place. He was not a man to dally with thoughts when there was an easy and sure way to find out. His brother's fifth wife received him cordially. She was decidedly the most loved of all the medicine man's wives. Probably this was because of the way he had married her.

She had been a hotly-contested-for girl, and extremely beautiful. So when this elderly and partly deformed medicine man had come to woo her, she had refused him outright. There were many other suitors who were handsome, rich and young. He went back a few days later but she told him in no uncertain terms that she would not change her mind. He had then sent some respected go-betweens to approach her parents but again she had refused. So he had gone there again personally to entreat her for the last time. He had told her that he would do anything within his powers to ensure that he married her. She had sent him off again.

Soon after he had left, she had started feeling funny. She developed a very strong urge to go and pass urine. She was feeling funny between the legs. So, before she peed, she looked. Alas, her privates were not there. An exuberant growth of mushrooms, of the small white type, had sprouted where the pubic hair should have been. When she investigated further, she found that what the pubic hair should have surrounded had also vanished. It had been sealed flat. Only a small hole for passing urine was left.

The poor girl had rushed to her mother for guidance. The mother in turn had run to her husband with the woeful tale. The three of them had run to Migayo to divine the cause of such a horror.

'Yes,' Migayo had said, blinking rapidly, supposedly equally surprised. 'I can make whoever took them return them to her. But it is rather complicated.'

'How much will it cost us?'

'I cannot tell until after I have returned them.'

'What should we do now?'

'Leave her with me for now. I must keep her in my sight for these next three days or so.' He looked at them with a convincingly deep concentration. 'She will return as soon as she is back to normal.'

She had returned home two weeks later as custom demanded. Migayo's brothers had already been to her father to report possession of the girl. She was not different from those who eloped. Migayo paid the bride price and she came back to him as a willing wife this time. And she had never regretted it. He really loved her and that was all she cared about. Ruteera looked up at her face. She avoided his eyes.

'He is busy but he will be coming soon,' she said shyly.

'I will wait. Even if he spent two years there, I would gladly spend them waiting in the presence of such beauty,' he said, adjusting the skins with a shrug of the shoulders. She laughed and walked out to hide her embarrassment. Ruteera always gave her this feeling. Probably she knew that he knew how Migayo had forced her into marrying him.

II

Migayo limped in from his shrine not long afterwards. His young son, Muhimbuura, followed closely, carrying the medicine man's bag. He put the bag in its place, greeted his younger father and left.

Migayo's deformations were not actually serious. He had fallen from a tree when he was young. He had suffered a dislocation of the left hip joint and the thumb of the left hand; and he had bitten off part of the lower lip, also on the left side. When he recovered the leg remained stiff and shorter than the right one. The left thumb remained almost pushed to the back of the hand and could not stretch. As he walked he bobbed up towards the right and down towards the left. Otherwise he was quite handsome.

'You slept well, child of my mother?' he greeted as he entered.

'*Yeego*. And you, how did you spend the night here?'

'It was well.' Migayo sat on a stool opposite his elder brother, scrutinising him. 'You look as if you did not sleep at all last night,' he observed. 'Are you playing at being a young man again or is there something disturbing you?'

They laughed loudly but Ruteera stopped suddenly. He looked across at the medicine man seriously. 'But largely, there is something disturbing me.'

Migayo became serious too. 'I thought as much. Otherwise you would not have honoured us with your most rare visit, so early in the morning.'

'That is not true, the bit about "rare" I mean,' he said jokingly. 'Ask your beautiful wife if I am lying.'

'Well, if you choose to visit me here only when I am not in and my most trusted wife thinks it best not to tell me, you would remain rare to me. As we say, "when a tree falls in a place, it can only fall on those who are in its immediate vicinity".' He looked at him quizzically. 'Can it fall on me when I am not there?'

'Decidedly not. But today it is your turn to feel the impact of the tree.' Then he told him about his dream.

'Yes, it could be very significant,' Migayo said thoughtfully, his face furrowed. He blinked rapidly. 'Come this evening just before the sun disappears over the edge of the earth. We will have to consult with the gods.'

Ruteera returned to Migayo's home shortly before sunset. A large red sun was hanging a few arm's lengths above the edge of the earth. A few thin clouds scattered near it had taken some of the red colour out of the sun. As they entered the shrine, Ruteera cast another glance at the sun. It reminded him of a bull being slaughtered, splashing blood in the grass around it.

In the shrine, Muhimbuura handed the bag to his father and stood attentively. He would be asked to do this and hand over that. He had long known that his father could not ask for the same thing twice. So the boy had to hear everything and do precisely as told.

Muhimbuura was a special boy. He had been chosen by the gods to inherit his father's bags and medicinal powers. Proof of this was the fact that he was born holding a gourd seed in his small right hand. Naturally, he was looked after with special care. He was so disciplined he could not misuse his powers. And as soon as he could differentiate between two herbs, his father placed him under apprenticeship, to learn everything that he himself knew. Muhimbura was only fourteen, but he already knew almost enough to be left on his own.

At any rate he had the gods of the clan to guide him.

The sun had long disappeared when they emerged. Ruteera's dream had been a premonition. Danger was imminent unless it was dealt with immediately. The source of the danger was so evasive that it could not be pinpointed. But the required sacrifices were very clear. The source was not so important now. It would be revealed after the sacrifices had been performed.

Three sacrifices had been indicated. These had to be performed the next day. The first one at sunrise was a general one to the gods of the clan and their attendants, the spirits of the clan. The second one would follow at noon, to the Nyabingi of the family. The final one would be at sunset to the sun, Kazooba Nyamuhanga, the god of all creation. It was all going to be very expensive; but Ruteera had to do his duty. He had the whole clan to protect.

As Ruteera walked home under a bright maturing moon, he was satisfied with his action. He was equally thankful to his ancestors. He was sure it was they who had warned him. He was glad he had always fed them well, a bit more than custom demanded.

Now that the sickness had been diagnosed, it could be treated, successfully too.

III

That night he jumped out of his bed again. This time, his second wife was shaking him hard, forcing him to wake up. She could not tell him much. She was hysterical. He swung his skins into place, grabbed his spear and matchet and walked out into the cold night. There was already quite a gathering outside his kraal. He heard his bull, Ruhogo, groaning before he got to the crowd. A cold shiver went through him. Somebody wanted his blood. He prayed quietly in the time he took to be swallowed by the gathering. He did not want vengeance. His clan was too small for that. He prayed that the blood his beautiful bull had shed would be enough for his enemies.

Ruhogo would die before morning. Both its hind legs had been slashed above the knees. There was another gash on the neck. They had certainly made sure.

They did not know how the attack had been carried out so successfully until the next day. Migayo found the tell-tale remains of the powerful charm used in the morning. It had been sprinkled through the gate, into Ruteera's compound. Some more had been sprinkled over the fence at the back of the compound. In this way the whole household was bound from the front and the back.

Migayo gnashed his teeth and shook his head. He regretted very much that he had not done something to prevent this. But he had not believed that they would strike so soon.

When the enemy had sprinkled the charm everybody had fallen into a very deep bewitched sleep. Even the family dogs and cows were affected. The men had come quickly, done what had brought them and gone away.

Only one young man had seen them and he had not recognised them as it had been very dark. He had been calling on a widowed in-law. The young moon had already set when he left. As he passed Ruteera's home he heard the bull give a terrible groan of pain. He hid in the fence and scanned the area. Of one thing he was sure, the attacker was not a wild animal. It would not have attacked the terrifying massive bull first. And the bull would have fought back.

His eyes were used to the darkness. He spotted three young men with spears and machetes. They were standing waiting as if on guard. Soon, a fourth one joined them. They disappeared in the darkness quietly like shadows. That was when he realised that his heart had been pounding so loudly. At first he did not believe his eyes. He thought that he was dreaming. But the continued groaning of the bull galvanised him into action. He blinked rapidly to clear his foggy brain. Then he raised the alarm. The dogs were the first to respond. As he knocked on the door of the nearest house he considered his position again. He was lucky they had not seen him. He would have been killed along with the bull.

By morning word of the incident had got to all the nearby ridges. Ruteera had sent special messages to the elders of the clans around. But his immediate plans had shifted. Of course they would go on with the sacrifices. As we say, "an appointment with the gods cannot be broken". But this time, they would not be asking only for protection. They would also ask for the gods' assistance in their endeavour to defend themselves. The bull, Ruhogo, would be the major ingredient in the sacrifices.

Chapter Eleven

I

Bugeiga was seen to smile that morning. His springy walk was real. But there was something cold about his smile. He had gone out in the mid-morning. When he came back just before noon, he wanted to see only his son, Ndemire. He sent for him.

At first he had been rather secretive about his mood. But now the truth was out. Migayo's horns had pinpointed him. He was the mastermind behind the raid. The occasion was worth celebrating.

Of all his sons, only Ndemire had agreed to take part in the raid. Those he had asked he had approached most discreetly. Some would have leaked his plan to Rwecurenga. That had to be avoided. His mind went back to a night some three weeks back. It had all come to him unexpectedly, from the least expected people.

An old man, Rukandema, accompanied by two young men, had called on him at his home. He was the same old man who had talked of doing something to the Bajura at that party, long ago. It was just after dark. They were his close clansmen. Quickly they had told him their story.

Essentially they wanted the Bajura uprooted from Nyabigyi. They wanted to force them into war. It was Bugeiga who had planted this idea into their heads some years back and it was only fitting that they should come to him. He could provide them with a good plan of action. They had talked at length. In the end they had left it to Bugeiga to investigate the case and its feasibility.

Bugeiga consulted many medicine men in the weeks that followed. They were all of one accord: that what Bugeiga asked for was very difficult. Ruteera was very strongly protected and they could not do anything to the Bajura through him. Eventually he found one from across the lakes who promised to try. He said that it would be very costly but possible. The Bajura would move. But the price the Bagirakwe would have to pay would be too high to justify the whole plan. Bugeiga jumped at this. He did not mind the price. He wanted the means and the end. After some instruction Bugeiga had gone home.

Now he was overjoyed to know that many other Bagirakwe wished to fight the Bajura and chase them out of Nyabigyi. For them, it was not because of the bull fight. No. As a matter of fact, they did not even hate them. They only wanted land. They were becoming a bit too numerous for the ridges and many of the young men would have to move in search of new land. But if the Bajura, the smallest clan, moved then these young men would not have to move away. They would simply take over the ridges of the Bajura. But they needed a leader, an elder who would champion their cause.

Bugeiga shook his head and came out of this reverie. The events of the previous weeks gave him something to dream about. He had spent quite a number of goats and two cows in those three weeks. These had gone to the medicine men and sacrifices. All this was an attempt to neutralise the strong medicine of the Bajura. And now the first part of the operation had been carried out successfully. Ndemire stood in front of him.

'You have come.'

'Yes, taata.' The two of them contemplated each other with mutual admiration.

'That spotted, castrated goat …'

'Yes, father …'

The father looked up at his son and smiled. 'Bring it. And do it quickly, quickly.'

Rwecurenga came home to find Ndemire pinning the skin of a large goat on the ground to dry. Everybody had always known the boy to share the same ideas as his father. Rwecurenga knew what was to be celebrated. He did not greet him. He went straight to his house.

Kenyangyi was lying on the bed with a headache. She had been weeping quietly since morning. Rwecurenga joined her with a heavy heart. He had gone to his father-in-law's home as soon as they had learnt what had happened. He had become very troubled when he got there. All the people seemed to be looking at him with accusing eyes. It was as if he had committed the crime and now he had come to mock them. He hoped that their eyes accused him as a Bagirakwe but not as Rwecurenga.

He was comforted later by his friend Kubiriba. He believed Rwecurenga when he said that he had known nothing at all. How could they understand that he grieved bitterly about his father's act?

'What hurts me most,' he whispered to his wife, 'is that I did not know in time to warn my friend.'

'Do not blame yourself,' she murmured tearfully. 'I hope it will end at the death of the bull.'

'You know it will not. Not with the people who have been keeping him company of late.'

'Do you know them?'

'I have ears and eyes. I should have wondered. Only that it had been so long ago and we had all assumed that everything was over.' He lay there quietly for a long time. He heaved deep sigh after deep sigh. He infected his wife who started sighing too. There had to be something that he could do.

He got up and put on his side skins again. He picked up his matchet and stick. He went hunting for his brothers, his mother's sons this time. He needed solace from them.

II

That evening Busaahu called on Bugeiga. He was accompanied by another old man. By then everybody knew the full story. The elders even knew the individuals who had carried out the raid. Bugeiga received them with profuse cordiality. He was very happy with himself. The two elders took their seats coldly. They refused everything they were offered to eat or drink.

'We have not come to celebrate with you, Bugeiga,' Busaahu started coldly. 'We shall not partake in a feast to celebrate evil deeds. You talked of doom long ago. Now you seem determined to bring it about.'

Bugeiga's face clouded briefly. He contemplated the two elders. 'My younger father,' he started happily, suppressing laughter, 'It really pleases me to know …'

'Cut out the madness, Bugeiga, and listen to me,' Busaahu interrupted sharply. 'You shock me beyond words. This thing of the bulls happened long ago. You have harboured it this long to bring evil to the clan. A man of your status to endanger a whole clan only because you want to satisfy your sick head!' He gnashed his teeth before continuing coldly. 'We talked to you soon after the bulls had fought. We were deceived that you had seen some sense. We talked to you again when your son was seeking to marry Ruteera's daughter. You agreed with us that you were in the wrong. You admitted that Ruteera had never wronged you at all. And now you have gone and done this thing!'

'But you do not …'

'Shut up and hear me out,' Busaahu interrupted, his old voice quavering with anger. 'Ruteera is father-in-law to your son Rwecurenga. To all intents and purposes, he is as good as a brother to you. You have betrayed and broken the relationship which the union of your two children had created.' He stopped and looked Bugeiga in the eye. Bugeiga was looking at him with an amusedly mocking eye. Busaahu was appalled. 'I see I am talking to a tree.'

'Not so,' Bugeiga countered. A strange smile was lingering on his face.

'All right, Bugeiga. I will be brief.' He looked at his companion as if to say 'you will be my witness'. He then looked straight at Bugeiga. 'We have always known you to be a bad man. But we never believed you to be really a curse to the clan. Maybe it is because the gods have been so good to you. "When a man makes a dog so used to him, it may start to think that it is his cousin".' He stopped briefly and looked down. 'Be careful, Bugeiga. You are starting to think that you are "cousin" to the gods. You want to direct the future of the clan. But instead you are heading it towards doom.' He shook his head slowly. 'The gods will not permit it. The curse you are trying to bring to the clan will come back to you.'

The two old men got up to leave. Bugeiga did not get up to see them off. They would have refused his company, anyway. When they were in the doorway, Busaahu stopped and looked back at Bugeiga. He was still seated there as if in a stupor. 'Only a bull which has never met with danger licks an axe.' After saying this he turned and went away.

'Is Bugeiga's head really straight?' the other elder asked thoughtfully as they went through the gate.

'No, his head cannot be alive. A man with a head which is alive, full of thinking, cannot provoke war just to see people suffer. Unfortunately, the world is full of such evil men. They thrive on the suffering of others. They cannot bear to live with peace. They would sooner plunge the world into war than see people live in peace and harmony.'

'Like a bad boy who cannot pass by a beehive without throwing stones at it, just to make the bees mad.'

'Do they not often go home swollen with bee stings?'

'That is right.'

'You only have to wait. The eyes of the gods are never closed to evil for long.'

III

The whole of the next moon was very tense. The Bagirakwe were divided. Rwecurenga and most of his father's sons had condemned their father's action. They were vehemently against any further provocation. They desired to live happily with the neighbouring clans. They wanted no war. After all, Nyabigyi was still large enough for them all. So, why fight for what was enough for them all? Those who felt that they did not have enough should have been the ones to move. They could go and jump over the edge of the earth if they wanted. No one would stop them.

Their anti-war crusade was led by Busaahu. Most of the other clan elders were with him. This crusade had by far the largest backing. The other group was led by Bugeiga. These wanted war with the Bajura. They wanted to force them to flee never to return to Nyabigyi.

All the other clans around saw one thing: time for such wars was over. Unlike their forefathers, they had become civilised. They had learnt to live together in full respect of their neighbours, despite their clan differences. At any rate, the Bagirakwe, led by Bugeiga, were completely in the wrong. Nature demands that man should defend his brother in all his troubles, even if he is in the wrong; then, after he has come out of danger, deal with him at home. The clan would then punish him to teach him not to be in the wrong in future. But how could any sane person side with such gross wrongness? How do you side with a wrongdoer who does not want to listen, and insists that he is right? There is a saying: "When you tell your brother to cover his shameful foreskinless penis and he refuses, you join the laughers and laugh at him".

'The world is turning upside down,' one man observed. He was one of a group of middle-aged men who were sitting in the shade of a tree, relaxing. It was in the early afternoon. None of them belonged to the two feuding clans. 'We have all seen clans fighting,' he continued. 'We have even seen a clan being forced to flee from this land. But this provocation beats them all.'

'You cannot compare this with those other wars,' somebody objected. 'They never fought without a very strong reason. Unless you are talking of those of long, long ago. But if you are talking about our fathers or their fathers, they would not act until they had caught someone in the wrong. Then they would use that as an excuse to chase him away.'

'That is right,' another man observed. 'That is why it was always easy for a whole clan to fight together. But now, even Bugeiga's family is not with him. The whole clan is divided. And yet Bugeiga insists on war.'

'Most surprisingly Bugeiga's son married Ruteera's daughter,' the first man commented. 'The two clans are generally very closely related. They have intermarried more heavily than any other two clans. This is like a man running mad and cutting down his own brothers with his matchet.'

'It is truly a mad world,' a short man, who had not said anything yet, started. 'In all truth, you have lived with these people for generations. You have eaten together. Your children call each clan home. Their parents come from both sides. You have sworn to be friends in numberless ceremonies. You have shared in almost everything, happily together. How do you close your eyes to all these and go to war? How do you fight the peace you have lived with and sworn to keep?'

'Very easy,' a cynic in the group said. 'You only need a few bastards like that mad Bugeiga and his followers. Nothing good can come of them. They think evil, feel evil, breathe out evil and …' He was interrupted by a horn. It was being blown from Nyamiringa across the valley.

'Taliiiiiiiiila,' the sorrow-laden message floated across the valley. 'Tilalaaaaaaaalali. Talilalalaaaaa.' For a few breaths they could not speak. The short crisp message was still echoing across the valley, in between the ridges. They looked from one to another enquiringly.

'What was that for, now?' The first one to recover asked. 'Is it the beginning of war?'

'Yes,' the cynic answered. 'Somebody has been murdered. And it is a Mujura. That horn is unmistakable.'

This was the fourth day after the death of Ruhogo. A young son of Oribariho had just been found murdered. He was the first son Oribariho had produced with the wife he inherited.

The young man's body had just been found in a disused chalk pit. He had failed to come home the previous evening. His parents had not been so worried. It was best for him to sleep where night found him. These were bad days. There was a threat of war in the air. But when by mid-morning he had not yet come home, they had got very worried. They had sent enquiries all over the place. Reports came in that he had last been seen leaving his maternal grandfather's home, a Mugirakwe, just before sunset the previous evening.

A search had immediately been mounted. The horn blower was announcing to all the other searchers that he had been found. And that he was dead. And thus to inform everybody that a Mujura had been murdered. That he had been strangled was indisputable. The killers had not bothered to hide the fact. The broken neck had human scratches on it.

The body could not be touched until the medicine man had come. Migayo soon arrived, closely followed by his son Muhimbuura. By the time he arrived there was a large gathering. A cold lull accompanied him to the mouth of the chalk pit. He mumbled a prayer before going down into the pit. He sprinkled a brown powder on the body and came up.

'All right,' he said with a tremulous voice. 'We can carry him home now.'

The men did not cry as they carried the body home. But they looked very severe. They were almost bursting with anger and hatred. The women followed closely behind. Many were crying quietly but the very close relatives were wailing. The young children trailed behind, not sure whether to cry or not.

A council of elders was already in session when they got the body home. Migayo did not join them right away. He headed for his shrine first. He had to be guided by the gods in this. Some young men wanted to cross the valley and exact revenge right away. But the wisdom of the elders prevailed over their emotions.

'No, my children, you cannot do that,' one elder advised. 'Let us bury this one first. As it is, one Mujura murdered in cold blood is one too many.'

'But are we going to let them get away with all this?' a brother of the murdered man asked.

'Certainly not. But there is no reason why any more of us should blunder across there to be murdered. Let us wait to hear the counselling of the gods.'

'No mourning,' Migayo announced coldly as he rejoined the group. He did not sit down. 'We shall have to give a sacrifice tomorrow morning. Then we shall give him a quiet burial just before the goats are taken out to graze.' He looked round at all the eyes focussed on him. 'Meanwhile every man should attend to his Nyabingi. Pray for protection. Also pray that, if the gods will, this war may pass us by.' He stopped and looked around to see whether they were all following what he was saying. 'Let me repeat this: no mourning at all.' He walked away fast, head down.

Only the immediate members of the family would sit by the traditional death-fire throughout the night. And they would continue to do so for four days after the burial. For the four days at the very least they would not go to their gardens.

Chapter Twelve

I

The next day was dry and cloudless and the whole clan turned up to bury the dead kinsman. Sympathisers and other relatives from the other clans around came. Busaahu, accompanied by some elders and a few young men from Bagirakwe, also came. Rwecurenga was with them. They had come to show the Bajura that they were on their side. This was to show their protest against Bugeiga and his followers. It was a great risk for them to come. But they were innocent. Fortunately many Bajura knew this. The small group braved the eyes of hatred through the burial.

There was no ceremony and no mourning. Even the women managed to remain almost dry-eyed.

After the burial people did not stay around to console the family. They went back to their homes straight away. They were all too grief-stricken to talk. They knew that this killing would lead to worse things. They were dead to the surroundings. If anybody had been observant, they would have seen a small, dry, light cloud floating towards Nyabigyi. It was coming from the direction of Butumbi. It was slow. Most of them were just settling down in their houses when it struck.

The whole sky exploded in a near simultaneous cracking of lightning and a deafening thunder. It was a dry thunderbolt. A few breaths later, another one rumbled. It had a hollow and deep roar. Even its lightning was slow. It was the stand-by thunderbolt. It had just collected the first one which had been weakened by the hit it had made. The small cloud disappeared suddenly. It left behind a rumble, reverberating in the ridges.

All those who were indoors came out stunned. They expected to see destruction outside their houses. To each of them it had sounded as if the lightning had struck the nearest neighbour's home.

'It has touched down,' one man stated loudly to his brother. Each person stood in front of his house surveying the neighbourhood.

'Yes, it has touched down indeed,' the brother shouted back. 'But where? Has it really gone with nothing?'

People were starting to recover from the shock. Everywhere people started calling out loudly, enquiring about neighbours. 'This is extremely rare indeed,' one observed. 'A thunderbolt striking when there is no rain, and not even a cloud!'

'It has been sent. And to whom? We shall know soon.' Some inaudible words came, addressed to them.

'Eh, listen!' Someone was calling from the opposite hump on the same ridge. It was quite some distance away.

'What have you said?' the younger of the two brothers shouted as loudly as he could. 'Repeat. We have not heard.'

'Are all of you there well?' the question came. The words were being blown away by the wind, but they were still clear enough.

'We are all right,' the young man shouted back. 'What about you over there?'

'We are all well.' The two brothers looked at each other puzzled. 'Where has it struck?'

A horn answered them. It had struck a home on the opposite ridge. The Bagirakwe were relaying a message of death.

The full story was told that evening. While the Bajura were burying, some Bagirakwe were celebrating. They were drinking at Rukandema's home. That is where it struck. Two people had been killed right there, Rukandema himself and one of the visiting young men. All the others had been immediately treated with fresh human dung. A few had recovered. But several more were critically ill. They would have to be treated more intensively by a powerful medicine man.

It was public knowledge that the dead young man, together with some others, had carried out the raid that killed Ruhogo. The dead Rukandema was the same old man who had first called on Bugeiga wishing to fight the Bajura. Now it was clear that the two had killed the Mujura youth. Otherwise, this would be a bit too coincidental to be credible. "Why was it that when my sheep got lost the hyena defecated sheep fleece?" everybody wondered. And of course the gods of the Bajura had not been sleeping. Migayo would be in constant contact with them. They would be doing everything possible to protect the clan.

Before morning a third victim of the thunderbolt died. Then a low-intensity war started in earnest. The next day another Mujura was found murdered, by the wayside. Many days of raids and ambushes followed. Clashes broke out whenever the two groups met. They even fought in the communal places, like the watering place. In such places, the Bagirakwe always lost. All the other clans were in support of the Bajura.

Normally these people would move around with a matchet and a stick. And sometimes a pointed staff as well. But these days they moved around with a sharp spear, instead of a pointed staff. Some even carried around with their bows and arrows. Seeing this development the Bagirakwe stopped crossing the valley. They even stopped taking their cattle across to the communal watering place. Instead, they intensified their night raids. The Bajura had to do something.

A group of young Bajura vigilantes was formed. They organised themselves into night patrols. They scouted their ridge throughout the night. Any Mugirakwe caught there was never seen again. By the time the Bagirakwe realised this, they had been badly hit. Some six men had gone on night raids in two groups and had failed to return. Very rarely, these young Bajura ventured across the valley. Twice they scored and once they lost a friend.

Meanwhile, Ruteera had summoned a council of elders. Not Bajura only this time. The leaders of all clans converged on Ruteera's compound. Even a group of elders from the Bagirakwe came. They were led by Busaahu. They gathered around the huge kitooma tree, Heirembo. They sat, some on stones, others on logs and yet others on the ground.

Ruteera stood up to speak. He was sad, angry and desperate. He looked around with a miserable face and looked down again, as if at a funeral. At first he was tongue-tied. He shrugged his shoulders to adjust his skins.

'Brothers, cousins and in-laws, I greet you all.' He seemed to have found his voice at last. It was a touching tremulous voice. 'Are you all well?'

'*Yeego*,' the gathering replied, sadly too.

'Are you thoroughly well?'

'*Yeego.*'

He fell silent and looked down. He swallowed twice and breathed in deeply to control his emotions. Then he looked up again to face the gathering. He scratched his short curly hair.

'We have met here to feast many times, celebrating one good thing or another. Those were the happy times. But now, we meet here to deliberate on a far more important issue than those feasts.' He paused and looked down again. A cold murmur went through the gathering.

He violently brought up his head to face the opposite ridge. Equally violently he thrust his staff towards the ridge.

'Bugeiga across there is after my blood. I have called you all to help me. I do not want war. I want peace and justice. I want you to help me escape Bugeiga peacefully.' Then, slowly, he gave a detailed history of the feud. The gathered elders nodded their heads in agreement as he told the story. They knew it as well as he did. When he finished he faced the elders again. 'One day, a few moons after the bulls fought, two elders called on me. I had just received a message from Bugeiga's son, who had not yet married my daughter. But he had heard his father planning evil against me. He had endeavoured to inform me.' He looked around for the two old men. He pointed at them. 'Zikanga is there. You can ask him.' People turned to look at Zikanga. He was nodding his head in confirmation of what Ruteera had said. 'They assured me that Bugeiga would not be allowed to do anything and that the elders would stop him. Now look!' He gnashed his teeth and spread his arms.

'When they killed my bull I informed the elders. I received assurances from all sides that this madness would be controlled. Then my kinsmen started being strangled. Those of the Bagirakwe who have died were caught here heavily armed. They came at night to kill and destroy. Now they want total war against us.'

Then, quietly as if talking to himself, 'Tell me, friends, what do I do?'

He looked slowly around at all the elders. Then slowly he sat down. Nobody talked for some time. They were all moved almost to tears. Some of them were as sad as Ruteera himself. It was as if they were in the same predicament. At this very moment they could imagine the same thing happening to them and their clans. After digesting it thoroughly and thinking thrice, they started talking. Old men, sure of themselves, set out to find a solution to the problem. They were the cream of Nyabigyi. In their combined heads they knew everything. What they did not know was not worth knowing. And a problem they could not solve was not solvable.

Many men spoke. And their words were good and heartening. They were all of one accord: Bugeiga and his followers were so very wrong. They condemned him in the strongest terms. Now Zikanga's own words highlighted what everybody else generally said.

'We should do everything to stop this band of mad rascals. We should deal with them as a united Nyabigyi. If Bugeiga is allowed to get away with this, only Nyamuhanga knows who will do what and get away with it in future. The dangers which threaten a hunting dog are the same dangers which threaten the hunter moving with it. It may be someone else's turn next.' He stopped and looked around for effect. 'After all, we are all brothers,' he resumed less violently. 'Who is not related to whom in Nyabigyi? Why should we kill each other? And why should we allow one clan to fight another? If Bugeiga and his followers want war, I suggest that he fights us all. If he cannot face that, then let him cool down. Let him learn that there is a community which now wants to live in peace and justice. If he cannot stand peace let him go and look for animals to live with.

'In this very meeting,' he continued with a pleading tone, 'we should plan what to do and see to it that we do it. Those who are not with us, let them stand up and tell us so. They are entitled to their views. We shall listen to their reasons.'

All clans pledged their fullest co-operation. The whole of Nyabigyi was to deal with that small band of Bagirakwe. They set up a powerful council of elders. They were to direct the clans and advise them on what to do. All clans were represented. This council was empowered to deal with Bugeiga as they saw best. But they were to try and solve the problem by peaceful means first.

In the meantime, the whole of Nyabigyi was to have absolutely nothing to do with Bugeiga and his followers. They were all known. Busaahu and his anti-war group knew which camp every Mugirakwe belonged to. If Bugeiga insisted on war, then all the clans would unite and fight him.

As the clans went home they were convinced that they had done a good job. Even Ruteeramareingwa was almost convinced that his problems were over. Of one thing he was sure: they had to follow through with all the resolutions they had passed.

III

Bugeiga reacted to all this indifferently. He had foreseen the possibility of his enemies leaving Nyabigyi. He would not change. Instead he went back to his medicine man across the lake. He wanted reassurance and the necessary reinforcements. His followers were not ready to change either. And they had greatly increased in numbers. That land of the Bajura was too tantalising for them to give up now and the sorghum of the Bajura had never done better. It was almost ready for harvesting. It needed just over one more moon.

'They are all joking,' one young man commented to a group of his friends. 'They cannot fight us.'

'What do you mean "they cannot fight us"?' someone enquired.

'I mean exactly that. They are only threatening us. They were only drunk with emotions at the time. If we act cowardly they will have won. But if we continue ...' And then as if to himself, 'Tell me, who in those other clans will take up arms and fight us? They are not involved in this quarrel.'

'Yes, indeed, who?' another young man commented. 'They talk of not dealing with us. But many of them are still dealing with us openly. But even the few observing this will not do so for long.'

'Anyway, it is all talk and no action. If we ignore their threats we are sure to beat them. And anyway we can always pull out when things become too hot. If we see all the clans preparing to fight us as a "united Nyabigyi", we can always stop. But it would be futile to stop now.' 'That is very right,' someone else put in. 'Never start anything you are not going to finish. Eh, brother?' he said, tapping his friend on the back excitedly. 'That small bird Kanyaamunyu

jumped high up and hard in an attempt to kick the blue sky. When its foot
failed to connect it came back. "You have tried," it told itself, patting itself on
the shoulder. "We should never give up without trying," it observed. I want a
piece of that land,' the young man concluded. 'I am not going to stop until I
am absolutely sure that I cannot get it.'

Chapter Thirteen

I

The Bagirakwe did not give up. They intensified the raids. A day barely passed without a body being found either in the sorghum fields or by the wayside. On all ridges there was one meeting after another. The council of elders moved to and fro. Here they advised, there they asked for advice, somewhere else they consoled. And the Bajura continued to bury their people.

Ruteera's hope for the promised peace started to wane. He realised that the Bajura had to fight to defend themselves. It was their war. They had to fight it themselves. The elders continued to tell him that they were doing the best they could. But he could not see anything useful that they had done. The situation got worse. Many members of the other clans did not follow the resolutions agreed on in that first meeting. They did not see why they should, they said. Others gave some weak excuses.

'I entirely agree with you in principle,' they would start. 'But my son marries there'; or, 'My daughter is married there'; or 'My mother came from there'; or 'My grandfather was a blood-friend to the grandfather of so-and-so there and as such my personal obligations mean that I cannot break the relationship with them.'

Ruteera realised that the concerted effort of a "united Nyabigyi' was largely talk and very little action. These were his feelings when he finally received notice of war. The Bagirakwe were challenging them to open war. They gave them four days to prepare. If the Bajura did not come out to fight on the appointed day, the Bagirakwe would cross and attack them all the same. They asked the Bajura to suggest a venue of their choice. The Bagirakwe suggested Hakiko kya Muhamangabo, in Nyamiringa. By then some fifteen Bajura and thirteen Bagirakwe, excluding the three victims of the thunderbolt, had died.

Ruteemareingwa rushed to the council of elders. They reassured him that they would do everything they had promised.

'You have promised us so much,' he tried to complain. 'But you have already failed to do most of what you promised.'

'This is of utmost seriousness,' the elders assured him. 'We have to deal with it most urgently.'

'But don't you see that these people have gathered the confidence to come out openly from your failure? From the fact that you did not carry out the empty threats you issued?'

'They were not empty, and we have not yet failed. You will see. Bugeiga will be surprised and he will not know what struck him.'

A day passed. The second day also came and went. There was no visible sign of negotiation or action. Bugeiga continued to swing the threatening axe of war over Ruteera's head.

The Bajura had their own sources of information. Their many daughters were married to the clans around. They found out what was happening in their husbands' clans and sent messages back to their fathers. No clan was preparing to fight the Bagirakwe to defend the Bajura. Individuals told their wives openly: they simply would not fight. The Bagirakwe had not quarrelled with them. It was difficult to fight for a cause that was not theirs.

'I am sorry,' one man told his wife, 'but let the Bajura fight their own wars. We will fight ours when it is our turn.' The problem was that these people could not come out openly and declare their non-intention. They did not want the Bajura to know that they would not get the co-operation they had been promised.

On the third day the Bajura elders had an extraordinary meeting. They decided to appeal to the gods for their final advice. Migayo invited fellow medicine men from his clan to his shrine. The rest of the elders were left behind deliberating further on the problem.

As soon as they returned everybody could see disaster in their eyes. Migayo, with his head downcast, led the others back into the meeting. 'We must flee Nyabigyi,' he said, almost tearfully. 'The gods have directed so. We must not wait to go to war.'

It was as if they had all been thrown into the darkness of a bottomless pit. For a long time they could not find their voices.

'What do we do now?' someone asked quietly, as if in a dream. It was as if he had suddenly hit the bottom of the deep pit and the impact had shocked him into realisation.

'We pack and go. There is no alternative. And the sooner we do that the better,' Migayo affirmed.

'Yes, we must go,' the other elders echoed.

'We should make some plans, then,' Ruteera said, looking down.

They sat there planning until after dark. They planned the whole escape route to the last detail. They worked out the best direction to follow and the approximate place they would end in. They would follow the route passing through areas where the inhabitants were most friendly; and on this particular route they would find some scattered Bajura, who would help them. Then, they sent a message to the Bagirakwe suggesting Hakicwamba as the battle field. This was across the swamp, on the ridge of the Bagirakwe.

That night they sent out a message for all families to start packing discreetly. They should not let anybody from any other clan know what was happening. You never knew what they could do. They should pack only the most essential things. And they should carry as much of the dry food as they could. Otherwise, the rest of the family should go about their daily routine as normally as possible.

They should not destroy any of the food that remained in the granaries and the fields. This should be offered as a sacrifice to the gods and ancestors of the clans. Migayo himself would perform a very complicated rite in which he would present all these as the sacrifice. It would offer all the granaries and the gardens of Nyamiringa to the gods and ancestors of the clan. Before they left they should all plant a special talisman at the graves of their forefathers. They would leave soon after dark.

II

The next day was quietly busy. Those grazing the cattle and goats were advised to take them in a particular direction. That was the direction they would follow in their flight. The very old and the ailing had moved that same way discreetly, in the early afternoon. Those who were too old or too sick to move would be carried on litters. Nobody would be left behind for the Bagirakwe to scorn and torture. By the evening all the families of Bajura in Nyabigyi were ready. Very few individuals had opted to stay behind. These were the gamblers. They happened to have some friends among the enemies.

That night saw many hundreds of men, women and children setting out on a long, dangerous trek. They all carried very heavy loads. Many of them had started off with loads they could not possibly manage to carry. It was most painful to watch them decide on what to throw away. It was imperative that they travel as light as possible. They had to cross the Nyabigyi boundary by morning. The night was extremely cold. But they could bear it. It forced them to walk faster. They would be catching up with their herds by midnight.

When they crossed from the land of the Bajura, Migayo and Ruteera fell back. They stopped and looked back at what they had left behind. It was too dark to see anything. But their minds groped in the dark and gave them a vivid picture of the Nyamiringa that they had lived in all their lives and that they loved so much. They could see the large expanses of sorghum in the fields, almost ready to harvest. They had not seen sorghum to do so well in many years. Indeed, as someone had commented before, by doing well this sorghum was foretelling doom. Then they thought of the hunger that lay ahead for many long and cold days. They were tearful.

'I am very sorry about all this, son of my mother,' Ruteera started. He swallowed hard to stop the tears from choking him. 'That bull should never have been born.'

'You must not blame yourself. It was not of your doing.' Migayo knew that Ruteera blamed himself for this catastrophe. He had to console him. 'I would say that Bugeiga should never have been born. And, indeed warmongers like him should never be born in this world at all.'

'Where is the world heading to?' Ruteera asked miserably. 'These people pledged so much. They swore by what is sacred to them that they would do what they had pledged to do. But now, look!' He gnashed his teeth. 'Not a thing. The unity they talked about never existed. Why should a man make a pledge that he is not going to keep?' He paused. 'Why should one condemn anything anyway, if one knows that there is nothing one can do to change it? If we sincerely believe something to be an evil and against our society, we should fight it and defeat it.' He stopped and looked at his almost invisible brother. 'I told these men long ago,' he resumed dreamily, 'that if Bugeiga really wanted to do something, nobody would raise a finger to stop him. They said they would. In that meeting they talked of all the clans of Nyabigyi uniting against this evil. I would never have believed it all to be sham unity. It is so sad that all the clans of Nyabigyi could fail to solve such a problem. And they will continue to fail to solve their problems. Unless they find a way of truly uniting. He started moving slowly. 'You see,' he continued before Migayo could interrupt, 'if all the clans of Nyabigyi, or the tribes of the whole world for that matter, sincerely united against one evil, they could not possibly fail to defeat it. But man is so hypocritical. When he talks of unity, he means part unity. That which will make more advancement will exploit the others even more, under the cover of unity. But not a unity to bring the two together to the same level. You would find a Mukiga saying "the Banyabutumbi and us are united all right. But they are so backward. How can we share everything with them?" A Munyarwanda would say "the Bakiga even eat sheep like the primitive Batwa. How can we unite with them?" And the Bahororo would say "the Banyarwanda are absolutely untrustworthy hypocrites. How can we trust them enough to unite with them fully?"'

'But you see, Ruteera son of my mother,' Migayo started quietly, in response, 'unity is a very difficult thing to achieve. If we could find a formula on which we could unite, forgetting our clan and tribal differences, then we would be truly peaceful. But man by nature happens to be selfish. And we have to live with this selfishness. Why, for instance, should you be happy when I am not and I allow you to continue being happy? Or why should I help you to be as I may be, to bring you into competition with me? No, son of my mother, nature happens to be like that. Equality is simply impossible with man. Each one of us is afraid of losing his identity as an individual.'

'Then it is a great shame,' Ruteera started gnashing his teeth again, 'that man should be such a negative animal. Why, for instance, should he be so self-destructive over small things? Why should Bugeiga have been ready to sacrifice his kinsmen only to get my bull killed?'

'And this is not the end, I can assure you,' Migayo said very thoughtfully. 'Did you notice that I went back to consult with the gods when the other elders had left, the other day?'

'No, I did not. I was too downcast to notice.'

'I did and I sacrificed a pure white hen.' He stopped for some time, as if he were tongue-tied. 'The hand of the gods is very heavy in this.'

Ruteera could not see his face but he could hear the sadness in his tone. 'What exactly do you mean?'

'These are just the beginnings of a terrible bloodbath. It is very obvious. I wonder why the advisers of the Bagirakwe do not see it.'

'Is our blood going to be shed?'

'Only very little of ours. It is as if the gods have chosen Nyamiringa to use in a demonstration of something known to them alone.'

'Why, son of my mother,' Ruteera said sadly, 'why should man be so set against peace?'

Chapter Fourteen

I

While the Bajura were secretly preparing to flee, hundreds of Bagirakwe were secretly preparing for bloodshed. There were very few old men in this group, old men who had fought in some bloody tribal war and come back. All the others were too young to have fought in the last war. But they had all the training they needed. They were very anxious to try it out.

They had pulled their weapons down from the roof and sharpened them. The spears, the matchets and the arrows were all razor-sharp. They inspected the straps on the hard dry skins they would wear. They tested the handles on the shields. That evening many of them spent a long time shadow-guarding with the shield and fighting ten imaginary men all at once with the spear.

The first war horns were blown just after early cockcrow the next morning. It was a long time since that special war horn had been heard in Nyabigyi. It was that time so long before when the Batwa had attacked Nyabigyi from across the lake. Then Nyabigyi had united and beaten them back. But this morning, the sound of these same blood-curdling horns shattered the morning sleep of thousands with a terrible purpose. They were waking up the natives of Nyabigyi to go to war with the natives of Nyabigyi. The warriors did not need any waking, though. Most of them had hardly slept at all.

The horns were blown for the second time just before the birds started twittering. The hidden sun was just starting to throw fingers of yellow light across the dark sky. It was promising to be another bright and sunny day – to be marred by blood.

Just after sunrise the whole of Kabisha ridge broke into war songs. Warriors came in groups of five, ten, twelve. Such groups came dancing vigorously, shadow-fighting and singing their blood-chilling war song. They were converging onto a hump nearby and facing Bugeiga's home. It was a short walk away from Hakicwamba. This was further down Kabisha towards the valley.

Each warrior wore a hard dry cowhide. It could hardly be pierced with a spear. A bow and arrows were strapped to the back. A deep skin pouch hung from the neck. It contained a long-handled matchet, talismans and other safeguards. The large shield was carried in the left hand and the spear in the right. The vigorous men shook the ridge as they went down to Hakicwamba.

Ahead of the singing, dancing and shadow-fighting troops brisk and invigorating horns were blown.

Some of the men noticed that there were no horns announcing the Bajura warriors. It was probably a new strategy in warfare not to announce your approach to the battlefield. Or perhaps their horn-blowers were too cowardly to go to war.

They were even more surprised when they got to Hakicwamba. There was no enemy in sight. They all stopped the war-song. They started looking around, puzzled. The commanders came together to consult. They wondered, indeed, what this new strategy would be.

'We shall cross over and fight them on their ridge,' the spokesman announced. 'But let us go most cautiously. Be particularly careful when crossing the swamp. There must be a trap.'

When they got to the swamp, only a few people crossed at a time. After several groups had crossed safely, they realised that the trap was not in crossing. The rest rushed across.

Many more Bagirakwe than had been expected had turned up. When they realised that the other clans were not going to join the actual fighting, others joined up. These were mainly the neutral ones. But several had deserted the anti-war group and sharpened their spears. They had realised that Bugeiga and his followers just might win. They did not want to sit by and watch the others sharing all that land. They wanted their share too.

The forces of the other clans did not come out to stop Bugeiga from leading his followers to war. But they were seen watching from safe vantage points. They were not armed. They had only come as observers. If they could not learn anything from watching the fight, they would find something to criticise. They would certainly have an interesting story to tell in future. Some of the elders who had pledged unfailing support to Ruteera were among the observers.

The warriors got to Hakiko kwa Muhamangabo without meeting a soul. Only then did it start to dawn on them that there might not be any fighting to do. The Bajura must have fled. The horn-blowers blew the tunes of victory. Then they really went berserk.

Everybody forgot that they had come as a group with one purpose. They ignored all orders and started running in all directions. The commanders tried to call them to order without any success. A few responded to the commanders and stayed behind. They soon realised what was happening and rushed off in an attempt to overtake the first ones. Their commanders were the last to follow. Bugeiga alone was left on the might-have-been battleground. He was jumping up and down with happiness. He could have been mistaken for being insane at the time.

When the plans to fight got under way, each one had started thinking of the land he would claim. By now, everyone knew the exact piece of land he wanted. This was all secret. Nobody could confide in a friend. Now, when the victory horns blew, everyone rushed for that land he had had his eye on. Whoever lay claim to that land first would take it. Or so they hoped.

II

'Our brothers are ransoming our clan, my children,' Busaahu said bitterly. 'The gods certainly cannot overlook this.' He was with five top-ranking anti-war members. They were going to Kaabya to visit Busaahu's old friend, the medicine man of the Baamungwe. He shook his head dreamily and continued, 'We must not sink with them. We must attempt to save as many with us as possible.'

'But we have tried our best, grandfather,' Rwecurenga pleaded. 'Unfortunately, we have won over very few of those who were strongly in favour of going to war.'

'That is all right, my children. As long as we know that we have done the best we possibly could.'

'We people are very strange indeed,' Rwecurenga observed. 'We can identify good from evil. We will then knowingly follow evil, well aware that it will lead us to no good.'

'Like a child who will put his finger in the fire to see whether it will get burnt. And yet he can see the wood in there burning,' an older man commented.

'You see,' Karwemera started, 'evil is more appealing and fascinating. It takes a man of strong integrity to refuse to do evil. The fisherman evil dangles such a beautiful bait on a deadly hook in front of you. It will be so tantalising that most of us cannot help but swallow it.' Then more slowly and quietly, 'Like all that land of the Bajura. What a beautiful bait! And the good? What does it have to offer? Only peace and a clean conscience. It offers nothing that is obviously tangible. Who will live on peace? Who will feed his wife and children on a clean conscience?'

'When you talk like that, Karwemera, I wonder whether you are really with us with all your heart.' Busaahu sounded troubled by Karwemera's outburst. 'You make evil sound like such a good choice that one would think that you condone evil. It is for such reasons that we must continue to condemn and fight this apparently beautiful evil. There is danger that evil might override good.'

'But it offers such enticing choices and you cannot deny it. That is why there are more people willing to die in an attempt to achieve evil than those dying for peace or good,' Karwemera persisted. 'Evil is more rewarding, and faster too.' He looked at his grandfather seriously. 'Look at the evil spirits! Are they not more powerful than the good spirits? Do they not strike their enemies at a faster speed than the good spirits take to reward the do-gooders?'

'Look here, my child,' the old man insisted. 'Let us study a practical example. Take a man like you. You have your land and some children to bring up. Your neighbour also has his land and his children to bring up. Between you, you have a long established boundary. Euphorbia trees, establishing the boundary, were planted long before you by your forefathers. This was to make very sure that you would not quarrel over it.

'Suddenly your neighbour decides that he wants to expand. He uproots the euphorbia trees and he plants them two fields deeper into your land. He declares the new boundary. What would you do to him?'

'I would certainly spear him,' the others answered, together.

'What if he pushes you completely off your land and he annexes it to his like your father, Bugeiga, has done? How can you defend that type of evil? Indeed, evil dangled your land so tantalisingly in front of your neighbour's eyes that he took it? No, my children, evil is evil and must be fought. And such greedy expansionists, as you have all observed, end up being speared.'

'That is true,' the other old man added. He continued to give vivid examples of such people who had been speared over their expansionist practices. The young men knew a number of them.

'The little partridge bird saw its friend die in a trap because of its greed. As it walked off, shocked by this, it said, "I would rather eat a little and keep my shin red." That bird,' Busaahu said, 'had a better outlook on life than most of us.'

They were approaching Kaabya. When they got there Busaahu went ahead to explain what he wanted to his friend.

While the Bajura had been preparing to flee, not all Bagirakwe were preparing for a dastardly war. The anti-war group was busy somewhere else. They were still looking for a way of barring their brother from going to war. Like Ruteera, Busaahu had soon realised that the consensus arrived at in that meeting would not work out. But he knew something else. The council of elders as a group had actually tried hard but when they got back to their clans their people did not support them. So many excuses were given, even by some clan elders.

Seeing this, Busaahu had prepared a response. He organised those against war into campaign units. These visited every house dissuading people from going to war. They could not convince everybody but they did a good job. Their efforts were frustrated by the hardliners and that big bait of land.

So, when some of their brothers were sharpening their spears, Busaahu and his most influential followers headed for Kaabya. Apart from being very close friends, Busaahu and this medicine man had fought together in that war against the Baatwa. They were not going there to ask him to use his powers to stop the war. They could not, and they knew it. If anybody could, then Migayo would have stopped it already. He was irrefutably the most powerful. They only wanted a general survey of the consequences.

'That is just about all, my friend,' Busaahu concluded his long tale, 'so now, where will this end? How will the fighting go? And what happens to the clans thereafter?'

'Let us go and find out.' So saying, the old man reached for his big goat-skin bag. He led them to his shrine. It was a round, small grass hut. It had a front room and an inner room. Patients and other customers would never enter the inner room. It was regarded as a very high risk. They could not wish to look the gods in the eye. One never knew whether one would meet a cool or angry god. Busaahu and his group sat facing the entrance to the inner room. There a row of short stools were already placed in position. The doddering old mufumu went to the inner room. The young men looked around at the display of medicines in all forms. There were liquids in gourds, dry twigs, leaves and tree bark, there were animal skins, bones and skulls, there were whole wings and other parts of unidentifiable birds. There were others which they could not possibly know. It was a wonder that any one person could know all the uses of each of those things.

The old man came back and sat on a shorter stool facing them. He spread out the skin of a spotted animal in front of him. Then he brought out his horns. He put three small ones on the skin. He then took the leading one, placing it on his lap. He started shaking it, slowly. His face was very serious, deeply concentrated. But his lips could be seen moving as if in conversation. But no words came from him. Then the horns on the skin started to dance very slowly. He stopped to watch. The men sitting in front of him also watched, thoroughly awed. When the horns stopped dancing he shook them again. There were some rattly things in them. He repeated this four times before he could get an answer. And when it came they all heard it.

A squeaky voice answered him from all over the hut. It sounded like someone who had lost his voice trying to make an alarm. It was a frightening voice. They could not make out what the gods were saying. But they could tell from watching the man's face as he sorted out the message. It was troubling news.

'Two things,' he said, after the voice of the gods had stopped, 'both of them are very bad.' He looked down sadly. Then he brought up his eyes to face Busaahu. 'There is going to be no fighting tomorrow. The Bajura are fleeing. The gods have advised them to. But they are leaving a thick cloud hanging over the ridges of Nyamiringa and Kabisha.' He himself was deeply troubled.

'What type of cloud?'

The medicine man shook the horn again. 'I cannot tell now. But it is a very heavy and dark cloud. And no sacrifices will divert it. Unless the whole situation could be reversed to unshed the blood which has been shed.'

'Is it a curse, then?' Busaahu enquired miserably.

'It looks like it. Yes.'

'Could Bugeiga be sacrificed?'

He shook the horn again. 'No, he is a sick man. The gods would not accept him.' After he had exacted a promise from them not to mention the fleeing of the Bajura, the Bagirakwe left. The divination had cost Busaahu three expensive anklets.

'I am going to join them,' Rwecurenga announced bitterly, as they went home.

'Who?' asked the shocked Busaahu.

'I am going to join the Bajura.'

'No. You cannot,' Busaahu advised. 'It is never heard of. It would be like denouncing your clan and giving yourself to another.'

'But I cannot live with my clan after this.'

'But who will guide the clan if all the sensible men like you abandon it to the Bugeigas? No, my children, you must stay. We must do something. It is our duty to reconcile the Bajura with the innocent Bagirakwe.'

III

As soon as the victory horns were blown Ndemire ran for Ruteeramareingwa's home. It was very well positioned. And the whole of that fertile land! He convinced himself that he deserved it most. After all, it was through his father that this had been made possible. And he, Ndemire, had always been in the forefront throughout the whole campaign. But all the same it was imperative that he got there first.

He was shocked when he got there. Two other young men were already there, in hot argument. Each of them claimed to have got there first. One was stoutish and of average height. The second one was a smaller man. Ndemire stood there thinking hard and fast. He could not hope to get to any other land ahead of others. He made up is mind: it had to be this one or none.

'Hey, you people, what are you quarrelling for? The whole of this land has already been taken.'

The two men stopped their shouting. They were taken aback. 'What do you mean "already taken"?' the stout one asked. The first two looked at each other enquiringly. Then they looked at Ndemire. They could not understand.

'The whole of Ruteeramareingwa's land and that of his sons have been taken by Bugeiga and his sons. He stated this most strongly. 'You are wasting your time here. You might as well go and try your luck elsewhere.'

'A bad spear,' the smaller man swore. To emphasise it he drove his spear into the ground hard, blunt end first. It quivered in his hand. 'May I sleep with my mother. You will not drive me off this.' He had actually been the first to get there. At least he had got to Ruteera's inner compound first. The stout one had come in through the older sons' compound. And since his brother had been killed in a night raid, he also believed that he deserved this particular land. So the two of them had failed to agree on who would take which part.

'When did you, or Bugeiga, get here to claim this land, then?' the stout one asked.

'We did not have to. It was a precondition for my father to agree to organise the whole war campaign.'

'Take that precondition and shove it up your father's you-know-what. There was no such thing and you know it very well,' the stout one said angrily. 'So leave us alone while you still can.'

'You do not know what you are doing,' Ndemire pressed. 'You will regret this before morning.'

'Who are you threatening, eh? You want to kill us at night the way you killed the Bajura, eh? Why do you not kill us now when there is daylight, eh?' The stout one was becoming rough. He was roaring now. 'Are you taking us for the cowardly Bajura who fled without a fight, eh?' So saying, he posed in an offensive position, his spear raised. Ndemire was forced to take guard. He was in a defensive position.

'What do you think you can do to me?' Ndemire asked. 'Do you think that your testicles are larger than mine? This is our land. I am not leaving it.' They started circling each other.

'You men, what has got into your heads? Do not fight.' The smaller man, who had stopped talking when the quarrel threatened to become a fight, tried to separate them. 'Do you forget that you are brothers? This land is big enough. We can all have a share.'

'Brothers!' the stout one spat, lunging with his spear at Ndemire.

'Share?' Ndemire growled. He warded off the blow.

'Would he be threatening to kill us tonight, if he was a brother?' He thrust his spear furiously. Ndemire executed a perfect guard with his shield. He sent in an equally furious thrust. His opponent stopped it an inch away from his breast.

'I did not say that I was planning to kill you,' he growled, teasing with his spear tentatively. 'I only said that you would regret it if you did not leave this land.'

'We shall not. Let us see who leaves it first.' The stout one attacked more furiously.

'Stop fighting, you men. Have the evil spirits possessed you?' the smaller man shouted. 'This is not what we planned to fight for. We were armed to fight the Bajura, not among ourselves.'

The fighting men ignored him. Their spears got closer each time. Each of them had already drawn blood from the other. The sight of blood on their opponent's spear drove them madder.

'Stop, stop you men.' He tried to get between them but the spears were crossing each other so fast that he drew back. 'The elders will judge. After all the land is enough for us all.' By then he was yelling at the top of his voice. Other people came running to see what was happening. They came too late. Before they could get to them and grab them, the stout one struck a mighty blow. The spear went through the hard skin as if it was flesh. Ndemire fell, fatally wounded.

Chapter Fifteen

I

Ndemire was one of the first people to die. But quite a few others died that night too. This marked the beginning of hatred and bloodshed among the Bagirakwe families. The elders among Bugeiga's group attempted to solve the problem. By then some twenty-five men had already died. Most of them died trying to defend the land they had acquired. Others died trying to get a share from those who had acquired too much. And vengeance within the clan had scarcely started.

Their leaders decided on a solution. The fruits of war acquired from the Bajura were to be shared equally among all those who had come out to fight. But this caused a major problem. Some claimed to have done more in the war than others. Some were accused of having joined right at the end. Others felt that some never came out to fight and only came to share in the land. Therefore, they could not possibly be given an equal share. Violent clashes continued to occur in Nyamiringa and sometimes in Kabisha.

Bugeiga, the source of all this, was not available to help solve these problems. He was dead to whatever was happening around him.

It had taken the news of the death of his son to make him go home. His affliction started on that fateful day. He set out walking with no particular purpose in mind, talking rapidly to himself. By then he had already thrown away his skins. He walked home with his buttocks shamefully bare. His children and grandchildren covered their faces in shame. But still, he refused the skin one of his wives brought out for him to wear.

The next day he slaughtered a bull and declared a big feast. When he started shouting unintelligibly, people thought he was drunk. But the man was instead mad. From then on he rejected his skin completely. After that he took to roaming between Kabisha and Nyamiringa. When he got tired of going to Nyamiringa he would roam around Kabisha. He moved very fast, not entering any home. He did not talk to anybody. Sometimes the spirits possessing him would turn violent. Then he would start bawling incomprehensible words.

At first his wives followed him around. They tried to bring him home and care for him. But they failed. Soon they realised that their husband was truly mad. They had to do something about it, however much it cost them.

The first wife, Keigwisagye, called a meeting of the three wives. They had to make a joint effort to find a way of helping their husband. They decided that they should go and see a medicine man. They sent Baanuza, the second wife, who soon found one who could listen to her.

'It is not possible to treat your husband now,' the medicine man said, after divining the cause of his illness.

'Why not?' she enquired.

'That is not a normal illness. Some foreign gods have taken over his body. There is nothing much we mortals can do about it.'

'How long will this go on?'

'Who knows the wishes of the gods? Until their purpose has been served, we cannot really tell.'

'Could you not give me something to give him? At least something to bring him home to eat?'

'All right.' The medicine man disappeared into another room: 'Take this and put a little in his food if you can.'

Baanuza went home with the powder she was given. She did not approve of what Bugeiga had done. After all, Ruteera was her uncle. But she could not reject him when he needed her most. Whatever he was, he was her husband.

The drug was shared among the three wives, so that wherever Bugeiga went to eat he should be given the drug. But he evaded them all. Sometimes he would come when he was least expected and head straight for the pot. Before anybody knew what was happening, he would be eating. And if anybody came to serve him, he would walk away without talking.

When they failed to administer the medicine, the wives decided to try another medicine man. They chose Keigwisagye to go this time. She went to the *mufumu* of her clan. She was told the same thing as Baanuza: Bugeiga was possessed by foreign gods. Keigwisagye had also been against his action and intentions. She had even openly supported her sons who led the anti-war crusade with Busaahu. And she had tried to talk Bugeiga out of his anger. But he could not listen. Once, he even almost beat her, which was unheard of – to beat a first wife, at that age, with grandchildren!

'What do you women know, after all?' he had roared with anger. What he was doing was for men only. Women had no right even to comment. But she, too, could not abandon him, at his time of greatest need. Above all he was her husband. And he had not been a bad husband at that. Her sons would understand why, she hoped.

II

The evening was cool. The dry season was just round the corner. It was needed to dry the sorghum. Bugeiga had just passed his home without going in. He now hurried past Busaahu's home. He did not call out a greeting. His naked body looked ashen. The shoulders were getting more and more stooped.

'You see, my children,' Busaahu commented, pointing at Bugeiga. He sat outside his inner compound with a group of his followers. They had formed the habit of meeting at his home. Here they would often just discuss the current situation. Nobody planned these meetings. They would often just find their feet leading them there. Not many of them, only the very close followers. And they enjoyed learning from Busaahu.

'Evil is evil indeed,' he continued. 'And the gods have their eyes open wherever they are. They never fail to punish those who deserve to be punished.' It was almost a complete moon since the Bajura had fled. None of the Bagirakwe had managed to settle in the land they had picked. 'Karwemera, where are you? How many of them have managed to make their home across there?'

'Give them time, old man. They will settle down. After all they knew what they were going in for.' Karwemera defended his original argument. 'They did not expect peace right away. But with some luck, it will come to some of them soon.'

'You are wrong, my child. Do you think any peace is going there?' He shook his head resignedly. 'You will be telling me that we are involved. And where are we going to go?' He considered this last statement very seriously. He was a very old man and the good gods had given him a really long life. He wondered whether he would still be with them for long. 'Do you think, for instance, that it is Bagirakwe killing Bagirakwe across there?'

'What do you mean by that?' Rwecurenga asked. He was a sad man these days. His wife was broken-hearted.

'Have you ever heard of so much uncontrolled bloodshed in a clan?' Busaahu said slowly and quietly. 'And why do you think that the gods told the Bajura not to wait to go to war?'

'You mean,' a young man chipped in, unwilling to believe the implications of this, 'you mean their gods are fighting their war for them?'

'And the spirits of their ancestors, too,' an old man added. 'No. Bagirakwe will never settle across there peacefully. They will have to conquer the gods of the Bajura first. Then they will have the spirits of their ancestors to battle with. Only then can they claim to have defeated the Bajura. But by then there will be none of them left to settle there.'

'And they can defeat neither their gods nor those spirits,' Karwemera observed.

'I hear the spirits have chased some of them out of the houses at night,' Rwecurenga said.

'That is very true,' Busaahu confirmed. 'In some cases the houses have talked, advising them not to enter.'

'Is that why many of them have built new huts outside the inner compounds?' a young man asked with wonderment.

'What else!' Busaahu replied laconically.

'What surprises me is why they are not harvesting all that sorghum,' another young man added. Everybody else had already cut their sorghum. It lay in neat piled rows. One row ran from one end to the other of the field, the stems laid directly on the ground and the sorghum heads on top. These heads would be cut off after half a moon or so. By then the sorghum would be dry. 'Are they going to leave it to rot in the fields?'

'Listen to this young one also! Do you think the Bajura left their crop just like that, undefended?' Busaahu said, smiling.

'Do you mean they will come to harvest it?'

'Certainly not. But they must have left it all to their gods and ancestors in one way or another. There are some rites that could be performed to ensure that. And I can assure you, that Migayo did not overlook or neglect anything. He is too powerful a medicine man to neglect the slightest detail. And if Bugeiga had not used very expensive, reckless and powerful charms – without thinking of the consequences – he would not have managed even the bull in the beginning. And, by the time he struck, they were already on him. They knew he was planning something. He was quiet for some time. And their gods ...' he shook his head thoughtfully. 'The cloud that my friend divined that time has only started to gather. You wait. You will see.'

'Can we do anything to help the situation?' Rwecurenga asked quite seriously.

'Nothing at all. Those who are dying are a necessary sacrifice to the gods. Their blood will cleanse the clan. When eventually they realise their folly, we will not need very expensive sacrifices.' He surveyed the young men around him. 'You see, peace must be wooed and kept, like a woman. Like a woman, it has an unpredictable and sometimes a very bad temper. But we must always woo it to come back among us. We cannot afford to let it desert us for long.'

'I hate my father.' Rwecurenga shook his head sadly and gnashed his teeth. 'He is the one who started all this.'

'Do not waste your emotions on him, my son. He does not deserve them. Am I not his father's real brother?' Everybody mumbled an agreement. 'I have given up on him. And anyway, it is useless to hate someone unless you can do something about it.'

'I could kill him,' Rwecurenga hissed.

'Death would not be a better punishment for him. As it is, the gods are hating him enough for us all. We could not do more to him than that.'

'It is not quite enough,' the other old man said. 'Do you know how many people have died as a result of his evil deeds?'

'Very, very many,' the others answered.

'Do you think his punishment is small?' Busaahu objected. 'To live your life as a house for many evil spirits? Many of which do not even belong to the ancestors of your clan? A man like Bugeiga, with all the prestige and riches, having to go round with his buttocks bare? Having to go to the houses of his wives to steal his own food from the pots? Having to suffer the cold at night on some abandoned ashy fireplace when any of his wives would have willingly given him a good night of warmth and love?' He looked at the quiet group. 'You think that is better than death?'

They were all quiet for some time.

'Poor father,' Rwecurenga said quietly, shaking his head. 'When I picture him going through all that I find it difficult to hate him. After all, he was not a bad father to us at all. I do not know what got into him.'

'That is why I advised you to leave him to the gods.'

'These spirits must have entered him when they crossed to Hakiko kya Muhamangabo,' the old man wondered, 'from the time he threw away his skins, shouting and rejoicing, he never put them on again. We thought it was because of happiness. When his son Ndemire was being buried, he was naked and shouting. People thought it was because of grief. When fools like him were eating the bull he slaughtered to celebrate catastrophe, he was naked and shouting. Everybody thought that he was drunk. But the man was instead mad.'

'Oh, but the spirits entered him before that,' Busaahu corrected. 'Do you not remember the medicine man's divination? Bugeiga could not be sacrificed because he was already sick. Some spirits had already entered him. Crossing to Hakiko kya Muhamangabo only activated them. And of course some others entered him then.'

'It is a sad situation, indeed,' the old man continued. 'Can you imagine your children covering their faces for shame every time they see you, instead of running to you happily?'

'You see,' Busaahu remarked, 'we have a proverb that says that "the animal which is destined to die will not hear the horn-blowers summoning the hunters". Bugeiga got more than enough advice. As Karwemera has pointed out, he knew what he was going in for. A young boy who forces his father to give him a wife before he is of age must consummate his marriage. He cannot start saying that he is too young or that she should wait. We have done what we could. We would be justified in joining the laughers and laugh at him too.'

Chapter Sixteen

I

The Bajura had made some progress. It was slow and hard. But they were moving. They had been on the move for almost a full moon. They had not yet got to any place they could settle in. The problem was that they were too many – too many people, too many cattle. They needed a large expanse of land that was completely unclaimed. They hoped to find this on the edge of Rukiga, so they were heading towards Butumbi and where the wilderness started. They were tired of battling with their fellow man. For a change, they were prepared to battle with wild animals for existence.

They had had quite a number of setbacks. The greatest of all was that they were too many to find passage easily. When they were outside Nyabigyi, it was as if they were in a foreign land. They were still among the Bakiga but even the way of speaking had changed. They could not afford to antagonise the people there in the slightest way. They could not afford to have even one goat straying into some garden, for instance. So finding proper passage was very difficult.

A group of elders always travelled at least a day ahead. They would endeavour to make friends with the owners of the land. They would then seek permission to go through. When such permission was granted they would carry out a survey for a suitable route. They had to find a corridor where there was enough uncultivated land for them all to pass, along with their animals.

Sometimes the elders made enemies. Then everybody would wait for many days camped in one place. The advance group of elders would take another direction to seek friendship and passage. It was during such a time that Tindikahwa tackled his grandfather again.

The elders had made enemies with the clan they had approached first, so they had come back to report their failure. They had then gone in another direction, but only that morning. That night over one thousand people anxiously sat around a hundred and one fires.

When night came they gathered into groups, usually of their families. They sat round their central fire. Children and the very old would be nearest to the fire. Those far away would be shivering from the cold. Meanwhile, the men took turns to move around the camp. They had to guard against raiders and wild animals. They had been camped in this place for four days and nights. The longer they stayed in one place, the more dangerous it became. Fortunately, this time it was in the mountains, far away from any homes.

The area was bare, rocky and unproductive. These mountains did not belong to anybody.

Tindikahwa sat far away from the fire. There were many children smaller than his thirteen seasons. They needed to be closer to the fire than he did. He was shivering violently. The big goatskin he wore could not keep out the cold. Soon his teeth started chattering uncontrollably.

'Is that you, Tindikahwa?' his mother asked.

'*Yeego*,' he answered with a quavering voice.

'We are really suffering, my child,' Ruteera mused. 'Why do you not come nearer the fire? Do you want to wait until your teeth have knocked each other out?' Tindikahwa went to his grandfather. He squeezed in and sat in front of him.

They had had a very light meal indeed. Each one had fed on half a small calabash of hot millet gruel and one small sweet potato. They all felt hungry. Tindikahwa was very miserable. When the warmth came back to him he brightened up a bit. He looked up at his grandfather's face. He thought the old man looked very miserable too. He snuggled closer to him. He rested his arm on his grandfather's thigh reassuringly.

'I think we are not as brave as our forefathers were,' Tindikahwa said in a slow, serious voice.

'What makes you think so?' Ruteera asked, jerked out of his thoughts.

'Why did we not stay and fight?'he asked, with bafflement in his voice.

'We fought, my child, we really fought. You cannot fathom how much we fought. Only it would have been a terrible error for us to go to the battleground. You or me or your father would not be sitting together like this around this fire.'

'Indeed, we would probably be at home sitting around a better fire in the house.' Others laughed at this before they stopped to consider it.

'Not so, Tindikahwa,' Ruteera started patiently. 'I meant that some of us would be dead. Either killed on the battleground or found at home and massacred wantonly.'

Tindikahwa was thoughtful for some time. He resumed his inquisition heatedly. 'Is this how the Bajura always fought their wars?' He did not hide his disappointment. 'They always fled before they got to the battleground?'

'Oh, certainly not. Sometimes they stayed on the battleground and fought for days. But, as I told you, the odds were always against them. They were always outnumbered by far.'

'All the same, I wish we had stayed and fought.'

'Me too,' another young boy put in.

'I think it is better to fight and die fighting at home,' Tindikahwa persisted, 'than to live your whole life roaming all over, looking for some place to settle. You would run away from there also if someone threatened to challenge you to war.'

'Let us be patient and wait for the gods to act, my child. We did not choose to flee, remember? The gods directed us to. They know best what is good for their children.'

'All the same, I do not think that we should have fled without a fight. Those Bagirakwe must take us for the most cowardly people alive. And anyway, if the gods knew what was best for us, they would not have allowed the Bagirakwe to force us to flee at all. They would not have even allowed them to start the quarrel.' He looked up at his grandfather's face. It looked more troubled than it had been at first. 'Could they not have helped us to defeat them had we stayed to fight?'

'We are only human, my child. We cannot start questioning the acts of the gods.'

'I will go back one day. If I die before I go back, my body will refuse to enter the grave,' he declared strongly. 'I must be buried in Nyamiringa where my great grandfather is buried. I will fight the Bagirakwe single-handed if I must.'

'I'll come with you,' a younger father said.

'Me too,' a few other boys said in unison.

'Eh, their bows,' Tindikahwa's mother swore. 'Are you going to take away all the Bajura young men to your dream war?'

'If I am still young, I will come with you too,' Kubiriba said. He had come from scouting in time to hear the last part. 'Tindikahwa, you are a man. I think I want to be buried in Nyamiringa also.' His wife looked at him from across the fire. She almost said something but checked herself.

Ruteeramareingwa got up. He walked off towards the cattle. His eyes were not yet used to the darkness. But he could hear and smell them. Thirty strides away he stopped. He leaned on his spear and peered back. Yes, he mumbled to himself. Tindikahwa was right. He continued into the darkness.

II

Back at the fire there was a heated argument. Some thought that they had done the best thing to flee. Others supported Tindikahwa. Others were still undecided. The older people had also joined in the argument. Around many other fires similar discussions were going on.

'Why should any reasonable person go to fight a war he knows he certainly cannot win and in which he is likely to die?' a young man asked.

'How does he know that he cannot win it until he has gone to the battlefield and fought?' another one asked.

'Oh, some things are obvious. If one man was to fight three men each of whom was as strong as he was, or a small boy was to fight a big man, what would you expect? It would only be an accident if the lone man or the small boy was not killed.'

'But surely, we cannot talk in support of war, whether we win it or not,' somebody else said. 'It has such drastic consequences that it should always be the absolute last resort. For instance, supposing we had fought the Bagirakwe and defeated them. But in the process we had lost two hundred men – fathers, brothers and sons – would Nyamiringa be worth the exchange?'

Here again the young men were heatedly divided. 'I could say,' the first young man started, 'that people should go to war only if, by not going to war, they would lose as much, mainly in terms of human life and human dignity, as they would have lost by going to war. But if by going to war they would lose so much and still not get what they fought for, then war should be ruled out.'

'But how can war be ruled out when you have clans like the Bagirakwe who will force you to go to war?' Tindikahwa said heatedly. 'I still think that it is best to fight and die defending yourself and what is yours than submit and be treated like a dog.'

'Thank you, my son. You are a man,' his father, Mazima said from across the fire. He thrust his hand at him. 'Take my hand. Shake it.' The boy proudly shook his father's hand. 'War may be so wasteful but there are situations where only fighting can solve a problem. Like in this case of ours. If we could have fought back and not been defeated then we would not have been here regretting that we did not fight. But again, fighting when we were so outnumbered ...'

'But,' Kubiriba interrupted, 'if they had not known that they were so much stronger than we were, they would not have bullied us. You never hear of a man ambushing and attacking three men single-handed. The weaker person does not have the opportunity to use war to solve problems.'

'War is very bad, my children, let me tell you,' Keirigyirwa, Ruteera's first wife, started. 'I was already married to your father when the Baatwa attacked Nyabigyi from across the lake.' Everybody listened attentively. It was very rare that women told stories of war to men. 'Ye, ye, ye, you women of skins! Oh mother,' she slapped her skin skirt several times. 'Our men would go in the morning. Sometimes they would stay away for many days. Then you would hear that so and so and so and so had died. Then others would be brought home with stabs and cuts too terrible to look at! Ye, ye, ye! You earth and soil!' She covered her mouth with one hand. She made a strange sound with the side of the tongue pressed against the teeth. She removed the hand and clapped her hands wordlessly. 'Do not tell me. May wars be thrown away, my children. May they be cursed. I …' She was interrupted by someone raising the alarm at the place where the herds were.

'Give me arms. Give me arms. Raiders, raiders, raiders,' the person shouted. It was Ruteera calling for help. All the able-bodied men from all the families rushed to the area. Their dogs joined them, barking madly. Tindikahwa followed against his mother's objections. He was determined to act like the man he had claimed to be: the man who had sworn to fight the Bagirakwe single-handed, if it was necessary.

A band of raiders must have been in the area, watching the movement of the patrols since dark. Somehow they must have missed Ruteera or assumed that he had gone back to the fire. In fact he had been sitting among the herds not very far from the edge. His concentration had also been on the people on patrol. He had not been surprised to see some four people walking towards the sleeping herds. He had stayed hidden, just to see whether they would see him. Then other things occupied his thoughts.

He was aroused from these thoughts by the movement of a group of cattle. The people were quietly pushing and hissing at them. Then he raised the alarm right away. Realising that they had been found out, the raiders drove the cattle harder. They still did not shout but they forced the cattle to run down the steep slope.

Soon many men came from the camp and chased them down the hill. They had to go cautiously. They did not know how dangerous it was to chase, carelessly, an enemy that they could not see. The raiders, realising the odds against them, abandoned the cattle and ran away. The men then scouted the area to make sure that they had recovered all the cattle. They also made sure that the raiders had left the area. They went back congratulating themselves.

This was the first time they had been attacked by human raiders. They had been expecting them all the time. But when they were attacked tonight, they were not quite prepared. If Ruteera had not been disturbed by the discussion with Tindikahwa, he would not have gone that way. Then the raiders would have succeeded.

Twice before they had been attacked by leopards. Each time a goat had been taken. They would hear a muffled bleating but by the time they got there the leopard would be gone, with the goat. And of course they could not follow it during the night. And the dogs barked running away from the sound, with their tails between their hind legs.

III

The weather was nasty the following morning, foggy and cold. Light mist made everything damp. Everybody was breathing out smoke as if they were smoking a pipe. Mornings were by far the worst time of the day. Then everybody, young and old, fought to get close to the fire.

All nights were cold throughout, but the worst time started not very long before cockcrow. The absolute worst was around the time when the stars started falling from the sky. Those hours were almost unbearable. Time seemed to move even more slowly than a snail.

When deciding on a camping place they had to be very careful. They had to look for a sheltered area. It had to be on the leeward side of the hill. If possible there should be trees growing there. And of course there had to be enough water for them all. Then babies and young children would have comparative comfort.

Most of them slept in the open around the fires. The young boys, however, had found a better place. They slept among the cows. They would go right into the centre of the herd. Each of them would wedge themselves in between two cows. The heat generated by thousands of animals was so much that the boys would not feel any cold. They only had to be careful not to oversleep because they could easily be trodden on or squashed by a restless cow.

On a good day the fog cleared very early and there would be no mist. But on a bad morning like this morning, it did not clear until far into the morning. This was a bad day, indeed. Everybody realised it when the milkers went to milk the cows.

Some two calves were released from their temporary shed. But they did not find their mothers outside waiting. They mooed and ran around anxiously searching. No mother mooed back to call them. They ran around the thousands of cattle, mooing and searching desperately. But the lowing replies from their mothers were not forthcoming. Instead they were kicked and butted by the other cows. Only then did the people realise that some cows were missing. They gathered around, utter disbelief on their faces.

'How could they have got away with them?' Bagambirelyo, who had been on the night patrol, asked, baffled. 'We chased them down the slope and recovered all the cows they had taken.'

'We shall know soon,' an elder replied. 'Let us scout the area around first. Maybe they strayed off on their own.'

'How many do you think are missing?' an anxious owner asked.

'That, too, we cannot tell just yet. Every family will have to take count first.'

They sent off groups of young men to search the area. The possibility that some hungry cattle could have strayed off on their own could not be completely ruled out. So the men had to be careful and find the right tracks.

They took quite some time to cover the whole area immediately surrounding the camp. But they found the tracks all right. They followed them for a long distance. The human footprints were unmistakably fresh. They were made following the cattle. The place they were taken to was indisputably established.

'It is those evil men who refused us passage through their land,' they announced when they returned to the camp.

'Have you seen them, those who sleep with their mothers?' the old man who had lost most cows cursed. 'They refused us passage so that they could steal our cattle? May they be struck by lightning.'

'But how did they manage it?' Bagambirelyo persisted. 'I still do not see how. After we had chased them away we tripled our patrols. Did they use witchcraft to lure away the animals?'

'Of course they used some charms for their protection and success,' an elder answered. 'They could not attempt such a dangerous operation without using some strong charms. But that is not what took away the cattle.'

'What was it then?'

'We tripled the patrols too late. The cattle were already taken.'

'That is right,' another elder said. 'The group we chased so overwhelmingly was only a diversion for the real raiders. Did you not notice how quickly they abandoned the few they had taken?' He did not have to explain any further. Even the blind could see it. While the Bajura were chasing after the decoy, the real raiders had attacked from the other end.

After the count, the number established was some thirty cattle. If gathered in a large group from different areas, cattle also form family herds. So almost all of them belonged to one person. This was treated as a loss for all. The richer people contributed to the losers. Nobody imposed it or even suggested it to them. They saw it as the normal thing to do. The loss could have been anybody's.

IV

From then onwards they strengthened their patrols heavily. The herds were forced to crowd very closely together. The fires were made at short intervals all around them. Several men and older boys sat by these fires throughout the night. This also reduced overcrowding around the family fires. They were not attacked by human raiders again on this journey.

The trek was very well organised. They did all things communally. They only broke down into families when it came to eating and sleeping. They cooked and ate in families. The food depended on their resourcefulness and what they had managed to carry away with them. A group of elders went around making sure that each family had something to eat. If they found any that did not, they made arrangements for its members to be fed. But these were very special cases and rare.

Groups had been set up to graze the cattle and goats. When their turn came, these went off to their duty without being told. Young boys and girls went off to the bushes to hunt for wild fruits, mushrooms and vegetables. Sometimes they even found honey. Men went off to hunt for game and set traps for guinea fowl and partridges. This was the only meat eaten unless a cow or a goat happened to die. Even then it would be too small to go round.

Some other men and women went off to the villages near their camp to barter for food. They took ghee, bangles and other metal products. In exchange they were given all sorts of foodstuffs. Sometimes they were given a place to dig for an agreed measure of foodstuff. But as a rule everybody had to be back in the camp by mid-afternoon.

Food acquired in this way was very rarely shared out. Anybody could have got it in the same way. Only the sick and the old could not and they were the responsibility of all. Firewood was also never shared. Every family had to collect enough to last them till morning. If they did not, they would learn to – before morning. Cold was the best teacher.

Of all the people in the camp Migayo was the busiest. He was to be seen limping from family to family, closely followed by his son Muhimbura. The young son carried his big bag for him.

Many diseases attacked these people. Some were the result of a combination of hunger, coldness and being tired. But others were serious ones. Most of the children suffered from fever. At another time a dysentery epidemic broke out. But Migayo, with the help of the gods, managed to control it.

Every adult knew quite a number of herbs and roots for treating the ordinary ailments. Also, there were several other medicine men in the clan. All these treated the sick. But for the really stubborn and serious cases Migayo had to be called. On top of treating the sick, he had to be in constant touch with the gods and the ancestral spirits. He had to ask for general protection and guidance.

As the gods willed, they did not lose as many people on this trek as they would have lost had they stayed.

Chapter Seventeen

I

The day had started very badly, what with all that cold and hunger and the raid! But everybody eventually got back into their daily routines.

It was the middle of the afternoon now. The boys had just taken the goats out to graze. The cattle had finished drinking from a muddy stream farther down the mountain. Most of the people had just had the lightest of a light meal. Quite a few had had to do without any food at all. The weather had greatly improved. Many people were relaxing under trees near their fireplaces. Some were sleeping, with others actually snoring.

A young boy saw a group of armed men coming up towards their camp. 'Look,' he shouted, pointing down the slope. 'Who are those people coming up this way?' The intruders were already within calling distance. Everybody got up to see for themselves.

It was confusing. These people were armed. But they were not attempting to conceal themselves. They were not in a hurry like people who had a long journey to make. At any rate, around here there was no road leading anywhere. And yet they did not show any fear in their approach. Some young men suggested that they should go and repel the intruders right away. They were all still angry about the raid.

'No, children,' an old man advised, 'you should never attack a person who approaches you openly, without fear, unless you know him well and what brings him. There has to be a very important reason why he does not fear.'

'And anyway,' another old man started, 'we have condemned violence so much that we should not be the ones to provoke it.' By now people from all parts of the camp had arrived. The women and children watched timidly, keeping a respectable distance from their men. Some young men came fully armed with their spears and shields. The intruders were getting closer.

'What could they want?' a young man asked, confusion in his voice. 'They are definitely coming straight for us. Have they come to ask us to surrender the cows peacefully this time?'

'Let us just wait and see,' Ruteera said, pushing through to the front. He had been napping under a tree on the other side of the camp. 'They do not look dangerous to me. But they will tell us what they want soon enough.' He was trying to reassure the people though he did not feel reassured himself.

The intruders were eight in number. Their leader was an old man. Six of them were strong young men. They could not have seen thirty full seasons yet.

The eighth one was completely wrapped in skins. Only his feet were visible. They all stopped some fifty strides away. They drove the ends of their spears hard into the ground, with the sharp end pointing to the sky. They all looked very serious.

Their leader came forward. He was a stout man, quite a few seasons younger than Ruteera. He proceeded to display an expert's fighting skills. He guarded his body with the shield against numberless invisible spears thrust at him from all directions. He moved forwards battling and spearing his way through uncountable invisible enemies. He was very fast and accurate. Bagambirelyo made to detach himself from the gaping Bajura. He wanted to go and fight him. An elder grabbed him by the elbow and restrained him.

'Don't,' he ordered. 'You do not know what he is doing.'

The elders looked at each other in quiet consultation. Ruteera nodded at a man the intruder's stature and age. The others nodded their approval gravely. He was a brave warrior. They trusted him. The man grabbed a shield from a nearby young man. He moved towards the intruder. He did not even have a proper spear. He carried only his staff.

As he moved forward he performed an equally expert warrior's display. As the two got closer their tempo quickened. Their movements were so coordinated that they seemed to be moving to the beat of drums. The men and women watching were tense. They were just about to see the most furious fight of their time.

Each man seemed to be fighting twenty enemies at a time. When they met they struck their shields together very hard and violently. At the same time they made as if to spear each other. But each made his weapon pass over the opponent's spear-carrying arm. They narrowly missed the flesh. They coiled their arms together and strongly shook each other. They looked each other in the face furiously. Each seemed to approve of the other.

Meanwhile the watchers waited to hear a terrible groan of pain or to see one of the two men fall. Instead the two men pushed each other away violently. Each staggered backwards, steadied himself and posed in a position for throwing the spear. Some women screamed. The elders smiled inwardly with approval.

The intruder was the first to break the silence. When he did, he made sure that everybody heard what he was saying. He chanted his ancestry backwards for very many generations, deliberately leaving out the nearer ones:

'I am Rutetiina son of Beijuka

He who cannot flee, of Kaakyenaga.

I am great-great-grandson to Kajura

Kajura son of Komunobi

Komunobi son of Ruhandagazi

Ruhandagazi son of Mpanju
Mpanju son of Tabaro
Tabaro son of Nyeimaza
Nyeimaza son of Bihengyeri
Bihengyeri son of Nyarubamba
Nyarubamba son of Bebwa
Bebwa son of Karemera
Karemera son of Nzobikyi
Nzobikyi son of Kahaya
Kahaya son of Murali.

What can you do to me?' he concluded, jutting his chin. It was covered with a short greying beard.

The gathering of the fleeing Bajura could not believe their ears. This had to be a trick.

It was the turn of their elder to reply:

'I am Tibeijuka son of Bebwa
The brave of Nyabigyi
Who has fled Nyamiringa.
I am great-great-grandson to Kajura
Kajura son of Komunobi
Komunobi son of Ruhandagazi
Ruhandagazi son of Mpanju
Mpanju son of Tabaro
Tabaro son of Nyeimaza
Nyeimaza son of Bihengyeri
Bihengyeri son of Nyarubamba
Nyarubamba son of Bebwa
Bebwa son of Karemera
Karemera son of Nzobikyi
Nzobikyi son of Kahaya
Kahaya son of Murali.'

As he finished chanting his ancestry the enwrapped intruder unwrapped himself. He was one of their elders who had gone ahead to seek friendship. The truth dawned upon them. It was not a trick. The intruders were also Bajura. They had at last found their clansmen.

Everybody stampeded towards the eight visitors. Very soon they engulfed them, shouting and screaming with joy. The eight were carried, shoulder high, back to the camp.

The story of the newcomers unfolded later. These people, the Bajura of Kaakyenaga, had in fact already heard about what had happened to their brothers in Nyabigyi. They had even vaguely hoped that they would come their way in their flight. So, when the advance group of elders got to Kaakyenaga they were received very happily. They were not even given time to finish identifying themselves. A huge castrated goat was immediately wrestled to the ground. Beer was brought and a feast was held.

Very soon everybody in Kaakyenaga had heard of the coming of their brothers. The forerunners gave all the details of how they had come. Their numbers, the problems they had met, everything. The feasting people therefore could not forget those still suffering up in the mountains. They planned how to go for them the next day. This group of eight had been chosen to come and guide them home. The seven knew the way because they had come this far, hunting.

'So here we are,' Rutatiina, the leader, concluded. 'We have come to lead you to Kaakyenaga, our home. There you can eat and rest for some time. Meanwhile we shall scout for the best direction you can follow. For you must continue. Kaakyenaga is not big enough for one thousand more people and their herds.'

'We are most grateful,' Migayo responded. 'We will only delay for as long as it will take us to gather our things. And if you could give us some general directions, then those with the cattle and goats would start moving. The herds can move slowly, while eating.'

'One of us will go to show them the way,' Rutatiina assured them. 'We shall catch up with them later.'

They took quite some time packing their property. The women had learnt to be slow. Fortunately, most of the things had never been unpacked. And it was good that everybody had followed the clan regulations, because all those who had gone on errands that morning had already returned. While the older people packed, the children chased and caught the chickens.

The day which had started so badly had taken a turn for the better. It was promising to be the best since they had started on this long journey. The Bajura of Nyamiringa were moving again. But this time they were going to a welcoming home.

They got to the outskirts of Kaakyenaga just as it was getting dark. The guides knew the most direct routes. And it was down-slope most of the way. Kaakyenaga turned out to be surprisingly nearer than they had imagined.

Many young men came to meet them. They relieved them of their loads and led their herds home. The cattle and goats were taken to a central hillock, which had mainly trees growing on it. It was a central place for collecting firewood.

Everything had changed for the better. Even the evening was warm. Kaakyenaga was gripped by a festive mood.

II

Their first night in Kaakyenaga was like a dream to the travellers. For a whole moon they had been living in the wilderness. They had lived a life of absolute hardship day and night. When they were not feeling extremely hungry they would be feeling extremely cold. Then there were the illnesses, exhaustion and their anxiety about the future. Not until they had settled and established themselves in some place, would they get some real rest.

Then, suddenly, to find themselves enjoying all this! It had taken them by such surprise that many of them did not recover enough to enjoy anything that night. The way they were received was simply overwhelming. And yet not so much had actually been done for them. The men at home had put up a camp for them in a central place. They had even built as many small huts as they could in that one day. They were simple ones but they would be improved on later. They would be used by the married people. The unmarried girls and boys were not a problem. They would share the sleeping quarters of their agemates in various homes.

Every family in Kaakyenaga had cooked extra food. It was unfortunate that this was the period of plenty. As soon as the visitors had settled in, the women started bringing food. Each house brought a basket of food and an earthen bowl of sauce or vegetables. There was so much to eat! Some women even brought calabashes of *bushera*. It is only fair that if you give a person food you should also give him some water to chase it down. And this cannot be plain water from the river. It is simply unheard of.

The people ate their fill without making any dent in the food. The women put the rest of the food in their own pots. The children would have this for breakfast. Everybody had eaten as if they had never seen food before or would never see it again. Indeed many had stomach problems that night. And yet, not many had managed to eat as much as they used to eat before fleeing.

'This stomach is very stupid,' one man grumbled angrily. Everybody around him had stopped eating. 'Does it not know that I have not had a tenth of a full stomach in a long time?'

'If I were you, I would take a stick and cane it to teach it manners,' an elder advised.

'I could, too. You just wait. Has it already forgotten the number of times it asked me for food most painfully? And those times I had nothing to give it. But now look!' He shook his head, rubbing his stomach. 'It is telling me, most painfully, that it is very full after only a few mouthfuls.' His family laughed at themselves too. They were all feeling the same way.

'Have you never heard about the man who cut it out to punish it for the same reason?' the same old man asked.

'How do you mean?'

'He had got stranded in the wilderness for many days without food. At one point he had to eat baby rats and baby birds. He collected them from their nests. He was too weak to catch the older ones. All the time he thought of his goats, cows and the food his wives cooked at home. "If I ever get home," he promised himself, "I will cut up a whole bull, and I will eat so much." When he got home, he indeed killed a bull and declared a feast. But like you, some ten mouthfuls was all he could eat.'

'Aaah, what a shame!' his companions commented.

'It was a shame indeed. He was so angry that he accused his stomach of all sorts of things. But above all how could it reduce a grown man to eating a mere baby rat or baby bird yet when he killed a bull for it, it could not even let him eat enough to satisfy his appetite. He took a sharp knife and cut it out.'

'Did he not die?' a boy nearby asked.

'Tell this young father of yours here to show us. I can see he is equally angry with his.'

That night, those whose stomachs could allow them to, slept as if they were drugged. They all had full stomachs, the night was warm and there were no raiders to fear. The young Bajura of Kaakyenaga had volunteered to do the patrols.

III

The next morning they woke up to a different reality. The climate was different from what they were used to. The morning was quite warm. The atmosphere was only slightly hazy. Even the physical features and vegetation had changed. The ridges were generally low, more rounded and undulating. They were covered with rich grass suitable for cattle. The valleys and lower areas were covered in endless banana plantations. It was a wonder how anybody could know where his plantation ended and his neighbour's started. People here sang that if a kite tried to fly over a plantation it would get tired before it could manage to cross it.

It was very beautiful. But it was differently beautiful. Nyabigyi was more beautiful. To many of them, Tindikahwa included, Nyabigyi was the most beautiful place of all.

In the middle of the morning a horn was blown. It summoned the people to a meeting. The meeting place was near where the visitors had camped. They started arriving around midday. Only men turned up. The Bajura from Nyabigyi had another surprise. There were more Bajura in Kaakyenaga than there had been in Nyamaringa. The men who turned up were more than double the number of the men from Nyamiringa.

They gathered in a big clearing just outside the Kaakyenaga spokesman's gate. They did not quite mix in their seating. Banturabusha, the spokesman, got up to speak. He was a very old man but his voice was still very powerful and commanding. A slight shakiness due to his age made it even more compelling. He was one of the head elders.

'Brothers, I greet you all,' he roared. 'Are you all hard?'

'*Yeego*,' they roared back in one giant voice.

'Hard and well?'

'*Yeego!*' they repeated.

Banturabusha inspected the crowd as if he was looking for someone. He seemed to find him. A smile lit up his wrinkled face. He faced the direction with more Nyamiringa Bajura in it. 'And you,' he started, spreading his hand to embrace them all, 'our brothers from Nyamiringa, I greet you especially. We indeed welcome you here. We are very happy to have the opportunity to help you. We absolutely abhor the circumstances that have brought you here. But now that you are here, we are really happy to be here to give you a rest.

'We may not have enough to give us all a full stomach for ever. But, as our saying goes, "you eat that which is small with the person who is really yours". So when you see small baskets starting to come only half full, do not scorn them. Where they will have come from they will have been given with a whole heart.' He looked at the side having more men from Kaakyenaga. 'Do I not speak for us all?'

'*Yeego*,' his brothers answered emphatically.

'Are we not ready to share the last bit with them?'

'*Yeego*,' they answered again, more emphatically.

'May you all produce more children,' he said. He followed this with a history of the two groups of the same clan. He went through how they came to live in different parts. He recalled the suffering the Bajura in different places had gone through. Eventually he got to Nyamaringa and the current suffering of these Bajura.

'Some of you still think that you should have stayed and fought, that if necessary you should have died for Nyamiringa. That is a manly thought. It is both admirable and honourable of you. But I want to assure you of this.' He stopped for some time and his audience waited very quietly for him to continue. 'Sometimes it is a more important sacrifice to live for your people and your homeland than to die for them. If the gods had not seen your case to be in this category, they could not have advised you to flee. If our great-grandfathers – when they fled – had stayed to fight, would we be here to give you shelter?'

'No,' the gathering roared.

'You will stay with us for some time. We will send out our men together with yours to scout for places for you to settle. Until then your wives and children will find shelter with us.' He stopped again and looked around. 'Before I sit down I want to ask a few things of you. Is it only Bajura who have helped you since you fled?'

'Certainly not.'

'All right. Always remember this. If ever a man in trouble comes to you for help, never refuse him. Do not say, "You are not a Bajura. I cannot help you." And never add more trouble on top of his. Like those other people did to you in the mountains. As for a brother, I do not have to tell you how to treat your brother.' He sat down.

Ruteera got up to speak. He was not the oldest man from Nyamiringa and he had not always been the spokesman for the clan. But people talked when they were moved to, they only had to have something to say. But since the beginning of the feud, he had gradually taken the role of spokesman. This may have been because he still blamed himself for what had befallen the clan. He had not deprived anybody of their position. No. After all, he was personally one of the most highly respected elders.

'You are well, children of my father?'

'*Yeego*,' they roared.

'You are thoroughly well?'

'*Yeego*,' they roared again.

'It is very good.' A smile lingered on his face briefly. It was soon replaced by a mask-like seriousness. He went straight to what he had to say. 'If I say that my people and I are well, I will be lying. But if I say that we are not well, I will be lying too. Because you have made us feel well. So my words fail me. And yet my dilemma does not end there. We want to thank you very much. But we have nothing to thank you with. Thanking you with words cannot be enough. What should we do?' He really looked his dilemma.

'Do not thank us,' some people answered.

'One day we shall thank you in a fitting manner. If we die before we are in position to do so, then our children will. Will you not, young men?' he asked his people.

'We will, many times,' the young men answered.

'If you do not, you will have many angry spirits to answer to. It is not very often that anybody takes up the problem of housing so many people, whether they are brothers or not.' He then told the Kaakyenaga people the source of their problems. It was only fitting that their brothers should know in full detail the reasons that had led them there. He told the story in such a moving way that their brothers could visualise all the hardship they had faced. He brought the story right up to the present.

'Now we are at home. We have hope. At least we have a base. Again, with words only, we thank you very much. And, I can assure you, we shall intensify our search. We can spare more people to go and look for a place we can claim. We should not wish to be a bigger burden to you than you can carry.' He looked at the elders on his side as if to ask them for their contribution. 'Now, what more should I say? Maybe some of my friends also have something to say.' He sat down.

A few more elders from either side talked. They stressed the fact that they should not fail to help their brothers as those in Nyabıgyi had failed. They followed this with a fundraising request for food. Several people gave bulls, and many others gave goats. They would be eaten at intervals. The women would take care of the other foods. An inner organising committee of elders would meet that evening. It was charged with dealing with the welfare of the visitors.

That night they were given a proper feast. The first of the bulls given was slaughtered that evening. The elders had sent out for beer from all corners of Kaakyenaga. There were quite a number of pots of beer from bananas, *rwarwa*. There were also several pots of *muramba*. It was a night that would be remembered for a long time to come.

'Our elders were right,' one man said to a few friends as they left the gathering. 'Truly, people cannot fail to fit in a place. Who could imagine that Kaakyenaga could put up so many and feed them without feeling the pinch?'

'It is not the people who may fail to fit in a place,' another one explained. 'It is the hearts which fail. Only two men, both with bad hearts, would fail to fit on a whole ridge.'

Chapter Eighteen

I

'You may wonder why we asked you to see us,' Ruteera started, formally. The elders had been talking about general things. 'It is in order to thank you again that we wished to see you. We have absolutely everything that we need, thanks to you.'

'If you have called us only to thank us again,' one elder complained, 'I will start to doubt your seriousness.'

'He cannot,' another one said. 'Do you mistake him for a child?'

'Certainly not,' Ruteera resumed, 'but I will thank you again and again. Kick me in the back for it if you want to. However, something more pressing brought us this time.' It was the third day after their arrival. They had been resting and rejoicing; and they were being treated very delicately all this time. But their elders had asked the Kaakyenaga elders to give them audience. They were again at the home of Banturabusha.

'We have already been here for three days,' Ruteera continued. 'If we do not start our hunt for a home now, we might start believing this to be our destination. It is our forefathers who said that, unless a person has felt things biting him in his bed, he will not take the bedding out into the sun. If you continue to make us feel so much at home, we will not feel the urge to go and look for a home of our own. So we have decided that some of us should give up the enjoyment and go on. They will leave tomorrow by cockcrow.'

'It is good. And it is good that you have told us beforehand.' Banturabusha stopped and looked at his group of elders. 'We promised to help you in this and we shall. Our men know the people and the lands around well. Some of them have friends in the clans. We will give your men such men to lead them. But let me ask.' He looked across at Ruteera's group. He seemed to wonder at something. 'Which direction do you want to take? Where do you hope to settle?'

'If we went towards Butumbi, we hoped we might find some unsettled land just after Rukiga.'

'That is very true,' Banturabusha agreed. His brothers mumbled their agreement. 'My brother there can tell you more.' He pointed at a man who was not very old. 'He has been to Butumbi many times. He has friends there.'

'Yes,' the other man started. 'It is a one-and-a-half day journey.'

'So near?' Tibeijuka asked. He whistled with surprise.

'Not so near, as you will see. But the journey itself is not a problem. The problem is, will you manage to live with all those animals? That land is for animals only. Lions, buffaloes, elephants, leopards, hogs, man-sized apes – you name the animal, it is there.' Many turned to look at Migayo questioningly.

'That is all right,' he said. 'We have had enough battling with people. Let us go and try our luck with those animals also.'

'You seem very determined and sure of what you want,' Banturabusha resumed. 'It would be futile to try to persuade you not to go there. But there is a good place towards Mpororo. It is only fair that I should mention it. There are lions there also but there are cattle too. Some wandering herders who are not settled there go through grazing their cattle about once a year. And it is roughly the same journey. I know the place. I have been there.'

They all considered this alternative. They discussed the possible problems. In the end Ruteera rejected it. 'I think our best bet is towards Butumbi. In the other place we may find ourselves battling with those cattle-men.'

'They would not dare,' Rutatiina said. 'The land is not theirs. Nobody has settled there to claim it.'

'I do not doubt that but …' Ruteera started, but Migayo interrupted him.

'Since we left Nyamiringa an idea has been haunting me. Supposing that, now that we approach our destination, hopefully,' he stopped and looked straight at his brother, 'supposing that we split into two groups. Then we would go to lands which are not so far apart. If one group fails to manage the conditions in their land, they would go to the other group. At least they would find there a home to rest in while they looked for another one. And if both succeeded, then we would have two homes where we could expand easily.'

'That is true, indeed,' Banturabusha supported Migayo excitedly. 'People would have a choice on which way to go.'

This was also discussed at length. They agreed that two groups of people should set off the next day. The journeys were then planned.

Many young men volunteered to go along. They could not miss the chance of adventure. They knew that those who stayed behind would get terribly bored doing nothing. A number of strong men from Kaakyenaga were chosen to go with each group. These were men who had friends in the clans they would go through. Big quantities of provisions were packed for them. They had to carry their own food even though they were going to pass among friends.

That evening Migayo consulted the Kaakyenaga medicine man. Then each man went to his shrine to consult his gods. They both asked the gods for help and a successful journey. Just before cockcrow, the two groups set off. Each man had his ordinary protective charms and talismans. But now each had an additional special talisman. Its ingredients contained potent things such as a feather from the chest of a thunderbolt, a special hairy vomit of a lion, whiskers plucked from a living leopard and many others.

II

The people left in the camp were very anxious and expectant. At last they were approaching the beginning of the end of their biggest problem. Many of them got very restless, sitting around doing nothing. Ruteera's wife Keshakama gave many, especially the women, a reasonable example. She had boldly gone to Banturabusha's home. There she had confronted his oldest wife with her problem. This was his third wife. The first two had already died of old age.

'Sitting down the whole day without a thing to do is killing me with boredom,' she said, after they had been talking for some time.

'Yes, I can see your problem. But what can you do about it?' The older woman sounded really concerned. 'You have no garden to attend to.'

'That is why I thought I should come and see you. I was wondering whether you could lend me a piece of land. I would dig it and plant something. If I never come back to harvest, you would have it. Maybe it could become a woman's way of thanking you.'

'Cho, cho, cho, cho, you girl! Where will it be heard that you are now digging in my garden for your upkeep.'

'It is not really so. Consider, how long are we going to be here?'

'We do not know.'

'Supposing that we stay for three moons, for instance, something could be ready in that time.'

The older woman thought about that for some time. 'All right,' she said quietly. 'I see your point. Wait here. I will go and consult my husband.' She went to look for him. Keshakama was starting to fidget uneasily when the old woman returned. 'He has agreed. Let us go.' She led Keshakama to the gardens and showed her a strip of fertile land above her banana plantation. 'You may dig as much of that as you can. When you are ready to plant any crop, come and ask me for seed.'

Keshakama did not have much of a choice regarding what to plant, since it was now in the dry season. She would plant sweet potatoes. If they were still in Kaakyenaga when the time for weeding came, she would plant beans while she weeded.

The next day many women in the camp saw her go off with her children carrying hoes. The clever ones learnt what she had done, and before the end of the day, they went to some other elders' wives. By the third day after Keshakama had started, very many women had gardens they were preparing. Many would come to harvest their crops later. But some did not.

III

Young Tindikahwa had also become deeply bored and the only activity available to him was grazing the cattle. The day the men left he went out with the cattle but it was no solution. It was there that he thought of a possible adventure. But no sooner had he thought of it than he discarded it. It could not be done. Even if he could convince anyone that it was possible, they would not let him go. They would say that he was much too young to go on such an adventure. The thought of this really depressed him.

The next day he did not go with the cattle. It would depress him more to watch the gap left by the raiders. His father and his grandfather had not lost any cattle in the raid. But Ruteera had had to contribute to help the losers. 'But why?' he asked himself loudly.

It was then that his younger father, Kubiriba, found him. He was sitting on a stone in front of his father's hut. His elbows rested on his knees. His cheeks rested on the open palms of his hands. His mind was very far away from Kaakyenaga.

'What is it, Tindikahwa?' Kubiriba asked. 'You are gripping your cheeks as if you have lost someone.'

'Uwhm,' Tindikahwa muttered agreeing without opening his lips. 'Nothing,' he said quietly. Suddenly he became lost in his dream again. His face seemed to close like a wilted flower. Seeing this, Kubiriba sat on another stone near him.

'It is a boring period, is it not?' he asked, resting his hand on the boy's shoulder. He was more than seven seasons older than the boy.

'Uhmm,' the boy answered, again without opening his mouth.

'We are all bored. I wish there could be something exciting to do.' The boy looked up at his face. He did not answer. He went back to staring far off towards the mountains. 'Ah, come off it Tindikahwa.' The younger father tapped him on the shoulder. 'Surely you can confide in me. You do not trust me?'

'Uhm,' was all the boy could utter.

'All right, tell me all about it.'

'Will you help me if I tell you?' the boy asked, his face lighting up.

'Of course I will. What do you think?'

'Swear,' the boy looked suspicious.

'May I sleep with my mother!'

Tindikahwa looked up at Kubiriba seriously. Now that he had sworn by his mother he could not wriggle out of it. He had either to go along with him or have the other impossible, humiliating alternative.

'I am planning to go and collect our cattle.' He said this matter-of-factly. 'I wonder who else will come with us.'

'Which cattle?' Kubiriba asked, puzzled.

'The ones which the raiders took, up in the mountains.' It took ten full breaths for the words to sink into Kubiriba's head. When it did, it shocked him for some more breaths. It was replaced by anger. He vented it on the boy.

'You stupid little fool, you evil nit!' He got up and stamped his feet on the ground. He turned away to hide his angry face. He turned round and shook his fist at the boy. 'You are a big-headed, stupid little creature. What else do you think you are? Do you think you will just walk there and they will give you the cows? Why do you not let your elders think about the welfare of the clan?' Then with a shaky voice he added, 'Why did you have to make me swear on my revered mother over your childish dreams? Eh?' He looked at the boy as if he would kick him.

The boy stood up and looked him straight in the eye. 'I thought you were a man,' he said very coolly, with a completely controlled voice. 'I did not know that you were such a coward.' He started walking off. 'I will go and look for a man to tell my problem to.' He quickened his speed. Kubiriba was left standing there, stunned by the boy's belittling reproof. Let him go and sleep with his mother instead, the boy thought.

The boy had not gone a hundred strides when Kubiriba came running after him. 'Stop, Tindikahwa, stop,' he shouted. Tindikahwa looked behind briefly and ignored him. He quickened his pace even more. 'Stop. Wait for me. I will help you,' Kubiriba said.

By then a few people were looking at this man running and calling after this boy. Tindikahwa stopped. 'But first, let us hear how far you have thought it through,' he panted to a stop as he caught up.

'Simple,' Tindikahwa uttered, unconcerned. 'There must be some men and women from here who have married there. Such men will go to visit their sisters and their in-laws. In two days' time or so, they could find out all we want to know. Who has the cows, who planned the raid, the best way to get there and other things. Then they will come and tell us. We will go to the mountains and camp as close to their place as possible. From there we will plan the route of attack and that of exit. We could do it at night. But the best time would be when they are taking the cattle home, just before dark.'

Kubiriba was quiet and thoughtful for some time. 'Yes, you nit with that large head of yours,' he said excitedly. He punched him on the shoulder with approval. 'It could be done. Do you want me to swear again?'

'No. Now I know you will come with me.'

'But are you sure you want to go yourself? It is more dangerous than you can imagine.'

'Try stopping me and see. I will run ahead and warn them.'

'And you could, too.' He grabbed the boy's left hand which disappeared into his right. 'Good. Let us go and recruit a pack of raiders and find out who married who and who married where.' Then, more thoughtfully, 'I wonder why nobody else thought of it before.' They walked off briskly hand in hand. They were both excited about the prospect of adventure.

That same day the first two of their plans were accomplished. Some two young men went to visit their sisters. Three others went to visit their in-laws. They all had the description of the stolen cattle to the last detail. They were expected back in some three days.

They had also managed to convince the elders of the two groups to allow them to go through with the plan. Those of Kaakyenaga had to approve first. It would be terrible if that other clan invaded Kaakyenaga because of them. But the elders assured them that that could not be. That clan was much smaller than the Bajura. And they had always feared them. 'Had they known that we were related, or that you would end up here, they would not have raided you,' an elder concluded.

Chapter Nineteen

I

Tibeijuka and Rutatiina were nursing cuts just above their navels. They were deep enough for them to draw a mouthful of blood to drink. They had just finished the ritual of becoming blood-friends. A number of their very close brothers were present to witness the ceremony. A pot of banana beer, *rwarwa*, stood in the centre of the group. There were no tubes in the pot. Instead there were a few small wide-mouthed calabashes. A calabash would be filled for the next person. A young son to Rutatiina served the beer. Nine men were present. They were in the house of Rutatiina's first wife.

'We say that a person behaves according to the name he is given. My friend's name is Tibeijuka, "they never remember",' Rutatiina said, jokingly. 'Is he not going to forget, one day, that we are blood-friends?' He looked accusingly at his friend.

'I thought you knew what my name meant, my friend. It is not I who does not remember.' Then he thrust his finger at Rutatiina. 'It is those other people, like you, who never remember.' The others laughed.

'Somebody must have disappointed your father very much,' Rutatiina's brother remarked. 'His name was Bebwà, "they forget" and he called you "they never remember".' They laughed again. Tibeijuka took it all in stride. People had always commented on those two names.

'It was one of his blood-friends,' he started seriously. 'He forgot that when my father gave him a cow, he did not ask him to carry many pots of beer. He did not ask him for anything. Secondly, when this cow produced several times, he did not give my father the traditional return cow. The third thing, when my father went to visit him, he did not skin a goat for him. Instead, he only plucked feathers off a flapping two-legged one. Surely ...'

'That was forgetfulness of the highest order,' someone interrupted.

'Why did he not invoke their blood?'

'No. He could not. He was too good-hearted to do that. I would not have stood it all had I been the one.'

'Yes, your father was justified to give you that name. I hope I will not forget like that man when you eventually give me a cow.'

'We shall have to see who has got more than the other.' A lot of jolly laughter followed this. As they drank they talked about many things. They eventually got to the findings of the two expeditions. Those who had gone

133

towards Mpororo had returned the previous evening. They had been away for five days. Those who had gone towards Butumbi had returned that day, just before the noon meal. Tibeijuka had gone towards Mpororo.

Everyone was talking about who would choose which place. Some people had already decided that they would go towards Mpororo. The report about the place was quite fair. There was no formal report about Butumbi yet. But from the rumours that were spreading, it was not bad either. They only had to battle with and defeat all those animals. The place was more fertile than Mpororo.

There was to be a meeting of elders the next morning. The spokesmen of both expeditions would give their reports and their recommendations.

A brother to Tibeijuka commented thoughtfully, 'It appears that we will go soon. But Kazooba Nyamuhanga only knows how far from this stage we would be if it was not for your people's help, Rutatiina.'

'Haa, do not talk about that,' Tibeijuka started. He slapped his thighs with his hands lightly several times. 'Oh mother, oh mother! Stop there. Do not remind us of those conditions. And if we ever forget this and fail to thank you accordingly, then the whole clan should take up my name, Tibeijuka.'

'Thank us for what, and how, Tibeijuka? Have you not thanked us enough?' Rutatiina asked sounding hurt. 'Did we not do our duty?'

'No you have not. Just look at all you have done for us! Feeding a whole clan for weeks. Is that not going to leave your granaries very low for a long, long time? Not only that, you led us to the places we hope to settle in. You have even made friends for us along the routes. What more can a man ask of another man?'

'Very much more,' a young father to Rutatiina replied. He was quite an old man. He had not talked much that evening. 'The other day a fellow elder gave us this advice: "If a man in trouble comes to you for help, help him. And never give him more trouble on top of his". I will add something to that.

'It is of great importance that a man should learn to eat with his brother. All Bajura from all corners should learn to eat with each other. Not only that. From what we have, we should even provide for those of us who do not have, the ones who are less gifted than we are. We should always remember that they did not choose to become less gifted than us. They have as much right to be on this earth as we have. Sadly, instead of using our gifts to give them a share of the good life, we use our gifts to bar them from getting anywhere near the beginnings of a good life.' He stopped and looked across at Tibeijuka and his brother. He pointed a steady index finger without a nail. 'If we had not helped you, you would still have survived, no doubt. But in what conditions?'

'Terrible conditions,' they replied quietly.

'Now, by helping you, what have we lost?'

'Some food, probably,' came the answer.

'As a matter of fact, we have not lost the food either. Do you not think that Kazooba Nyamuhanga is happy with us for feeding his people? Will he fail to give us rain and strength when he sees us nearing starvation? And yet, we have made great new friends. I am sure I will not be the first person to say that the gods see everything and act accordingly.' He relaxed and picked up a calabash with *rwarwa* in it.

'You're very right, my young father,' Rutatiina concurred. 'Things of this earth can always change. Like drums can change rolls without warning. Unless you are the one playing the drum, you cannot know when they will change.' He seemed lost in what he was thinking about. 'There are some people who are born gifted. They grow up gifted but somehow lose their gifts when they are old. Their luck dies before they do. An epidemic could come and kill all their domestic animals. They could even be chased away from their homes, as you have been. They might not even get the chance to keep their dogs. How could they expect help from anybody if they helped nobody when they were still gifted? All they would get is promises from people who know what they used to be.'

'Promises! By earth!' the younger father swore. 'Who can feed on promises?' His forehead became wrinkled. 'When those clans of Nyabigyi fed you on promises, what happened? They talked of being united. They swore to combine their forces to fight evil. They condemned the Bagirakwe most vehemently. They promised you everything you needed to overcome them. And where are you now?'

'On the run, on the move and suffering.'

'Never feed your brother on promises,' the old man continued, heatedly. 'Give him what he has asked for but not a promise. If you cannot manage to give it to him, if you do not have it, tell him the truth. You cannot be hanged for not offering what you do not have, can you?'

'No, you cannot.'

'He who does not have, can he be killed for not having?'

'Certainly not,' the other men replied. The old man talked no more.

They continued to drink until very late in the night. A few more elders joined them. They had been attracted by the voices. As someone said, you cannot hide a pot of beer for long. The gate-crashers did not wait to be invited. They reasoned, if you wait for a brother to invite you before you can join him to eat, you may starve. And they were nonetheless welcome when they joined the group.

The next morning the elders met at Banturabusha's home. They started the meeting early, in the middle of the morning. They had not finished two deliberations when ululations interrupted them. The men who had gone for the cattle were returning. And they had cattle with them. Within a short time ululations were heard all over Kaakyenaga announcing their successful return. Soon fresh young men took over the driving of the cattle.

The group had captured about eighty head in retaliation for the thirty that had been stolen. This herd had only five of their captured ones. But all rejoicing was marred by one thing: Tindikahwa was hurt. They carried him in a litter improvised from a large skin. They found a proper litter only when they entered Kaakyenaga. The boy did not lie on the litter as he should. Despite the pain, he sat up. He went waving and laughing at people excitedly.

As soon as they got home, Migayo was summoned. Ruteera and Mazima, the boy's grandfather and father, were the first to get to him. The council of elders had temporarily postponed their meeting.

'It is not really painful,' the boy said, looking at his thigh. He was trying to comfort the old men. They looked very worried. 'It was not even painful when the arrow hit me.' Tindikahwa seemed to be enjoying himself. He had never received such great attention before.

'All right,' Migayo said, removing the skin covering the lower part of his body. 'Let us look at it.' The wound was big. The arrow had entered through the front of the upper part of the thigh and come out through the back. Fortunately the arrow did not hit the bone. 'Did the arrow go right through?'

'No, it was a barbed one. Here it is,' Kubiriba said, producing the two halves.

'Do not lose my arrow,' Tindikahwa interrupted, 'I want to keep it.'

'We had to cut it and push the remaining part out through the other end.'

'I see. You are sure you left no splinter in his flesh?' the medicine man asked.

'We are sure.'

'Ahaa. That was painful! Oh, mother,' the boy said, smiling, 'it was much more painful than when the arrow hit me.'

'All right for now. Grit your teeth for more pain while I work on you,' Migayo teased him. 'You are lucky it was not a poisoned arrow. Otherwise you would not manage to make that trip back to Nyamiringa.' Four men came to hold the boy down.

II

The initial plan of the raiders had suffered no hitch. Fifteen strong young men and one boy had gone, all well armed. On their first day they got as close to the grazing grounds as possible. They had closely watched during the last part of the day, up to the time when the cattle were being taken home.

After watering the animals most of the older people accompanying the young herders had gone home. They had left the cattle completely in the hands of the young boys. Some of the older men, however, stayed on. Most of the boys only had sticks, though one or two of them had a bow and arrows.

After their reconnaissance the Bajura had gone higher up in the mountains and camped there. Before they left, the relatives of the thieves had informed them that some of their cattle were in this area but most were deep in the land, so they would have to make do with replacements They had honed their plan to perfection.

The next day they had gone down the mountain in the afternoon. They had hidden most of their weapons. If anybody saw them so heavily armed, he could raise the alarm before they got what they wanted. They then settled down to work out which herd they would go for. There were many herds scattered around. They could not raid any one of them without alerting those looking after the others.

They did not take action until the sun was almost disappearing. The herds started moving in different directions, returning home. Then one large herd started moving as if it was coming their way. The cattle were moving very slowly, pulling up the last mouthfuls of grass. There were five boys with the herd and two men were nearby but were not helping the boys.

'Now is the time,' one of the Bajura said. They moved slowly, keeping under cover of the bushes. The herd was about three hundred strides away. A small valley separated them. The sun disappeared as they moved out of the valley.

The cows had veered away. The boys were driving them faster now. The Bajura wondered if they had been noticed. They also moved faster. Three of the Bajura were sent to deal with the two lookouts. Seven moved to the left and disappeared into the valley again. The boys did not notice anything until the cattle in front had stopped. They were being forced back. The boys went to see what was stopping the cattle. Then the six men who had stayed behind broke cover. They rushed for the boys from behind. They took them unawares, still confused and struggling to go through the herd. Tindikahwa was the first to get to them. At this time the two men had realised that something was wrong. They rushed in to help the boys. But as they got to them they were attacked from behind. After they had put up a short furious resistance they were overpowered and tied up.

It was all very easy. There was no more fighting nor the slightest resistance. The Bajura tied all the captives' hands behind their backs and took them along with the cattle. Speed was all-important. They had to put a lot of distance between themselves and the settlement.

They were just getting into the valley when Tindikahwa saw an older boy. He had a bow and arrows and he carried a large dead edible rodent. As he pointed him out the boy dropped the rodent and before anybody knew what was happening Tindikahwa was running for him.

Kubiriba ran after him shouting, 'Careful Tindikahwa!'

Two other men followed but they were too late. The boy managed to shoot just one arrow. Tindikahwa jumped high and landed on the ground while holding his thigh with both hands. Not a sound had escaped him. Kubiriba fell to his knees beside Tindikahwa, grief-stricken. Seeing this, the boy panicked and started running. The other men gave chase and soon caught him. They came back to where Kubiriba was kneeling by his son.

'Quick,' one man advised. 'We must remove the arrow while he is still numb.'

'It is barbed,' Kubiriba said, looking at the captured boy menacingly.

'The other man got out his knife. He measured off the part of the shaft which was sticking out. He cut it off carefully without leaving a splinter. He looked at Tindikahwa's sweaty face, clenched his hand into a fist and hammered the remaining part of the arrow through the thigh. Tindikahwa screamed once. He started shaking all over with pain. They pulled out the stump of the arrow through the other end. A stream of blood started trickling down his leg. It was getting quite dark but they could still identify a few herbs. Kubiriba collected them and chewed them. He used them to plug the two wounds and tied them in place with a string. They carried Tindikahwa and ran after their fellow raiders and the cattle. They dragged the boy who had shot Tindikahwa along.

They caught up with the other raiders near where their weapons had been hidden. They were relieved to hear that the injury was not fatal. They picked the largest cowskin available and used it as a litter, so that two men could carry Tindikahwa at a time.

From then on four men kept to the rear. They would follow at some distance. They were supposed to repel any attack which might come but, if they could not, then they would run and warn the others.

When they had covered some distance, and no sign of an attack had appeared, Kubiriba called for a halt. 'We leave these people here.' The men and boys were very frightened. They thought they were going to be killed. 'Tie them all up and gag them,' he said. 'We shall hide them around here. Then we will take this one along,' indicating the boy who had shot Tindikahwa, 'and when we get far enough we will let him go. He can then come back and untie the others.'

'You are letting him go after ...' someone started.

'Yes,' Tindikahwa whispered painfully, 'let him go. If I had been him I would have done the same thing that he did to me.'

They tied up the boys and the two men and hid them some distance from the track. Each one was then tied to a tree. They took a different direction from there. They did not go straight up to the mountains. They set the other boy free around the first cockcrow.

'Tell your people that we have forgiven you,' Kubiriba told the boy before he set him free. 'We could have killed the eight of you, particularly you.' He pinched him. 'But we are not like them. Tell them never again to attack or raid people who have not disturbed their peace. Do you hear me?'

The boy ran off blindly. He could easily get lost or even get killed by wild animals. The others had been left in even greater danger. If any hyenas went that way, they would have a feast. Whereas a hyena would not attack a standing man, it would not hesitate to attack one who could not move. It would assume him to be dead.

III

Migayo had finished treating Tindikahwa. The boy had fallen asleep immediately after the treatment. Many people were coming to see this brave boy. Word had already spread all over Kaakyenaga about how the small boy had made the whole plan for the raid. People believed, perhaps rightly, that Tindikahwa had led the men. They were suggesting that he should take most of the cattle.

Migayo could not stay there to stop the people from bothering him. The meeting of the elders was to reconvene after the midday meal. Before Migayo left, he gave explicit instructions on how the boy should be treated when he awoke. Under no circumstances should he be woken up and nobody should be allowed into the hut to see him. His father and mother sat on the stones outside their hut. They would make sure that Migayo's instructions were adhered to.

'How is the boy?' Banturabusha asked as soon as Migayo arrived.

'Oh, that boy is all right. He is lucky, too. The arrow went through flesh only.'

'He is a brave one, that boy,' another elder said. 'Did you see how he arrived smiling?'

'Yes. It was as if nothing had happened to him. And you should have seen him when I was treating him. Passage of the hot plant juice through his wound drew no sound from him. Not even when I started squeezing the wound with hot leaves straight from the fire. He only gritted his teeth and sweated through it quietly. I did not need men to keep him motionless.'

'A barbed arrow and the accompanying treatment would draw screams from many men,' another elder commented. 'Imagine him acting so bravely at his age.'

'And do you know,' Ruteera started conspiratorially, 'he has sworn to return to Nyamiringa. That he must be buried where his grandfathers are buried. That he is determined to fight the Bagirakwe single-handed, if need be.'

'And this boy is determined to go?' Banturabusha sounded surprised.

'Yes. At first I thought that it was childish talk. But now I can see that there is nothing childish about him any more. Look at the way he has carried out this raid through!'

'He is one to watch,' Banturabusha said admiringly. 'He may lead the Bajura to great wars and greater victories some day.'

Eventually they got back to the more important issues. The time the visitors should leave was the most crucial. In the end they agreed that the men should go first. They were to leave in four days' time, when they would have made up their minds about which place to go to. When they got to those places they would put up some huts. They would also clear some land which the women would cultivate as soon as they arrived. That would take about a week. Then they would come back for their wives.

'After all,' Rutatiina started, 'all your wives are busy cultivating some borrowed land. It is only fair that you should give them some time to plant their crops. That food might help us all in moons to come.' All the others agreed with him.

'Then when you come for them, we will hold one big feast to send you off. We must wish you safety from the hogs, the lions and the man-sized apes,' Banturabusha concluded.

Chapter Twenty

I

Seasons had passed. The Bajura had been in their new homes for five full seasons. The place lying towards Butumbi they had called Kitajo. Those who went towards Mpororo called their home Rwebicuncu. The beginning had been very difficult and painful. That had been expected. But they had not been well enough prepared for what they met.

The group which started Kitajo had it roughest. The animals gave them a tough time. They would plant something during the day time. That same night some animals would come and destroy it. If anything survived, the elephants and buffaloes would eat it as soon as it was tall enough. Lion's and leopards killed their cows and goats. And for some time a person could not move alone even during the day. The animals were trying very hard to defend their territory and enjoy the new diet available.

Soon people realised that they had to guard their crops day and night. At night they lit fires by the gardens. Many men had to sit there throughout the night, battling the animals. It was some relief that they had started off with big communally owned gardens.

Communal hunting had to be intensified. The men, along with their dogs, spent whole days hunting. They killed every animal they found, whether small or big and whether edible or not. Sometimes their traps caught animals alive – leopards, cheetahs, civets, antelopes, monkeys and even crows. They would strap bells worn by hunting dogs around the necks of these animals. They would use hard leather and sometimes large metal rings. Then they would release them. Other animals would run away from them, taking them to be hunters.

Meat from the many animals compensated for the destroyed crops. It formed the bulk of their food for months. But soon the animals stopped coming to their place. They learnt that straying there, whether by day or by night, meant almost certain death. They moved farther away towards Butumbi. Then some crops started growing. The maize and beans and potatoes were very healthy. This place was very fertile indeed. When the people saw this they intensified their vigil. However trying the place was, they were determined to succeed.

Driving away the animals started to affect them. Meat became scarce. Then they turned back to Kaakyenaga. Those crops the women had left were ready for harvesting. Some had already been harvested. The men organised themselves into groups. One group stayed at home guarding their families and crops against animals while the other one went to Kaakyenaga to collect food.

That, together with the little game they now killed, kept them in food till their crops were ready for harvest. Amid rejoicing and celebrations, they ate their first crop in Kitajo. Now that they had defeated the animals and famine, they were sure that they would be able to settle. Nobody now could come to bother them. It was only much later that they met the Banyabatumbi and, when they did, it was under friendly circumstances. But could anybody be friendly with those witches from Butumbi?

The Bajura who started Rwebicuncu had a very easy beginning. They did not have so many wild animals to battle with. Even the threatened lions were not so many and they followed the movements of the nomadic cattlemen. But once in a while they killed one or two of the Bajura cattle.

Ruteeramareingwa's fears about the place had come true though. When the cattlemen realised what was happening they came to the place in bigger numbers, along with their cattle. They put up some temporary huts in the area around the Bajura. In their first season the two groups had a few skirmishes. Some of them were serious, resulting in a few deaths. But after both sides had lost some relatives, they agreed to live together. After all, the land was more than big enough for them all. There only had to be a fair way of distributing the good fertile land equally to everybody. Fortunately, the cattlemen were not after land for crops. They wanted grazing areas. And when the season forced them to move away, the Bajura expanded their gardens. When the cattlemen returned the next year, they could not assess how much of the grazing land they had lost. But the fact was that the newcomers could not expand as much as they wanted. And, as they produced more children, they would need more land.

Several families had gone to neither of these places. They had been given some land in Kaakyenaga. These faced no difficulties at all. We say that a lucky kite strikes a rat which is salted. These people's rat was truly and nicely salted. There had been neither animals nor cattlemen to trouble them. And while they toiled on their first crops they were given a big basket of beans here, some millet there, a bunch of bananas somewhere else, and so on.

Only much later did they meet some problems. Their children had to migrate because there was not enough room for expansion in Kaakyenaga. When they migrated, they went to Kitajo and their brothers were there to welcome and nurture them.

II

None of this could be said for the Bagirakwe in Nyamiringa. They still went on suffering. They had failed to settle down in their newly acquired place. Their problems were not of the earthly type, such as wild animals and cattlemen.

They were worse. They had failed to conquer the gods and the spirits of the Bajura.

They had taken over granaries which were almost full and fields of sorghum ready to be harvested. But that first year they were very busy fighting each other to keep the land they had acquired. They did not even settle down in time to harvest the sorghum. A few did not get any land at all. Others ended up with poorer pieces than they had first claimed. These were not satisfied. They believed that they had been cheated. These went round burning the sorghum which was dry in the fields. They even invaded the homes at night and burnt down the granaries. A few Bajura had been left behind. They also went round burning fields, granaries and even houses. They would do this secretly, of course. Several times people were burnt to death in their own houses. But the Bagirakwe persisted.

A new season started. People had somewhat settled down. They started planting all their crops. But just before the beans and peas started flowering, small green insects attacked them. As a result only a few plants flowered. Unfortunately most of these died before the pods could fully develop. Most farmers did not bother about going to see whether there was anything to harvest. Instead they concentrated on weeding millet and sorghum.

Some two moons later, the millet was almost ready for harvesting. The sorghum had big seed heads. Most of it had finished unfolding from the last swollen leaf. Then a heavy hailstorm fell and pounded the two crops. It fell for two consecutive days, and came again three days later. Most of the fingers on the millet were knocked off and pounded on the ground. Those which stayed up did not have any seeds left in them. Some six days later, the millet fields seemed to have already been harvested. The sorghum also got badly damaged. And the hail pelted down about one moon later. Then soon after that, small caterpillars attacked the sweet potatoes. They ate all the leaves, leaving behind only bare stalks.

The Bagirakwe wondered at this. They could not remember any time before when such misfortune had befallen them. So they went to medicine men to find out the reason. Wherever they went they were told that it was the gods and the ancestral spirits of the Bajura. That they came disguised in these natural forms and attacked. The Bagirakwe did not believe it. At any rate none of them was ready to give up the land at this stage.

In the third year locusts attacked. The millet was still green and the sorghum would soon start unfolding its seed heads. The two crops were promising a big harvest. The locusts flew from the side of Butumbi. They had managed to overfly Lake Rwitanzigye. They passed over other places and swarmed in Nyamiringa. The millet and sorghum were greener than the areas around and attracted the insects most. They were stripped of all their fleshy green. Even the soft stems were eaten up. The people caught pots and pots of locusts but they could not finish them. And while they ate the otherwise delicious insect, they cried. All their gardens had turned a dead yellow. The locusts had harvested all the crops.

Again they went to the medicine men. They were told the same thing: It was the gods and ancestral spirits of the Bajura.

'Do you not wonder,' one medicine man asked, 'why all these disasters come to Nyamiringa but not to the neighbouring ridges?' Some people had wondered. But they had refused to connect it with the truth.

It was at the end of this season that Rwecurenga made his first visit to Kitajo. He went with some six other men, taking directions as they passed through Kaakyenaga. He was received with feasting and rejoicing. Some news of Nyabigyi and Nyamiringa in particular had been filtering through but had got there several moons late and greatly distorted. So Rwecurenga spent some time telling and retelling stories about Nyabigyi.

Rwecurenga stayed in Kitajo for one moon. But he was greatly impressed by his in-laws. These people had taken a very short time to establish themselves. And so completely.

The following year was no better. A cholera epidemic broke out in Nyamiringa at the time of planting. Those who were not ill were busy burying their dead relatives and could not go to the gardens for a long time. When their relatives heard of the epidemic they stayed away from Nyamiringa.

By the time the epidemic left the people of Nyamiringa, the other clans were weeding their millet and sorghum. All the same they went to their gardens and sowed some millet and sorghum, even if they knew full well that they were already very late. The crops which came up were poor and stunted. By the time the crops were ready everybody else in Nyabigyi had harvested theirs. So all the birds migrated and rested in Nyamiringa. They started eating the poor crops a full moon before they were ready.

The people tried to chase away the birds. They put large scarecrows in the gardens. But the birds got used to the scarecrows. They would even perch on them. It was too much. Some people would have gone back to Kabisha then but their land had already been taken by their brothers, who would not relinquish it.

And then, as if this was not enough, another epidemic broke out, attacking their cattle this time. Few people were left with any cattle at all. And all the time, they were told that it was the gods and the ancestral spirits of the Bajura.

A very old Busaahu now went to visit his even older friend, the medicine man of the Baamungwe. He was accompanied by Rwecurenga and other followers.

'There is only one solution,' the old man said haltingly. He had grown even frailer than Busaahu. 'They have to leave the place. Otherwise they will be finished. Only the Bajura who were there before can live there.'

But the Bagirakwe in Nyamiringa could not accept this. They said that this divination was false, that it was because the old man was more closely related to the Bajura. His grandmother was sister to Ruteera's grandmother. But many others accepted his divination. They had come to realise that their brothers had been grossly wrong. Otherwise the gods would not punish them so heavily and so repeatedly. They had spent so much in sacrifices and fees to medicine men. Surely, if any gods were going to listen to them, by now disaster would have been averted.

Rwecurenga planned another visit to Kitajo. This time he was taking Kenyangyi along. She had not seen her parents in a long time and the route was clear. It was necessary that the Bajura in Kitajo and Rwebicuncu knew what was going on in Nyamiringa.

III

A direct route from Nyabigyi to Kitajo and Rwebicuncu had been established. The places had turned out to be quite near. Rwecurenga and his companions had taken five days. They had found friends and relatives along the way who put them up for the night. But they did not feel really free from danger until they reached Kaakyenaga. From there they passed through friendly communities only, all the way to Kitajo.

They had arrived in Kitajo three days back. They had spent the first two days nursing their swollen feet. They did not enjoy the welcome feasts in those two days because they had not moved around much. For Kenyangyi it was a different case. She was not a visitor and had been moving around as much as her feet would allow her. She still received the same compliments about her beauty and good health as before. Her three children had not altered her beauty much. She had left the first two, a girl and a boy, with her mother-in-law and had come with the youngest one, a girl.

On the afternoon of the third day Rwecurenga at last moved around. His legs inevitably led him to Kubiriba's house. He always received a very special welcome from Kubiriba and his wife, far beyond that accorded an in-law. And always delicacies started to be put before him before his buttocks had even touched the seat. One had the impression that these delicacies had been prepared much earlier, in readiness for his visit. Later three men, Rwecurenga, Kubiriba and Tindikahwa, sat nursing their over-full stomachs.

'My in-law,' Rwecurenga called out to the inner room.

'*Yee*,' Kubiriba's wife answered gently, with full attention.

'Do you have enough ghee in your ghee calabash?'

'*Yeego*,' she answered meekly.

'Some of us are going to need it. I for one will need some to rub on my tummy. My tummy skin needs softening so that it can stretch out full. As it is, it cannot contain all the delicious eatables I have packed in it.' They all laughed at him.

'But my husband,' Kenyangyi complained. 'Do you mean I have never prepared meals that are this good for you?' She had joined him there from her mother's house and was in the inner room eating with Keishemeza and the children.

'Of course you have, my woman. Why do you wonder?'

'Why have you never asked me for ghee to rub in the skin of your tummy?' The others laughed again. She did not.

'Do you only want us to laugh?' Rwecurenga started, controlling his laughter and rubbing his tummy comically. 'Can't you see that our stomachs will hurt us if we continue laughing so much?'

'No,' the wife said heatedly. 'I am serious. Why never?'

'As a matter of fact, I have,' he said after some thought. 'But it is so long ago that you might have forgotten.' They laughed again.

This time Tindikahwa did not join the laughter. 'Tell me more about Nyamiringa,' he interrupted. 'I am dying to go back and fight for our land.'

'You might not have to fight to have it back,' Rwecurenga replied, suddenly serious too. 'You may end up only walking in there and repossessing your land. Just the way you left it, without a struggle.'

Tindikahwa was a big man now. In recent years he had proved himself to be even more daring and brave. For quite some time now he had been training many young men, and some older ones in fighting skills. He had learned these from old men himself. Then he tried them out with the young men, altering here and perfecting there. They had become experts in the art of fighting with all weapons – spears, bows, matchets and bare hands.

He had got the inspiration for this from that day in the mountains when Rutatiina and Tibeijuka had demonstrated their skills. He had practised tirelessly as soon as he had recovered from that cattle raid so long ago. And since then he and Kubiriba had become inseparable companions. They were more like brothers than younger father and nephew now.

'You see, I want to be able to beat somebody. I want to show those heartless rogues that the Bajura can stand and fight.' He was talking heatedly now.

'But you will not have to, I can assure you. Your gods and the spirits of your ancestors are doing it beautifully.'

'That may well be true. But they are not doing it fast enough. I want a wife very badly. And I must marry my first wife from Nyabigyi.' He sounded distantly thoughtful. 'I cannot be expected to marry a witch from Butumbi for a wife.'

'Ehehee, their bows!' Kenyangyi laughed and swore from the inner room. 'May I start looking for one for you as soon as I get back?'

'Yes, indeed,' the young man blurted excitedly, 'and I hope your eye is as good as the rest of you.'

'Do not worry, my child. As we say, when you send your mother to the inner room, you do not follow her with a torch.'

'I will reward you very generously. But when will that be?'

'You have lit the fire in his heart now,' Kubiriba observed. 'When will you present the meat to roast in it, then?'

'Very soon, I can assure you,' Rwecurenga added. He told them what had been going on in Nyamiringa. Again he started from the beginning and ended with the last divination Busaahu had got from his friend. He had already retold this story several times before. 'Many of them are already looking for a new place to go to.'

'Well, well, well.' Tindikahwa eyed Kubiriba sideways.

'Well, well, well indeed,' Kubiriba mimicked. 'We shall have to go to Rwebicuncu. Some of our brothers there will want to come too.'

'A great idea,' Rwecurenga said excitedly. 'I might have a chance to visit that place. How soon would that be?'

'In three or four days' time. We shall have to consult the elders first,' Kubiriba told him.

'Yes. Do that soon.'

'I will do it when we come back from the communal hunt tomorrow. Remember not to oversleep.'

IV

The next morning the communal horns summoned the men. In a short while, hunting bells were heard from all the areas around. They were converging upon the rendezvous. All the dogs had to wear hunting bells. A group of fifty or so men set off with their dogs. Some carried rope traps. They were going farther away towards Butumbi, where the animals had migrated.

The animals did not invade them very often now. But if, for instance, a leopard killed somebody's goat, it would be communally hunted the next day. They would make sure that they killed it. Still, they wanted them even farther away.

Kubiriba, Rwecurenga and Tindikahwa stayed close together throughout the hunt. At one time Rwecurenga almost got killed by a male cob. Several dogs came chasing it. They kept quite some distance behind, afraid to attack it. The same dogs had chased it over a long distance. The three men saw it running in their direction and hid behind a bush some twenty strides beyond a rope trap. Somehow the cob jumped over the rope trap. Whether it actually recognised the camouflaged trap, whether it jumped only accidentally when it got to it, or whether it was just by instinct, no one quite knew. But as fate would have it, the three men were directly in its way. When the animal jumped the trap Rwecurenga jumped out of hiding excitedly. The animal saw him. It came straight at him, very fast. Its coiled horns were aimed below his knees. He speared it when it was only about two strides away.

'My spear,' he shouted. He was announcing to everyone that he had speared it first. The largest share would go to him. The animal fell down on the spear. Rwecurenga thought it fatally wounded. It had even broken the spear shaft as it fell. He relaxed his attention briefly.

Suddenly the animal sprang up. In an instant it was on him. He had no time to unhook his machete. The injured cob brought up its horns, intending to skewer him savagely. He skipped to one side. A creeper trapped his leg. He fell down helplessly. The cob pulled its head backwards to take a careful aim for his belly. Tindikahwa jumped into the air. He landed on his knees between man and beast. In the same movement he grabbed its horns. The two wrestled for their lives. The animal flung him this way and that way. It even threw him to the ground once. It trampled him with its front hooves. But his grip on its horns was unbreakable. It could not disengage itself from his grip. It would have skewered him to death the moment he lost his hold.

Rwecurenga stood up and joined Kubiriba to help Tindikahwa. But they could not use their weapons. The two fighters were changing their positions all the time. By the time anybody hit out, Tindikahwa could easily be in the way. After a long struggle the animal started to weaken and slow down. It had lost a lot of blood. Only then did the friends manage to spear it. In one last tremendous effort it leaped into the air. It carried Tindikahwa with it. It fell back to the ground with a terrible last groan. Only then did Tindikahwa let go of the horns.

He sat on a stone wiping sweat from his face. He was shaken. Rwecurenga joined him wordlessly. He was awe stricken by the young man. Others started to gather round. Only then did they notice a number of dogs barking and struggling in the rope trap. Having missed the cob, the ready trap had caught the dogs which had chased it.

'The mother-fucker almost killed you,' Kubiriba said, much later, as they skinned the animal they had killed.

Tindikahwa whistled long and loud with wonder. 'And that is an understatement. Can you imagine what would have happened if those horns had got Rwecurenga?' he wondered.

'Oh, mother! Those mad Bagirakwe would never believe that it was an accident.'

'My mad brothers should have watched the contest.' Rwecurenga said. He wanted to veer the topic away from the Bagirakwe. 'They would not wish to meet you on the battlefield.'

'I was a dead man down there, my father. I could not afford to lose the only grip I had on sweet life.'

All the men had gathered around to skin and share the animals they had killed. Tindikahwa's fight was still the subject of talk. They still had some five more animals left to skin when three old men from Butumbi suddenly came upon them. Everybody started talking to them with strained friendliness.

'You did gives us meat,' one of them said, in their crooked language.

'No, we did not gives you meat,' someone answered, imitating them.

'You did refuses us meat, you didn't eats it, yous.' They turned to go.

'Come back, come back,' someone else called. 'We did gives you meat.' They selected a fat bush-buck and gave it to them. The men became happy. Everybody joined them in the laughter.

'Do you know what that man meant? He actually said that if we did not give them meat we would not eat it ourselves.' Kubiriba told Rwecurenga as they went home, each carrying meat heavier than a big goat.

'Oh, I did not know.'

'Just by saying "refuses" he had bewitched the meat. And had we refused to give them any, we certainly would not have eaten what we had.'

'But how could they stop us?'

'I can see you do not know these people at all. Do you think they asked us for some meat because they lacked meat?'

'Why else?' Rwecurenga was puzzled.

'Indeed you do not know them. Those people can get any meat they want, any time. One of them can get in among a herd of buffaloes alone, armed with only a sword. He will proceed to select a fat one, just like a man among his herd of cattle. Then he will slaughter it. As it falls down groaning and kicking, all the other buffaloes will run away.'

'They must be armed with very powerful charms indeed.'

'It is not only that,' Kubiriba continued. 'You see, they claim to own all these animals. They have mastered the skills of bewitching them so completely that you never hear of any of them being killed by a wild animal. Yet they live together with them.'

'Someone was telling me of an experience he had there,' Tindikahwa said. 'A friend had taken him to visit. That friend has friends there and one of them took him to visit an uncle. They arrived to find the family having their lunch. They were eating millet bread and smoked fish. "You did comes and we ates," the family head invited. So they washed their hands and joined in to eat.

'The visitor picked a normal-sized lump of millet. He manipulated it into a ball, pressed a hole in the ball with his thumb and scooped soup with it. The millet was well-ground and had cassava flour in it too. So it did not stay in the mouth for long. But when he swallowed it, it got stuck halfway down the gullet. It did not become painful or whatever. It only made him feel sort of stupid and uncomfortable. He struggled with it quietly for some time but it stubbornly refused to go down.

'When the others had swallowed some fifteen balls the man of the house looked straight at him and cleared his voice. "You are not eating, visitor," he commented. "What is it?"

'Suddenly the ball went down. He found his voice. "I am eating," he answered. He sent his hand into the basket to prove that he was eating. The basket was empty.'

Rwecurenga whistled with wonderment. 'What had happened?' he asked.

'The man had bewitched him so that he could not. They could not invite their friend only. But they bewitched their other visitor because they did not want him to eat their food. So the first ball got stuck in his gullet. When he asked him why he was not eating he was actually releasing it. And he knew that there would be nothing left in the basket.'

'They must be terrible people,' Rwecurenga surmised.

'Surprisingly, if you know how not to cross them, they are all right. They are essentially very simple people. But those who have made friends among them say they are good.'

'And yet I hear that those of Kyangwe kya Mbanibiri are worse.'

'Very true. Those are terrible.' Kubiriba turned to look in that direction. They could see Lake Rwitanzigye very clearly. 'Can you see all those small flashes of lightning beyond the lake?' He pointed them out. 'They seem to be playing in the lower skies just above where the sky and earth meet.'

'Yes,' Rwecurenga replied. 'They are playing around, like children learning to dance.'

'They are indeed playing around. All of them are tame thunderbolts. They are owned by individuals. If you anger the owner of a thunderbolt, he will send it to you. It will strike you dead that very day, if not there and then.'

They had got to the edge of the scattered compounds. The children had come running to meet them to help them with the loads. They were assured of meat for some eight days.

As soon as they got home, Rwecurenga, Kubiriba and Tindikahwa went to look for the elders. They had to go to Rwebicuncu within the next few days. That evening Rwecurenga would accompany Tindikahwa to watch the young warriors practising. They would find some other men who would make the trip to Rwebicuncu with them. But, of course, anyone in Kitajo who was interested in making the trip was welcome.

Chapter Twenty-one

I

The group of brave men stood by the great river, Ekyambu. It was still very early in the morning. The sun was just starting to get warm. They had left home at first cockcrow and had got to the top of the very steep slope, *enengo*, soon after the sun had come out of its hiding place. They had taken a long time to get to the river at the bottom of the valley. They had to move very carefully. It was not rare that people slipped or took a wrong step and were seriously injured from the fall.

The *enengo* was very steep indeed. In some places it looked like the face of a very high wall. If you looked up from the bottom of the valley you would think that you were in a great big house with massive walls. The blue sky high up looked like the roof. The giant trees looked like the poles holding up the sky. Nobody could shoot an arrow straight up and make it reach the top of the trees.

If all the plants were to be removed and a person fell down, he would roll to the very bottom of the valley. Going up was even more difficult. And that was why they had left home so early. They wanted to climb the *enengo* on the opposite side before the sun became very hot. Then Rwebicuncu was not very far away. They would get there long before the cattle were taken home.

'Who has no fear of water?' Kubiriba asked, uncoiling a long stout rope. There was no bridge. They had to use a rope tied across the river. One person had to cross with it to tie it on the other side.

'Who fears water?' Tindikahwa asked, coming forward. He was already removing his skins. 'Give me the rope. I will swim across with it.' The rope was handed over to him. 'Someone come with my skins.'

'Will you not tie the rope round your waist,' somebody asked.

'No. This is the narrowest part of the river. And you can see all those stones. At any rate I can swim very well.'

'Ahh, you man,' an older man said, 'have you forgotten our saying: "Water kills the man who insists he knows it?" We can swim, too. But we can also see that this water runs very fast here.'

'All right, I will take your advice. But it is really not necessary.' He removed his skins and tied the rope around his waist. Then he swam across. This place was only thirty strides across. But, true enough, the water was very fast. He did not use the rope but twice he almost had to. Instead he grabbed at and clung to the stones. On the opposite shore, he tied his end of the rope securely around a stout tree.

The other twelve people started crossing, their heads barely staying out of the water. Had it not been for the rope, some of them would have been washed away. The last person untied the rope from the other bank and tied it around his waist. He partly swam and was partly pulled across. The dogs swam across much more easily.

They had just started going up when they surprised a solitary hippopotamus. It fell and rolled down the slope. They heard it land in the river with a loud splash. Their dogs chased after it from a distance, barking timidly.

'Have you seen that cowardly animal? It simply rolls down,' someone started by way of conversation.

'Do not tell me about hippos. One of the beasts killed my stepmother only two moons back,' another man said bitterly.

'Oh, yes. That was sad, indeed,' Kubiriba agreed. 'It cut her in two and put the lower part of her body on this bank and the top part on that bank.'

'Yes. And when people came, they found her upper body still talking. She was saying that the stupid thing had eaten her but she had also beaten it.'

'Poor woman,' someone observed, 'she must have been bewitched.'

'Poor woman, indeed! She really suffered.' They walked quietly with sadness for some time. Each one was thinking about the woman and the hippo.

'The hippo that attacked her had to be out of the water, like this one. A hippo does not leave water to go and attack a person,' someone said.

'If the person has been bewitched to be killed by a hippo, anything can happen. The person will even leave home and go to the river to be killed.'

'What was this one doing outside the water now?' Rwecurenga asked. 'I thought they left the water only at night, in order to feed.'

'It must be a young male,' Kubiriba explained. 'It was looking for its father's footprints. It has to keep measuring its feet in the father's footprints.'

'Why should it do that?'

'You do not know?' Kubiriba asked with surprise. The other men were equally surprised.

'No, I do not know,' Rwecurenga said, puzzled. 'As you know, you left no hippo in Nyamiringa.'

'It must keep measuring. The day it finds that its foot is larger than the father's, or just fits tightly, it will challenge the father to a fight. If it wins, it will take over all the father's harem.' They digested this information quietly for a brief moment.

'But animals are very interesting. Imagine fighting your own father so as to take away his women,' another man observed.

'I do not think fighting the father is anything special,' somebody else argued. 'If you are going to fight over women, you can fight practically anybody who gets in your way.'

'In that case, it is not animals only that do that,' Rwecurenga concluded. 'We people do exactly the same thing. And why we should fight while there are many other women around beats me.' As soon as he said this he wondered at himself and his wife, Kenyangyi. And he remembered that, when his father had tried to stop him from marrying her, he had been prepared,to fight.

'We have escaped only narrowly,' somebody observed. 'We almost became animals. When it comes to women, food, and land or territories, we fight just like these other beasts.'

They continued to discuss men and women as they negotiated the steep *enengo*. And the topic had drifted far away from hippos and men fighting for women.

They rested for a short period in the early afternoon. They ate their lunch, drank some *bushera* from long-necked calabashes and continued their journey.

II

The travellers got to Rwebicuncu long before dark. They were received with happy feasting. They had not been expected. There was no way in which they could have informed their kinsmen about their coming. But before they could rest their legs, a large billy-goat was wrestled to the ground. And while they drank the sweet *bushera*, beer was being looked for.

They were first entertained at Tibeijuka's home and, during their week-long stay, their subsequent meetings took place there. But they could not all sleep there. They had their intimate friends who would put them up at night. Tindikahwa and two others were not married. They did not mind where they slept. Often they slept in the homes where night found them, if there was beer there. On other nights, Tindikahwa slept in the home of a younger son of Tibeijuka.

The older men went to the homes of their married friends, particularly those with two or more wives. It is our custom that a married man should not sleep alone, unless it cannot be helped. So, when such a man visits a very close friend he does not sleep alone, in a cold bed, unless the friend has only one wife. Kubiriba's friend had just whispered to his second and only other wife. He had instructed her to make a bed for the visitor. That night, Kubiriba started thinking of marrying a second wife. If this friend ever came to visit him, Kubiriba should be in a position to reciprocate this courteous welcome. As we say, "something is given to that one who will some day give in return".

The next day the visitors met the elders of Rwebicuncu. They met at Tibeijuka's home, just as the sun was getting warm. Kubiriba and some of his friends looked red-eyed and sleepy; and they yawned every so often. But as the sun became warmer, they also started to get brighter and more awake.

Kubiriba had hinted at the purpose of their visit the previous night. So the elders had enough time to think about it. They had seriously wrestled with it through the night. Many had concluded that it was a mad idea but they were ready to listen to the young men. Maybe there could be something in it after all.

Tibeijuka stood up and greeted them all. They were sitting in his inner compound. They were not many, only about thirty altogether. He welcomed them to the deliberations.

'Our young sons have come to visit us,' he continued after the greeting, 'but they came on a very important errand too. Whether it is a good one or a bad one, whether it is feasible or not, we shall see after they have spoken. But let us listen to what they have to say most carefully. Then we shall give it our most serious consideration.' He looked at the elders, entreating them to be absolutely honest with themselves when they got round to discussing the issue. 'If we make a mistake here, it might cost us the lives we have suffered to save.' He looked at the young men invitingly. 'Tell us how you plan to go back to Nyamiringa.' He sat down.

Kubiriba got up. He greeted them all in a low tone. Then he called upon Rwecurenga to stand up. 'You all know him?' he asked. Most of them agreed that they knew him. A few hesitated. 'The time is long ago. He is Rwecurenga *wa* Bugeiga.' There was some significant mumbling. It was in favour of Rwecurenga. They all remembered him well now. 'You may remember that he married my sister, Kenyangyi.'

He briefly told them about their friendship, the part he had played in starting and organising the anti-war crusade and what the group, under the leadership of Busaahu, had achieved. 'It is not the first time that Rwecurenga has made the long, dangerous trip from Nyabigyi to Kitajo. But this time, we had to bring him here so that you may get information about Nyamiringa right from his mouth.'

Rwecurenga told them a long story. He gave them an account of everything that had happened to the Bagirakwe in Nyamiringa. He even gave the verdicts of the medicine men the Bagirakwe had gone to.

'So, right now,' he concluded, 'they are looking for another place to go to. Some of them have been trying to come back to Kabisha but nobody will have them back. Their brothers who were left behind will not give them back their land.' He stopped and looked around. His tale was having the desired effect. The elders had heard such stories but the news had got to them in such fragments that they were often meaningless. But now …

'I have seen Tindikahwa's brave warriors in action,' Rwecurenga continued. 'I am sure only fifty of them would defeat and chase the Bagirakwe out of Nyamiringa. They are too demoralised and too weak to defend themselves.'

Next Tindikahwa got up to speak. He told them about his army and part of his plan. He even had four of the men who were in his army demonstrate their martial prowess. Even Tibeijuka, from whom he had got the whole idea, was impressed. He watched the five men, mesmerised by their expertise. Had he only been told about them, he would not have believed that a boy of eighteen could know so much about fighting. He would not challenge the boy to a fight himself.

'As you may well know, we have not come to ask you for permission,' Tindikahwa said. 'Nor have we come to ask for help. No.' He stopped and adjusted his skins importantly. 'If we get any help from you, our fathers and brothers, it is most welcome. But we came to tell you that we are preparing to go back to Nyamiringa. Whatever happens we must go, and very soon, too.' He looked around dreamily. 'But Nyamiringa belongs to us all together. So we found it only fitting that we should come and see whether any brothers here would like to come with us. Then they can have their rightful share.'

'Some blood will be shed. But it will be very little and worth it in the light of what we shall achieve for the future generations of Bajura. Never will anybody think of going to war with the Bajura again, simply because they are few. Nobody will hunger for our land again and decide to throw us out. Any number is welcome to come and join us.' He sat down.

There were some murmured comments on the young man. They could all remember the boy who had been shot with a barbed arrow. That was five full seasons back, during that cattle raid. They continued to discuss the issue until the afternoon and left Tibeijuka's home as the goats were being taken out to graze.

Although the elders still had some reservations about the whole adventure, they decided to train young warriors just in case it became necessary. They had had some training but it was inadequate.

When the elders left they took a message calling upon all the young men to start training the very next day. Tindikahwa and his friends would start them off and have some two days with them before returning to Kitajo. If any of them wished to return to Nyamiringa, they would have the blessing of the elders. If the journey never materialised, then Rwebicuncu would still have benefited through acquring well-trained warriors. The Bajura were now ready to start defending themselves against fellow man.

III

'*Iwe* Keijumeeza,' Rwecurenga called out to his wife with exaggerated tenderness. He used her pet name this time, which he rarely did.

'*Yee*,' Kenyangyi answered with matching meekness.

'Bring a pin and save me from jiggers.'

'*Cho*,' Mazima exclaimed, 'where did you get the jiggers from?' Mazima had not gone to Rwebicuncu with them. 'There are no jiggers in Kitajo.'

'I thought my feet were eating me because of being tired,' Kubiriba said, rubbing his foot on the edge of a nearby stool. 'And I was afraid to talk about it in case you laughed at me because I had jiggers.' Three of the others also said that they believed that they had jiggers.

Kenyangyi came and knelt in front of her husband. She lifted the foot her husband indicated and placed it in her lap. She had come with a sharp needle used for making small baskets.

'Eh, their bows!' she swore as she saw the small fleas halfway through boring into her husband's flesh. 'Come and see, you people. They are following each other in a line like cows going home.'

'Then those are foretelling riches to come,' somebody said.

'Is that why the others are not complaining?' Mazima asked.

'Why should we complain about a foreteller of riches?' one of the others said. 'Have you forgotten that a messenger is never killed?'

'You will be like Rwomire. He left them until they invaded even his elbows and buttocks,' Mazima said, laughing. But the riches never come. Instead, well, you all know how he walks.'

'But where did you all get the jiggers from?' Kenyangyi asked, squashing the young jigger she had just extracted. It was already starting to swell.

'It must be from that dilapidated hut where we sheltered from the rain,' Kubiriba said.

'That is right,' Tindikahwa said, 'That must be the place.'

'Did it really rain?' Mazima asked. 'Where?'

'Why do you think we got back so late?' another young man asked. 'The rain started falling just as we had crossed the river, so all the way up the *enengo* it was raining on us.' He looked at Mazima. 'As you know, there is no place there where a man can take shelter. But when we got to the top, we came to this abandoned hut. We took shelter there.'

The group of brave young men had just returned from Rwebicuncu. They had arrived as the cows were being milked and found a small reception party waiting for them at Kubiriba's home. Everybody was eager to hear the news from their brothers in Rwebicuncu. And while they drank they told stories about what they had seen and how they had been received. They had quite a number of tales to tell.

Some few elders joined them later. These included Ruteera and Migayo. The elders had been informed about this drink much earlier. But they had stayed at home to see to it that their cows were milked and locked up in their kraals first. Soon the elders started enquiring about their friends in Rwebicuncu.

'How is Tibeijuka's father?' Migayo asked.

'He is fine. He sent warm greetings to you all,' Kubiriba said.

'How is he now?'

'He has grown very old. He needs the support of a stick when he walks now. Most of the time he is at home, sitting or lying down.'

'Old age is bad, my children,' Migayo said, shaking his head. 'Old age will wrinkle even the anus without shame. That was a very brave and very active man. To imagine that old age has immobilised even that one! I wonder how he copes with an inactive life.'

Very briefly they received all the news they needed to know about their friends and relatives. Some looked healthier while others had become poorer. Others were richer and yet others had died. Quite a few of them had married from among the cattlemen, and that aroused a lot of interest in Kitajo.

"How are their wives from the cattlemen?' a young man asked. He was Kubiriba's brother, of the same mother.

'They are not like our women. They are lazy. They do not know how to dig,' someone answered. 'But they are very pretty.'

'It is not that they are lazy,' Rwecurenga corrected, 'it is because they are not used to digging. Their work is to look after calves, and to prepare milk for making ghee, churning the milk, and cooking. And they have to maintain their prettiness.'

'Eh! What do they cook if they do not dig?' Mazima asked.

'Not much really,' Kubiriba said. 'Only some meat and some few small things. They buy food from their neighbours with ghee. Otherwise, they say that milk and meat are enough for them.'

'That is very strange,' one old man mused. 'A woman who does not dig, what is she for?'

'You mean yours dig all the time?' a young man asked.

'Yes, of course.'

'Even when you go to sleep?'

'Listen to this young one, also! If a woman does not know how to dig in the field and she does not know how to dig in the kitchen, how can you expect her to know how to dig in the bed?' They all laughed.

'Actually, you are right, son of my father,' Ruteera supported. 'As we say, a pumpkin plant which will save you from famine, will start off by giving you flowers and small fruits.' He paused for breath. 'Likewise, if you show a woman a garden and she says that she does not know how to dig, when next you give her millet to grind, she will turn the grinding stone the wrong way round. You give her food to cook, she breaks the pot. What do you think she will do when it comes to going to bed?'

'She will probably turn the wrong way around, like with the grinding stone,' a young man observed. They burst into loud laughter.

'But actually,' someone remarked when the laughter had subsided, 'those people's customs are just as wrong-way-round as their women. For instance, I was told that a man can sleep with his son's wife.'

'Is that really so?' Mazima asked, casting a sly glance at his father.

'It is very much so. He goes to see where his cows went. He has to know whether the woman is worthy of the bride price.'

'That is the height of foolishness,' Ruteera reacted. 'How can a man sleep with his son's wife? She is just like his daughter.'

'But it is not very different from us,' another elder observed. 'If a son can sleep with his father's wife, I do not see why the reverse should be so outrageous. His father's wife is as good as his mother.'

'But he does not, until the father has died,' Ruteera argued.

'I think we should not laugh at them,' Migayo said. 'Every tribe has got something peculiar in their custom which other tribes would find outrageous. You will find that those cattlemen also laugh at some of the things we do.'

'That is very true, son of my father,' the elder continued. 'For instance, they laugh at us for eating grasshoppers. We eat mutton and we even fart.'

'You mean they do not fart!' a young man exclaimed.

'No, they do not. If for instance a married woman farts, she must go back to her parents. And if a man farts while wooing, the girl will never want to see him again.'

'That is very difficult to imagine. What do they do to it, when it comes pressing them urgently to let it out?'

'They simply make sure that it does not come.'

'This world is really full of all sorts of funny things,' Rwecurenga interjected.

The men continued drinking and talking about all sorts of peculiar customs found among other tribes. A few neighbours joined them. They had not been invited but they could not be refused a drink.

Later, in the middle of the night, talk veered back to Rwecurenga and his group. They would be starting their return journey to Nyabigyi in a couple of days' time. Ruteeramareingwa had given Rwecurenga a young heifer, only recently weaned. He would finally hand it to him on a rope, at a farewell party for him on the evening of the day before they were due to leave.

As Rwecurenga prepared to return home, the warriors of Kitajo prepared to follow, to go and claim their Nyamiringa. They had started to believe that they would simply walk in as Rwecurenga had tried hard to make them believe. After all, their gods and ancestral spirits had been fighting for them all those years.

This disappointed Tindikahwa. He had trained very hard in preparation for fighting the Bagirakwe. He would feel bad if they got there and there was to be no fighting. He really wanted to beat those Bagirakwe on the battlefield. That would convince all the other clans around that, although the Bajura were few, they were incomparably superior on the battleground. Then no clan would dream of bothering them again.

Chapter Twenty-two

I

Four moons had passed since Rwecurenga had gone back. Tindikahwa was becoming very impatient. He went through each day steeped in a reverie about Nyamiringa. He had managed to convince the others that they should leave for Nyabigyi right after Rwecurenga's departure. But the gods had advised them against rushing into war, advising that there would be a sign to show them when it was all right to go.

That had been almost four moons back. Then recently he had started again. Many young men readily agreed with him that two more moons would be the maximum period they would wait. Then they would go whether the signs came or not. They were thinking of sending a message to that effect to Rwebicuncu when events took a new turn. The sign was presented to them.

A messenger group arrived from Nyabigyi. It was led by Karwemera. The news they brought with them was woeful. But terrible as it was, many young men rejoiced. Unmistakably this was the sign they had been waiting for. The messengers were received first at Kubiriba's house. They therefore told the bones of the story to Kubiriba and Tindikahwa first. After hearing it and grasping the implications, they all immediately went to look for the elders. They could not possibly sleep on such news. Then Karwemera told them the whole story in detail.

Rwecurenga and his group of brave men had got to Nyabigyi safely. Nyabigyi had not changed at all. The Bagirakwe in Nyamiringa were still refusing to look for some other place to go to. Their brothers in Kabisha still refused to take them back. Bugeiga was still roaming around the ridges naked. His children and grandchildren no longer covered their faces with shame when they saw him. To all intents and purposes the bony hulk that wandered around naked, caked with mud and with hair like the fleece on the tail of a sheep, was not Bugeiga, their parent.

But unhappiness continued to reign in Nyamiringa. Some five men had decided to pack their mats and pots and go to look for some unclaimed place to live in. That had to be very far indeed. They had to go right outside Rukiga. Their friends had looked at the pitiful group with miserable wives and children heading for the unknown. Many of them must have wished that they could be brave enough to make a similar move. But instead they had adamantly refused to budge. Many of them had been heard saying that they had nowhere to go to. They were ready to fight to stay in Nyamiringa. They would die there if need be. This was very troubling to their friends in Kabisha. Although they had all now turned around to blame them, they did not wish to see the clan continuing to suffer.

Rwecurenga started to become worried about the assurances he had given his in-laws and the elders of Kitajo. He had hoped that by now Nyamiringa would be free, waiting for the rightful owners to come and occupy it, without a fight. But now the settlers were even more determined not to leave Nyamiringa. With such worries, Rwecurenga had gone to Busaahu. Both the Bagirakwe in Kabisha and those in Nyamiringa had seen many medicine men. They had all said that the Bagirakwe had to leave Nyamiringa. Some had even vaguely foretold some of the catastrophes that had befallen the invaders. But they had all forgotten one important medicine man. And when Rwecurenga went to see Busaahu, he had this very one in mind.

'Supposing we went to see the medicine man who gave Bugeiga the medicine in the first place?' he asked as soon as they had settled down.

'How are we going to find him?' Busaahu said after a few thoughtful moments. 'Bugeiga was very secretive at the time. And the only son who could have told us, Ndemire, died long ago.'

'We shall find him. At least we know which direction he took. There cannot be many powerful medicine men in the direction of the lake.'

They had taken a few days to locate the medicine man. The fifth day found four men heading for the lakes. A very old Busaahu led the way. He was still going strong. He did not wish any young men to think that he was too old to do what he used to do some seasons back. They got to the medicine man in the mid-afternoon.

'I have been waiting for you for a long time,' the medicine man said as soon as they were seated.

'But we have not yet told you where we come from and who we are,' Rwecurenga exclaimed.

The man did not even smile. He simply ignored the comment. 'But maybe you have come at the right time,' he continued. 'Let us go and confer with the gods.' He was not as old as Busaahu. He was dark, tallish and slender. His hair and even the eyebrows were completely grey. And he never removed his pipe from his mouth, except when they went to the shrine.

They headed for the small hut in one corner of the compound. Inside it was not very different from some of the shrines they had been in. But there were many more things in here than they had seen in other shrines. He laid out his horns and prepared to start divining. Busaahu handed him the big anklet that he had asked for. He put it down on the skin where the small horns lay motionless. The men, awed by the way he had known about them without being told, were confident that they had done the right thing.

As soon as he started shaking the leading horn, the small ones started dancing. And almost immediately a hoarse voice, like that of someone being choked, filled the room. The medicine man stopped and looked at the expectant group. They were used to this, having visited several medicine men in the last few years.

'Nyamiringa is about to turn upside-down,' he said, biting his lower lip. He looked straight at them as if he was looking at something deep inside them.

'What do you mean?' Busaahu asked slowly and quietly as if he were afraid of being heard.

The medicine man did not answer right away. Instead he shook the horn again. His lips could be seen moving quietly in consultation. 'It is turning upside-down and the people are getting finished.'

'What is going to finish them?'

The man shrugged his shoulders before answering. 'What more can I tell you?'

The men mumbled quietly, not satisfied.

'What can be done?' Busaahu asked when the mumbling had stopped.

'I told that man,' the medicine man started, 'that what he was asking for was impossible. But he insisted that he wanted it done. I explained to him explicitly that what he would achieve was not worth what it would cost the Bagirakwe as a whole. He still insisted that he wanted the Bajura uprooted from Nyamiringa. So I went ahead and arranged it. And now, I think they have had enough. And those who have not, will - very soon.'

'You mean,' Busaahu started haltingly, 'you knew all these things would happen?'

'Yes. It was obviously glaring at me.'

'And you went ahead and made it possible?' Busaahu was appalled and he could hardly keep it from his voice.

'First of all, I did not make it possible as you say. I only consulted with the gods and they did the rest. Secondly, it was very necessary. Look at how many of the Bagirakwe were behind Bugeiga.' He looked straight at Busaahu. 'The gods had to step in and punish them. Only that would solve the problem permanently.'

'Could the gods not have solved the problem in another way?'

'Maybe they could. But it would not have been as effective. For one thing it was not Bugeiga only. Hundreds of other Bagirakwe wanted it. So it would have happened by and by. For another thing, some other clans could have thought of a similar scheme against another smaller clan.' He was talking only slightly heatedly now. 'But now only the very mad ones would consider it. And the madder ones still would back them up. Even then, most cautiously. They would all remember what happened to the Bagirakwe.'

'So actually the Bajura were martyred as a lesson for the future?'

'That is more or less so. People should not be so bad to their neighbours. If you scheme to rob your brothers, the gods will not let you enjoy the fruits of your scheming comfortably. You should eventually suffer more than the one you robbed. You should not hate anybody. You created nobody. And anyway, the Bajura will emerge better off with Kitajo, Rwebicuncu and Nyamiringa.'

'Is there anything that we could do to stop or lessen this impending threat?' another elder asked.

'Yes, but no.'

'What do you mean?' he asked, again confused.

'Yes. But it would cause something worse to happen. And therefore no.' They all looked at him blankly. 'Well,' he resumed, 'have you ever rolled a big rock from the top of a very high hill with a very steep slope?'

'Yes,' they answered together, still puzzled.

'And you saw how it went down, hitting the hillside and bouncing off, leaping into the air and knocking down trees, smashing anything it found in its way?'

'Yes,' they answered again.

'Could such a rock be stopped before it got into the valley?'

'No.'

'I say yes and no,' the medicine man said triumphantly. 'If you got a thousand men to trap it halfway down with rope-traps and big branches and so on, they could. But it would kill many of them. So why not let it roll itself to a stop down in the valley and only crush a few more trees?'

'So there is absolutely nothing that could be done.'

'As a matter of fact, there is. The invaders must leave Nyimaringa. And immediately. Only that would save them.'

The four men hurried back to Nyabigyi. They spent that night on the way in the home of close cousins. The next day they informed the elders of Kabisha. These elders went to Nyamiringa to inform their relatives. But the men in Nyamiringa did not believe them. Instead they decided to seek out the medicine man and learn the truth from him. But when they called on him two days later, he refused to see them. He simply did not want to have anything to do with the Bagirakwe living in Nyamiringa. So they went back, more determined not to move than before.'

'So last week it rained very heavily,' Karwemera concluded, 'And a storm such as had never been experienced before in Nyabigyi whipped Nyamiringa. In the night, as the people slept, massive landslides hit many of the homes. Many of the homes were buried with everybody inside.' The listeners looked down in sadness. They were shaking their heads slowly.

'These people asked for it. But even then, the gods have been too severe with them,' an elder observed. Others agreed.

'Well, they were certainly a stronger clan,' Ruteera added. 'So they were sure that they could do as they wanted in this world. They did not know that strength alone was not enough.'

'Do you not know our saying that "knowledge eats strength"? I am not saying that we have more knowledge than they do,' Migayo said, 'but certainly their lack of foresight has rendered their strength useless. They should have realised that the gods would frustrate their mad schemes to oppress and injure an innocent people. After all we are all equal children in the eyes of Kazooba Nyamuhanga.'

Many old men shared his views. They wished their sons all the luck and success all right. But they could not see any sense in a man leaving a happy home behind and going to die on that battlefield, while he could be enjoying the company of his wife and children. They were ready to sacrifice many things, all their rights included, so as to live out their lives peacefully. To them Nyamiringa was expendable.

II

The young men started their preparations for the move immediately. The elders had given their consent and blessed the mission. Among the many preparations, they had to have endless sessions with their gods and those of the clan.

Miyago's son, Muhimbuura, was going with them. He would be their medicine man in Nyamiringa. Migayo would confer with the gods and ask to initiate another of his sons to take Muhimbuura's place. But this one would not be as powerful. It had not come to him naturally, direct from the gods.

Before they made the journey, Muhimbuura had to get final and most special briefings. He was out of circulation for ten days. He spent most of that time with his father in the shrine. They were only interrupted by short trips to the bush. He had to be shown everything that he had not been shown before. He had endless meetings with the gods and ancestors of the clan. There were times he almost believed himself to be a spirit too. He was shown how to invoke the gods, how to cool their wrath and how to thank them in the most sincere way. And when he emerged, he really looked changed. There were no traces of youth. He looked much older than his twenty seasons, and wiser too.

Meanwhile, a message had been dispatched to Rwebicuncu. Those of them who wanted to go back to Nyamiringa had to get ready. They should move on the eleventh day from then. Then the two groups would meet in Kaakyenaga. If they decided not to go, they should all the same send messengers to meet the Kitajo group and inform them about it. Otherwise, the two groups of brothers should leave Kaakyenaga together.

Those ten days were really hectic. The many young men preparing for the trip were feverishly excited. They knew that they would simply walk in and take back what was theirs without a fight. Only a handful of middle-aged men were going with them.

'We are comfortably settled here where we are,' an older man said to Kubiriba when asked whether he would be willing to go. 'Why should we leave peaceful homes and full granaries here and go to fight? Why should we subject our children to another period of famine and anxiety?'

'But the land is ours, and we should redeem it from those rogues, by force if necessary,' Kubiriba said heatedly. 'We must fight to get what is ours by right.'

'If you were going there to fight for peace, I would come with you. But to fight for your rights?' the old man said heatedly. 'Who has got rights and who does not? What makes it your right to live, since your life may be taken away from you in a most degrading way and you would not even lift a finger to object or appeal anywhere?'

But for Tindikahwa time was almost stagnant. A day seemed to take a full moon to end. Now that his dreams were about to come true he could not wait to get there. Yet, a new source of anticipation had been added. The messengers had carried a separate exhilarating piece of news for him. It was from his female father, Kenyangyi. She had found the girl for him to marry. She had even talked to her already. And apparently the girl was equally excited.

'You only have to get there and declare your intentions,' Karwemera had said. 'The wife is as good as wooed. The negotiations will take place at your convenience.'

'Is she beautiful?' Tindikahwa had enquired. 'I cannot live with an ugly woman.'

'Kenyangyi really scouted the ridges of Nyabigyi for the best,' another man said, 'I wonder what you gave her to make her go to all that trouble.'

'Have you seen her?'

'Yes,' two of them had answered. Then a barrage of questions had followed.

'What does she look like? Is she slender? Is she black or anthill-brown? Is she short or is she tall? Is she as beautiful as Kenyangyi? Is she …?'

All the answers seemed to indicate that she was very beautiful indeed. And this made him all the more eager and impatient to go to Nyabigyi. They had to beat those Bagirakwe very quickly so that he could marry that beauty.

Cows were not a problem to him. His share from the raid, years back, had been multiplying steadily. His father was not going to Nyamiringa, and when Tindikahwa had told him the news from Kenyangyi, he had become equally excited. Although he did not have many more cows than his son, he had given him four healthy heifers. They were at the stage when they could mate any time. These were his contribution to the young man's bride price. It was a father's duty to provide for his son's first wife. Of course it was not usual that a son of eighteen had as many cows as his father. Most did not even have one to contribute towards their bride price. But a man who failed to give his son cows could not rightly be called a father.

Two days before they were due to leave, Ruteeramareingwa called his son Kubiriba, his grandson Tindikahwa and the boy's father Mazima.

'You are going back to Nyamiringa,' Ruteera addressed himself to Tindikahwa matter-of-factly. In answer the young man fidgeted in his seat and looked down, foraging in his left nostril with the left small finger. 'When you talked about "going back some day" and being "buried in Nyamiringa", I did not doubt at all that you would go back some day. Many of us felt the same, but only a few of us could believe in the practicability of it all. We could not imagine that it would be so soon.' He then turned to address all the three of them. 'Your younger father told me that a catastrophe would follow our fleeing Nyamiringa. But then I did not understand what it would be until punishment after punishment started befalling the Bagirakwe.'

'You mean Migayo knew that these things would happen?' Kubiriba asked.

'Of course he knew. In what detail, I do not know. But he knew. Who do you think has been punishing them so?'

'The gods,' the young men answered.

'That is right. It was the gods. Then how could Migayo, their messenger, fail to know?' He looked straight at the two men who would lead their brothers to Nyamiringa. 'You have almost achieved your ambitions. You are both young men. And you Tindikahwa, although you nearly led your elders to war, you are still a snivelling little boy.' He looked at the boy with serious intensity. The young man touched his nose and sniffed. 'Who do you think has made it possible for you to go back? Is it you?'

'It is the gods,' Tindikahwa replied confidently.

'That is right. I am glad you know that it is the gods. Now my sons, I have got a piece of advice to give you. Tindikahwa, your father is here. I called him so that he should hear what I have to tell you.

'When you have conquered Nyamiringa and settled down, do not forget the source of your power. Do not be like the Batwa. When they eat a big meal and end up with very full stomachs, they burn the granary believing that they will not need to eat again. And what do you think happens to them the next day?'

'They starve.'

'They feed on the memory of once having had a full stomach.' He looked at them, intensely again. 'I will tell you a short story. You know that a lion gets its strength from its tail?'

'Yes,' they replied.

'All right. One lion went hunting. He soon came upon a bull buffalo. The lion attacked and the buffalo fought with all his might. As the lion strangled and sank his long teeth into the buffalo's stout neck, he internally begged his tail to give more strength to his powerful chest and stout neck and mighty jaws. He soon killed the buffalo. After a big meal, he sat on a big stone near the remains of the carcass. He roared, praising himself thus: "Me, who raises the mane, I am a man." He repeated it several times. Then his tail below him also said "Even me, the tail, I am a man". This annoyed the lion very much. He tried to stifle the tail by sitting on it harder, but it repeated with a smothered voice, "I am a man".

'The next day the lion went hunting again. After the kill he repeated his roaring and self-praise. To his utter annoyance, his tail also started praising itself. This time the lion took an axe and cut off the stubborn tail.' He stopped and looked at the young man significantly. 'The following day, he hardly had enough energy to get up. But hunger forced him to head for the forest. When he attacked a young antelope it kicked him to the ground and escaped. I am sure you know what must have happened to the lion next.'

They were quiet for a brief moment, digesting the conclusion. 'He died of hunger.'

'I speak to those down here, while those high above are also listening,' the old man concluded the story. He then talked about the marriage. He hoped that the young boy would be happy and live a prosperous life. He also contributed one cow and a bull towards his bride price. He gave the bull largely for sentimental reasons. It was young but large. But it was not free in Ruteera's herd. He had an older one which did not allow this young one any peace. But above all, the young bull had a remarkable resemblance to Ruhogo.

III

By the day before they were due to leave they had disposed of the property they were not going to take along. Some people had simply given away their land to their brothers. Others had exchanged it for cows and goats. Still others had not quite given it away. They had left it to their brothers after extracting assurances from them that, if ever they came back, their brothers would give the land back to them. On that same evening their leaders met the elders of the clan. They were given a lot of advice on how to conduct themselves and how to observe the customs of the clan.

'It is most important that you should observe and follow the rules and customs of the clan,' one elder said. 'Do not get there and think that you are far away from the eyes of the gods.'

'As a matter of fact,' Migayo pointed out, 'they are going to where the largest number of their ancestors are.'

'You are very right,' the other elder acknowledged. 'Your forefathers and their forefathers observed these same customs and followed these same rules. Remember that they were not put forth by man. They were brought by the gods to guide and supervise us. And if it were not for these gods, would you be preparing for this trip?'

'No,' they mumbled.

'After they have led you back safely, do not neglect them.'

That night, Kitajo reached the height of ecstasy. There were celebrations in every compound. Almost every household had somebody going back to Nyamiringa. They were given a grand farewell. Some of them would see their brothers again only when one went to visit the other. But most would never see their loved ones again. And as they celebrated they knew that this was the final farewell. They would next meet in the spirit world, in the womb of the earth.

The next morning, several hundred men, women and children started off on the journey. They were retracing their footsteps to Nyamiringa. They were all excited about the whole adventure, knowing that the journey back would be smooth. The only trouble they could possibly encounter was in Nyamiringa. And even then, they had been reassured that it would be minimal.

Their children ran ahead playing. They were not carrying anything. They seemed to understand very well the mood their parents were in. This time, the brothers helped their returning relatives to carry their property. They would take them up to Kaakyenaga and even beyond, if it was necessary.

'How long, do you think, shall we take on this journey?' Tindikahwa asked his uncle Kubiriba. They were half a day away from Kitajo.

'About ten days, I should say,' Kubiriba said confidently.

'Ah, why so long?' Tindikahwa was rather taken aback.

'Of course we cannot drive the children hard. And the women carrying such heavy loads … And do not forget that the cattle have to eat as they go. As a matter of fact, I do not think that ten is a conservative enough estimate.'

'I suppose you are right.' Tindikahwa had a trace of disappointment in his voice. 'I am only very impatient. Having started on the journey, I feel like I should fly and land at our destination right away.' He gnashed his teeth and shook his head slowly, thoughtfully. 'Do you remember those cold, hungry nights when we were fleeing?' he asked, looking up at Kubiriba.

'Do not talk about that time, Tindikahwa.' Some anger could be detected in his voice. 'Ahh, no! It is a wonder indeed that we should be going back so joyfully.'

'Yes, it is a wonder indeed. Kazooba Nyamuhanga is really great.' Then, even more thoughtfully, he added, 'If I die after I have conquered those rogues, my body will settle comfortably in its grave and my spirit happily in the spirit world.'

'Do not talk nonsense, Tindikahwa,' the uncle reprimanded. 'You are forgetting that the gods sometimes grant their children their wishes. You still have a lot of responsibilities to fulfil on this earth.'

'Like that beauty Kenyangyi has found for me?' They laughed loudly and walked briskly to join another group that was ahead.

Chapter Twenty-three

I

The journey took them twelve days. On the fifth day they had not travelled. They had decided to give the children and their cattle a rest. Then on the eighth day it had rained heavily. They had not travelled far either. They had all needed a rest anyway.

When they left Kaakyenaga, together with their brothers from Rwebicuncu, they had sent some five men ahead to Nyabingyi.

'When you get there,' they were instructed, 'believe yourselves to be visitors. See all, hear all, and keep us well informed about Nyamiringa and Kabisha. Rwecurenga and Busaahu will help you to plan everything at that end. They will even give you trusted men to send back to us.'

'But some of us could bring the messages back to you,' one of them suggested. 'Those Bagirakwe could very easily betray us.'

'That would not be advisable,' one leader said. 'You do not want to be suspected. A stray arrow could easily find a presumably unintended target. Remember you are going ahead just as visitors. So you have to stay there until we all get there.'

The advancing Bajura met the first group of messengers soon after crossing into Nyabingyi. It was still early in the morning. The fog had not yet cleared from the lowest valleys. The men had left Kabisha at the first cockrow.

There was not much activity in Nyamiringa. The Bagirakwe there were not preparing to flee at all. If they knew that the approaching Bajura intended to attack, they did not give this knowledge away. And this heightened the excitement in many of the young warriors.

'We might get a chance to avenge ourselves against the causers of our problems,' one of them said.

'That appears to be the case,' Tindikahwa said, quite excited himself. 'And if this is so, we should start putting the final touches to our triumph.'

An inner group of leaders convened to polish up the strategy of approach.

'We cannot go straight to Nyamiringa as we had planned to,' Tindikahwa started.

'No, we cannot,' Kubiriba agreed. 'And we cannot go straight into war with our women, children, and chattels. We will have to leave them somewhere when we get nearer.'

'And when we go to the battleground, who will look after them?' someone else asked. 'We could not possibly risk leaving them with only a handful of men; we hardly have any to spare. The fleeing Bagirakwe could go that way and wreak havoc. Those rogues might have their spies abroad watching us, for all we know.'

After long deliberations they decided on two plans of action. They would send the messengers back to Rwecurenga and Basaahu. These would select a group of trusted men from the original Bagirakwe 'anti-war crusade' to come and give protection to their families while the Bajura men went to the battleground. Then, that evening they would pass a message on to the Bagirakwe in Nyamiringa to prepare for the fight at the Muhamangabo, the battlefield which the Bagirakwe had themselves chosen some five long seasons back. But this was only a formality. They knew that the Bagirakwe would not wait to fight them. And every time the young warriors thought of it, they were very disappointed.

'But I still do not see why we should send any warning to these bandits at all,' a young man said, angry in his disappointment.

'Let us have the law of our ancestors on our side,' an older man persisted. 'They cannot possibly wait to fight us. So, let us give them a chance to flee honourably, or dishonourably, whatever you would choose to call it.'

'But why should we? They gave us no chance at all when they were on the giving end.'

'We should not be like them. Let us teach them to be a little more human in future. They could do with such a lesson.'

'You are very right, son of my father,' Kubiriba rejoined. 'We could not walk in on them without any warning at all. It would not be manly. We would be blamed ever after for fighting a man who was not prepared, and disgracing him in front of his wives and children.'

'I suppose you are right,' a disappointed Tindikahwa said, defeated. 'Although they broke all the laws of the land, we should not be like them. We should abide by the customs that our ancestors left for us to follow.'

'And you can all see how the gods have punished them for that,' another older man said.

'I suppose that is all right,' the young man gave in, 'but I fear this warning may prove to be a very costly one to us all.'

That evening they camped very close to Nyamiringa and Kabisha. As they streamed through the ridges, many people came out to watch these returning Bajura. They had all heard rumours about a possible return. And everybody knew only too well what had been happening in Nyamiringa.

II

Just before cockcrow, the men on watch noticed movement in the bushes, just a stone's throw away from them. A group of armed men were approaching their camp. A small quarter moon had just risen. It was on its way out. It did not provide enough light for them to be able to tell the numbers of the invaders or to recognise any one of them. But the eyes of the sentries were accustomed to the meagre light. They could see that the group was coming straight for them, and not stealthily either.

The Bajura were prepared for such a night attack. And an appropriate message was rapidly transmitted. All the men were already in the maximum state of readiness, since they were planning to fight that same morning anyway. They all waited in queit alertness, ready to smash the invaders, if the Bagirakwe attacked them.

The sentries called out to the group to halt when they were near enough. The men obeyed the order. But one of them continued to walk confidently towards the sentries.

'It is me,' he called out, not quite loudly.

'It is you who?' the sentry asked, puzzled.

'Rwecurenga. We have come to ... .' He did not finish what he was saying. All the hidden warriors broke out of cover. They welcomed the men who had come to look after their families. They were about twenty all together. Seven of them were some of the Bajura who had chosen to stay behind, when the Bajura fled. The rest were all Bagirakwe. With Rwecurenga himself leading them, the Bajura could trust the group almost completely to look after their families as best as was humanly possible.

There was no time for lengthy greetings. The situation did not call for it, much as the men on both sides would have liked it. Apart from Rwecurenga and some three others in the group, the rest had not met for the five seasons they had been apart. So after a brief consultation, the Bajura left for Nyamiringa. It was not far. They were sure to get there before sunrise. Then each group would take up its strategic position. Many of them were so excited that they could hardly restrain themselves from running.

When they were actually in Nyamiringa they went up higher into the hills, avoiding the homes of their enemies. A few dogs barked here and there. But the Bagirakwe did not suspect their presence. They could not suspect anybody else to be moving in that area at all.

They came to a knoll beyond which they could see the large tree, *ekiko*, which marked the battleground. Tindikahwa called a halt. The sky in the east was becoming pale yellow. The hidden sun was starting to throw streaks of light across the dark sky. The small moon was starting to wane under the power of Kazooba Nyamuhanga, who was coming on another routine check on his domain. The Bajura divided themselves into pre-determined groups and proceeded to take up their pre-planned positions. One group hid among the sorgum around the battlefield; another, led by Kubiriba, hid beyond the sorghum field; Tindikahwa's group was to lead the attack.

The sky in the east was rapidly getting light. The Bajura could hardly keep still in their positions. The coldness they had forgotten in the last five seasons was piercing through them. Everywhere teeth were clattering loudly. The men hugged the skins they wore closer to their own skin. But that could not help them much. Tindikahwa's teeth were almost knocking each other out. This brought back to his mind that cold night when he had made up his mind that he would come back some day, to redeem Nyamiringa.

When he started thinking about that night he forgot all about the coldness. His mind reviewed the suffering that accompanied their flight. His mind went through the hardships they suffered during the resettlement in Kitajo and the preparations for their return trip. He was almost back in Nyamiringa when someone nudged him with an elbow. The neighbour pointed out some men who were moving. It was the Bagirakwe secretly approaching the battleground.

This temporarily threw Tindikahwa off balance. That was not the way they had expected the Bagirakwe to come to the battleground, if indeed they did. They did not come confidently this time. They did not shake the hills dancing vigorously to blood-chilling war songs. They were not accompanied by horns to notify and scare the enemy. They came stealthily and started hiding in the sorghum around the battleground.

The Bajura had to change their plans. They could not allow all their enemies to hide in the sorghum, because of their own men hiding there. They could not wait for them to be discovered since they were almost too few to defend themselves.

The group under Tindikahwa's command was the one to come blowing war horns and all. He gave the signal right away. They left their hiding place, behind the knoll. There were only two horn-blowers with them. They blew the most frightening tunes they knew. They headed for the battleground moving at a vigorous canter. They were a small group of some forty men but they shook the valley enough to pass for double their size.

As soon as they got onto the battleground, a hail of arrows rained on them in one burst. They scrambled for cover before the arrows could land. Had they not seen the Bagirakwe hide and guessed at their intentions, they would have been taken by surprise. But now they were expecting some sort of attack. And they knew the direction it was most likely to come from. So they managed to get under some cover and dodge the arrows. They almost all managed. But two young men received a superficial wound each. One got the arrow in the arm and another one in the hip. The wounds were not serious and the men could even continue fighting.

Nobody stopped to examine the damage done. They expected another hail of arrows to follow immediately. They were very alert. They aimed to dodge all the arrows this time. Instead of the arrows they saw waves of violent movement in the sorghum. The movement was towards the open ground.

Suddenly Bagirakwe warriors broke out into the open, their backs exposed to the enemy behind them. They did not even risk a glance over their shoulders to see whether the ground before them was safe. Close in front of them, some young Bajura engaged them in close combat. Spears and shields were crossing each other very fast. The Bajura were out-numbered two to one by the Bagirakwe. But they were really pushing the enemy. Tindikahwa's group gave support to their brothers.

Soon after, another group of some hundred Bagirakwe warriors came onto the battleground. They were in close combat with the third detachment of the Bajura. Tindikahwa did not see them come. He was too busy defending himself to see anything else. He only noticed that the ground was becoming more crowded. The Barigakwe must have been several times more numerous than the Bajura.

Then he got one brief moment to cast a glance over his shoulder. In that brief moment he thought that he saw Kubiriba engaged in furious battle with three enemies. As he turned away, he believed that he saw one of them fall. Kubiriba was in command of the third group, the one that had been hiding beyond the battleground.

A spear scratched Tindikahwa on the shoulder. He subconsciously warded off the spear. But the near-instant pain sent a jarring shock through him. He had taken a blink longer than he should have taken to scan the battleground and it had almost cost him his life. He was angry with himself but he managed to control his anger. This was not the time to start blundering. He would have all the time he wanted for that after this war.

He turned and fought furiously. As he guarded himself with the shield and feinted to avoid blows, he furiously thrust his spear at the enemies. Once in a while he heard a groan as someone fell. He would continue to the next enemy. He could feel blood still trickling down his left arm. The whole arm was getting numb.

Then, through the corner of his eye, he saw two big men eyeing him intently. They cut their way through the crowd and came for him. Their faces wore a grim mask of determined fury. They looked rather familiar. But he had no time to drag their identities from the depth of his brain. They were upon him in an instant. Right away he realised that they knew whom they were fighting. And he knew that they were the best among the Bagirakwe and they were determined to kill him. He needed all the concentration that he could muster. Both men were much bigger and older than he was.

The spears were coming at him very fast. It was a furious fight indeed. Numb arm or not, he did the best he could. He whirled to the left and to the right and warded off spears at incredible speed. Once in a while he managed a perfect thrust himself. No groan came from the other end of his spear and spears kept on coming at him. If anything, they appeared to be coming faster. They were becoming more and more accurate. He was starting to be dazed by the speed at which they were fighting. Some warm liquid ran down the nape of his neck to his back. He wondered whether it was blood or sweat. He fought on, even more furiously. It was impossible to believe that all those spears were being aimed at him by only two men.

The two men were getting worried too. And they were losing grip on themselves. They were fighting more recklessly, like the desperate men they were. Tindikahwa's concentration could not have been better.

One of the men thrust a mighty blow. It went through the hide and canes of Tindikahwa's shield as if it was a banana leaf. He yanked the shield to the left with all his strength. The spear almost fell from the opponent's grip. The man was thrown right off balance to the left. At the same time Tindikahwa feinted. He dropped onto his left knee. The second man's spear swished through the air. It passed dangerously close to his head. From the lower position he saw an opening in the guard of the man in front of him. He did not waste this opportunity. His thrust went home. The spear was ensheathed in the man's groin and he gave a loud groan. As the man collapsed, Tindikahwa saw tortured disbelief on his face. He turned to face the other enemy.

The second man was not where he should have been. He was two strides away, shouting an order to his men. Those of them who could were alreay running for their lives. The Bajura chased after them triumphantly.

Somehow, Kubiriba and Tindikahwa found themselves running alongside each other. They had both sustained some stab wounds. They stopped to appraise each other's condition. Thin trickles of blood from some stabs had clotted. But some streams were still flowing from a few more. Tindikahwa tapped his uncle hard on the shoulder, excitedly. Kubiriba winced with pain. Tindikhwa had hit him on a wound. They looked at each other contemplatively.

'It is over,' Kubiriba said, a wide smile taking over his whole face.

And it had taken only a short time. The sun had barely climbed a whole arm's length since the first arrows were shot.

'Yes,' Tindikahwa replied while looking at the sun, with a similar smile. 'It is all over.' They looked at each other meaningfully. 'No more killings,' Tindikahwa continued, suddenly becoming serious.

Kubiriba shouted at the men to stop the chase. At first they could not hear him over the clangorous noise of battle. The two leaders went after them, shouting at the top of their voices.

'Let them go,' Tindikahwa declared when his comrades had stopped. 'I think they will never bother us again.'

The Bajura stopped the chase. They gathered around, exuberant. Only then did they have the time to look at the stabs they had sustained. Everybody had some injury and there were some rather big, frightening gashes. But they would all live. They also took this time to find out who was missing. Six of them.

'Let us go and check the battleground,' Kubiriba suggested. A few young men started off eagerly. They carried their spears poised for the final vengeance. Tindikahwa exchanged quick worried glances with two older men.

'Stop them,' one of them advised. The men were called back.

'Leave the Bagirakwe wounded alone,' Tindikahwa said to the confused men. Some of them looked at him with disbelief. 'Yes, the war is over,' he affirmed. 'Do not kill anyone else. The able-bodied ones have run. And we have let them go. It would demean us to kill a disabled man, lying wounded, after such a victory.'

'That is very true,' a few others murmured.

'But what shall we do with their wounded?' a young man asked.

'They have got relatives across the valley. We shall call them to take them home and nurse them. As for now, we still have some work to do.' He whispered to Kubiriba in consultation. Kubiriba nodded in assent.

'We have to make sure that all the Bagirakwe have left Nyamiringa,' Kubiriba announced.

They proceeded to organise the search parties. They could not search every inch of the big sorghum fields. But they did the best they could. At any rate, anybody who stayed behind would be making a terrible mistake. The searchers did not find anybody in the homes. Not even the wives and the children. The Bagirakwe had already planned to flee before the battle. And in fact when the men had headed for the battlefield, the women were already heading for the new unknown. The men would follow later. If they won the war, then they would follow and call them back.

By noon the Bajura were sure that they had put all the enemies to rout. A horn was blown to summon all the searchers back to the base. As if in answer Tindikahwa's young bull gave a youthful but fierce roar on the far ridge. They knew its roar. They had got used to it on their long journey back. They looked at each other excitedly. They were back home at last. And their wives and children were just across the valley, coming to join them after their victory. Cleverly, Rwecurenga had brought them back via Kabisha. This was to avoid any possibility of meeting the fleeing Bagirakwe. Only then did they blow the victory horns.

The brave Bajura gathered back on the battleground. They had lost three men in the fight. Three more were wounded. One was not in bad shape but one was in critical condition. He would need the blessings of all their gods to recover. For the first test of his medicinal powers in Nyamiringa, Muhimbuura had a serious challenge.

On the other hand, the Bagirakwe had lost heavily. Over thirty of them lay dead. A larger number of their wounded lay groaning all over the field. Many of them were near death and their brothers from Kabisha had to hasten to their help. If they took their time, more corpses would result.

III

Bugeiga heard the bull roar close by. He was standing under a big tree, not so far from his home. He was contemplating what other mad people contemplate at such times. The familiar bull roar shocked his brain into some terrible memory. He stood rooted to where he was. A great turmoil passed through him. Something spurred by that bull's bellow was trying hard to break through to him. But everything was too much for him to comprehend. For the first time, he looked at his ashen, naked body with disbelief. Filled with shame, he hid himself behind a bush. He was unable to believe that what he had seen was himself.

The bull roared again. This time he placed the memory. It was unmistakable. The roar was not very long but it was deep-throated. It reminded him of Ruhogo, that bull that beat his bull Rusiina. Then things started unfolding: he remembered everything that had happened up to that day, when they had gone across to fight the Bajura. It was all just like yesterday. It just could not be true.

He looked around him and at his bony body again. It just could not be true. This could not be he, Bugeiga, the brave one of Nyabigyi. If it was he in this state, with his buttocks exposed, then he had to be mad. When he came to that conclusion, cold panic seized him. He wondered whether anybody else had seen him in such a state. His wives, his children and grandchildren, his daughters-in-law and all those who had respected him

From his hiding place he saw a man passing by along the nearby path. With great effort, he partly exposed himself and called out to the man. He meant to send him to his first wife. The man went towards him inquisitively. When he saw who it was, he grinned with some fear and walked away. The petrified Bugeiga, with a shaky voice, tried to entreat him not to leave him like that. The man waved to him and went away hurriedly. Bugeiga felt like chasing him and violently shaking some sense into him.

One thing was now certain to Bugeiga. The man had recognised him. And the fact that he had gone away without coming to help him was most painfully puzzling.

Right then a victory war horn sounded across the valley. It awakened in him the memory of some other victory horns, not so long ago. Suddenly it all came back to him. He remembered how they had gone across to Nyamiringa and found no Bajura to fight there. After that he could remember nothing. How long ago that was he could not know. It could even be yesterday, as far as he knew. Then he wondered who now had defeated whom.

Suddenly he was overcome by the pressure of everything that was happening to him. He collapsed to the ground. He started weeping quietly like a woman. He could not know how long he lay there weeping. He fell into a shallow, nightmare-haunted sleep.

A bird in the branches above him awakened him. It was a *kanyonza* bird, which has a habit of sometimes talking like a person. It was saying, *"wakor'ekyaaci, wakor'ekyaci"*, "why have you done it". He believed that it was talking to him.

He rubbed his eyes and looked around him again. The painful memory had not been a dream at all. He was still naked. But now the sun was setting. The dusk would hide his bare buttocks as he went home. He would get into his first wife's house undetected. There, he would try to find out what had become of him. If it was not too painful to live through, he would grit his teeth and face the world. But if it was too much, then he would take the appropriate measures.

Avoiding the paths, he headed for home a determined man.

Chapter Twenty-four

I

Tindikahwa was going home. He had gone across to Kabisha to call on his female father, Kenyangyi. Rwecurenga had informed him that the girl she had found for him would be there and hoped to see him. After some semblance of settlement in Nyamiringa, Tindikahwa had gone across the valley with Rwecurenga's friends.

Kenyangyi had proved to have as good an eye as she had promised. Tindikahwa had right away known that this was the wife for him. The moment he had set eyes on her, his heart had seemed to fly out of him and rush out to her. And he could see that she had been equally affected. When he talked to the girl he had not a doubt that they were meant for each other.

He could not wait to start the negotiations. He wanted to have her as soon as possible. He would try to bring her home within a month or so. If any person or tradition got in his way, then he would convince her to elope with him.

After a delicious early supper Rwecurenga saw him off. The sun was almost disappearing when they left and the clouds above the horizon were a deep red. He had been asked to stay for the night but he refused. There was so much to do in the new Nyamiringa. His presence was absolutely essential. And with no more war to fear, there was nothing to stop him from getting home.

Rwecurenga left him halfway towards the valley. He had to go back and take Tindikahwa's wife-to-be to her home.

Tindikahwa's mind was preoccupied with visions of his wife, so he jumped a little when, a hundred strides away, a man moved very fast away from the path. Tindikahwa stood rooted to where he was. He tried to work out what was happening. Was the man running away from him? On watching more closely, he realised that the man did not look back. As his eyes were used to the meagre light, he thought he recognised the man. He looked like Bugeiga. But one thing puzzled him: this Bugeiga was wearing his own skins.

As Tindikahwa watched, Bugeiga stopped at a tree. He stood below it and looked up. Tindikahwa became inquisitive. Quietly he moved closer. The man was Bugeiga all right. Bugeiga uncoiled a stout rope. He proceeded to make a noose on its end. Tindikahwa had no doubt as to what Bugeiga intended to do. He realised that he had a very big decision to make. He could let the man hang himself. For all the misery he had brought to these ridges he deserved this death and more. But for Bugeiga to wear his skins again, he had to have snapped out of his madness. And that he should want to hang himself meant that he must have become ashamed of his deeds. So, for him to want to punish himself thus, he must have become repentant. In which case he should not die. Then Tindikahwa thought again. The man was the father of his best friend, Rwecurenga. What would Rwecurenga feel if he ever knew that Tindikahwa had watched his father preparing to hang himself and not moved a finger to stop him? What would he himself feel if it was his father? He made up his mind as Bugeiga started to climb the tree. He would not let him kill himself. He reached the tree as Bugeiga started to tie the rope on a stout branch.

'What is it, old man?' Tindikahwa asked, trying to be as friendly as he could. Bugeiga almost fell off the branch. But he ignored the intruder. He went on tying the rope, doing it even faster. 'Come down, please, and let us have an honest talk together first.'

Bugeiga stopped what he was doing. He looked down at the young man. 'Who are you?' he enquired in a calm voice.

'I am a friend of your son, Rwecurenga.'

Bugeiga did not respond to that quickly. He seemed to be having problems with his tongue. ' Wha... What do you want, following me around like this?'

'I was not following you around as such,' Tindikahwa said calmly.

Bugeiga suddenly jumped down. He stood facing Tindikahwa menacingly. The expression on his face was inexplicable. The young man felt like he was looking at the face of a bad spirit. But he was determined to save his friend's father.

'Go away and leave me to do what I must do.'

'No. I cannot allow you to kill yourself. I would not be able to face my bosom friend.'

'Leave me alone and go away,' Bugeiga said, with a far-off, quiet and shaky voice. 'Are you possessed by evil spirits?'

'I am not possessed,' Tindikahwa replied in a controlled voice, 'I am a Mujura. And we have forgiven whatever has happened. Go home, father-in-law, and live.'

'I see you are mad,' Bugeiga hissed. He pounced on Tindikahwa. They fell down struggling. Bugeiga was hitting him with desperate aimlessness.

Tindikahwa did not want to hurt him. He frantically warded off the blows. A plan started forming in his head: if he could disable him and tie him up, then he could go back and call for help. Once Bugeiga got home, he would probably see some sense in living. But Bugeiga did not give a chance to a man who wanted to stand between him and death. He was hitting out with mad fury, one arm groping for the young man's neck.

Tindikahwa disengaged the arm from around his throat. He twisted it hard to the old man's back. Bugeiga groaned heavily. His other arm flailed outwards. It landed on a fist-sized stone. He did not hesitate. He hit Tindikahwa with it several times on the head. Then Tindikahwa fell off him. He lay there limp. Bugeiga got up fast. He kicked the limp body aimlessly. Then, suddenly, he seemed to realise what he had done. He stooped to examine the motionless body. He touched the boy's head. It was moist and had several swollen lumps.

Bugeiga fell on his knees and wept. He had not meant to do the boy any harm. He had already done enough harm. He stayed there kneeling by the boy for a long time. When he left him, he was like a zombie. He remembered only one thing. His rope. After collecting it he left the place hurriedly, without looking at the young man again.

II

Tindikahwa regained consciousness much later. He lay there, hearing a million crickets chirping in his head. The head seemed not to be his. It was as if a heavy load had been tied to the rest of him, exerting a painful pressure where the head should have been. He could neither lift it nor any limb. He lay there in a kind of limbo, wondering whether he was dead or alive.

After a long time he started feeling cold. He realised that he was shivering. That was when he started thinking. The vision of his girl came to him. Then he knew that he must be closer to being alive than being dead. He tried to open his eyes. Sharp needles of pain drove themselves into the back of his brain and his eyes. He temporarily gave up the attempt. But the thought of his wife-to-be drove him to try again. After several painful attempts he managed to open the eyes. At first he could see nothing. It was so dark that he wondered whether he was not in a grave. After a very long time he was able to see some trees around him. Then he started struggling to turn over, onto his knees and forearms. He must go to her, he thought. It took him a very long time but finally he managed to get onto his feet.

The journey home was hell. He sank to his knees and lay down numberless times. The rests he took became longer and longer. Several times he almost gave up. But soon the cold would nudge his heavy head into thinking. Then the vision of his girl would come back. No, he decided, he would live long enough to marry her. Then he would get up again.

He did not know how he crossed the valley. As a matter of fact, he did not even know that he had crossed it. As if in a dream he saw a fire. And he dreamed that he heard voices around it. Then the thought of a fire and human sounds around it attracted him. He knew that ghosts made human sounds but he was beyond caring. When he got to the fire, many ghosts received him. The arms of many spirits grabbed him. He let himself go without a care. He was beyond caring whichever way he went.

He regained consciousness only once. He saw a horde of ghosts surrounding him. He thought he recognised a few. But he could not trust himself. These included Kubiriba, his wife-to-be, and Muhimbuura. He wondered how they had also come to the spirit world. But since his best friends were there with him, everything would be all right. Everybody seemed to be asking him how he had got there. With a jerky voice he told them, very painfully. Then he became unconscious again.

'I do not know,' he thought he heard Muhimbuura say as he went under again, 'The skull is broken in several places. I really do not know. But I will try.' As an afterthought he added, 'Let us put him in the hands of Kazooba Nyamuhanga.'